CLOSER
TO
OKAY

CLOSER TO OKAY

A Novel

AMY WATSON

alcove
press

Published in the United States by Alcove Press, an imprint of The Quick Brown Fox & Company LLC.

Alcove Press and its logo are trademarks of The Quick Brown Fox & Company LLC.

Library of Congress Cataloging-in-Publication data available upon request.

ISBN (paperback): 978-1-64385-830-2
ISBN (ebook): 978-1-64385-831-9

Cover illustration by Annabelle Sigmond

Printed in the United States.

www.alcovepress.com

Alcove Press
34 West 27th St., 10th Floor
New York, NY 10001

First Edition: October 2022

10 9 8 7 6 5 4 3 2 1

For Eric, Sam, and Isaac

CHAPTER ONE

I run my thumb up and down the length of the three scars on my forearm. The Blue Line train under the building rattles the windows. Across Division Street, The Coffee Shop is starting its day, turning on the Edison bulbs. I've been watching since I got here three weeks ago; it turns out I find their routine soothing, and I take comfort wherever I can find it these days. It first caught my eye because of its name, which is truly just The Coffee Shop—whoever owns it, these guys are confident or stupid. Or both.

The night nurse stands in my doorway. "Kyle, it's time to get breakfast started," she tells me. By the time I turn around, she's already continuing down the hall for her next wellness check.

"Thanks, Nancy. I'll be down in a few minutes."

The coffee guys are doing their prep: putting on aprons, making cups of coffee for themselves, stocking the counter with supplies. The guy with the shorter, dark hair never smiles. Why is he so serious all the time? He looks like someone pulled him out of a

J.Crew catalog with his long frame, tidy hair, and jeans that fit like they're custom-made. The other one is almost always smiling. I can tell, even from this distance, that he's trouble. He's all tattoos and muscles and long, wavy hair.

The Coffee Shop reminds me of the West End Bakery, where I worked for three years before I ended up in Hope House. Their slice of life is similar: moms with kids, commuters on their way to their jobs, workers needing lunch or a break-time pick-me-up.

Standing and stretching, I pull away from my Coffee Shop–watching and grab my toiletry bag. I head to the bathroom to brush my teeth, wash my face, and slap on lip gloss. It's a drag to share the bathroom, but I get dibs since no one else is awake. My baker's hours are a habit that just won't break. Today, at least, I'm grateful.

I head downstairs to the kitchen in my pajamas. Mental health facilities offer a strange alternate reality where it's acceptable to wear pajamas all day, sometimes the same ones for days on end. We have bigger problems than our fashion sense, after all; no one blinks an eye over fuzzy bunny slippers unless you walk out the front door in them.

Hope House is small, and cooking here is like cooking for family. We were living on hospital food before we got here, so most of us are happy as long as the food does not come from an industrial-size can or instant powder. Breakfast is my favorite, because I get to make something I love—something inevitably involving flour, baking powder, and measuring cups.

They volunteered me for kitchen duty before I even had a chance to put my bag in my room, which also means it was before I could tell anyone there's a difference between cooking and baking.

I don't like cooking. Cooking is imprecise. Throw savory stuff that tastes good into a skillet? Yeah, it'll taste good most of the time. Throw random shit in a baking dish and put it in the oven? Have the trash can at the ready.

Once the double ovens are on, I pull out two sheet pans and lay out a pound of bacon in neat, soldierly rows. Next comes the muffin batter. I go on autopilot, measuring and stirring the ingredients together. The bacon and muffins go into the ovens, and I move on to the eggs, whisking together a dozen before pouring them into the biggest skillet the kitchen has.

"Kyle, Dr. Booth needs to speak with you in his office," says Bruce the security guard, walking into the kitchen. "I'll keep an eye on things in here for you. He said it wouldn't take a minute."

I sigh. Always Dr. Booth, and always at the worst time. "Just pull everything out of the ovens when this goes off." I turn the knob on the timer and hold it out to him. "You can handle the eggs, right?"

Bruce ignores the question and turns toward the stove in answer. Wiping my hands on my apron, I trot down the hall and double tap the door frame as I enter the doctor's office. He's wearing a turtleneck today. I'm sure he thinks they make him look laid-back and nonthreatening, but no, he's just smug and uptight.

"What's up, doc? I'm in the middle of breakfast and need to get back to the eggs, so . . ."

"I've been reviewing your chart, Kyle, and I'm quite displeased with your progress. Please have a seat. The eggs can wait." He gestures at the chair in front of his overlarge Regency desk.

They actually can't. I don't know what Booth thinks happens to eggs when you just leave them on the stove, but it usually involves smoke. Still . . . his house, his call. Frowning, I sit and wipe my hands on my apron again, more from nerves than a need to get them clean.

"What's there to be unhappy with? I've been to every meeting, cooked every meal, taken every pill. I should really get back—"

"Your future health is more important than breakfast, Kyle. Bruce will take care of the kitchen."

"But—"

His expression squelches my protest. I don't talk back again. He holds my freedom in his douchey, doughy hands. Leaning back in his chair, he crosses his right leg over his left and leaves my file open on his desk. His hands steeple under his chin in what the residents call "Caring Pose."

"Nancy noted in your records that you're not sleeping properly. I'm unhappy with that, Kyle. If you're not sleeping during my prescribed hours, you're not doing what is being asked of you. If you're not open with me, I can't help you. You're a vibrant and capable young woman, and I'm here to see you leave Hope House and fulfill your potential."

"I *am* being open with you, Dr. Booth. I keep strange hours. I've had to for five years. I'm getting enough sleep, just not at the same time as everyone else. I kept these hours before the hospital, and I'm sure it'll be the same after I leave. They're baker's hours. Wouldn't it be more beneficial to maintain the same schedule? Make my transition easier?"

"I made the sleeping schedule with the optimal health of all my patients in mind. You need to adjust. I know what's best for you, Kyle. I'll get Nancy to provide a written record of your schedule for the remainder of the week so that I can reassess on Monday."

I put on my best fake smile and look him in the eye so he can't question my sincerity act. "I understand, Dr. Booth. I will adjust my schedule to meet your expectations. Will there be anything else? I would like to get back to my assigned chore and finish breakfast. I wouldn't want to let everyone down. That could be a real setback in my recovery."

I've only seen Booth a handful of times so far, but I've mostly got him figured out. Flattery will get you everywhere, and compliance with his instructions almost as far. What I haven't worked out, though, are his intentions. Put in the simplest terms: Is he a good guy or a bad one?

He looks at me over his glasses, breathes a sigh, and reaches over to close my file. "I suppose you're right. I appreciate that you're taking ownership of your place in the house, Kyle. You'll find that your recovery will accelerate once you embrace my program. We can review your progress together at your appointment on Monday."

Standing to leave, I smooth my apron back down and hustle toward the door. "Thanks, Dr. Booth. See you tomorrow."

The kitchen is a calamity when I get back. There's smoke pouring out of the oven. Bruce did turn off the stove and oven like I'd told him to but left everything where it was. The residual heat did a number on the eggs, now a solid brown-on-the-bottom disk that gives off the smell of burning sulfur. The muffins might be edible but are overcooked. I'd normally chuck them straight into the trash, but I have to serve them since Mary and Eddie will be here in five minutes and need breakfast if they're going to stay on Booth's schedule. I don't want everyone getting off-program and being forced to sit through the same talk I just did. We all know how important schedules are here. I'll make it up to them at dinner, maybe put some extra turkey on the lunch sandwiches.

"Oh my gosh, what is going on in here?" Mary asks, coming into the kitchen.

"Sorry, Mary. Booth called me into his office to talk as soon as I got everything cooking. You know how it goes. His two-minute talk turned into ten and breakfast burned. Bruce was in here tending the food when I left. I don't know where he went. I can salvage the muffins. I'll make it up to you guys, I promise."

"You don't have to make anything up to me, sweetie. Eddie was making a fuss; I'm sure that's where Bruce went. How can I help? Can I get the cups and milk?"

"I've got this, Mary. Go sit down and enjoy your horrible muffin. You've got to clean the bathroom, worst chore in the house. I will not have you doing my work, too."

She waves me off. "Nonsense. It's no bother. I've spent a lifetime cleaning up after my husband. One little chore is nothing. I'm glad to help. You go get those muffins out of the pan, and I'll get the drinks."

She hustles around me to the refrigerator and starts humming. I move over and pop the muffins out onto one of the red plastic trays, stacking them in tiers so they'll look good, even if they don't taste it. I put two muffins on a separate plate and carry them all into the dining room.

"What's up, Special K?" Eddie yells as I walk into the room. He does this every morning, and it always makes me flinch.

"It's a bad morning, Ed. You get muffins and milk. Sorry. The bacon and eggs got burnt. I'll make something extra-good for dinner tonight."

"Well, ain't that a bitch? You better make something really fucking tasty for dinner, then. I can't get through my day in this shithole with an empty stomach."

"Hush, Edward," Mary says as she comes in behind me with the glasses of milk. "It's not her fault."

"How's it not her fault, huh? It's her job to cook my food and keep my belly full. How are lousy fucking muffins supposed to keep me satisfied?"

"Eddie," Nancy warns as she walks into the dining room, stopping his rant. She has a slight accent, maybe something Slavic, that gives her voice more authority, sounds harsher to my ears.

Eddie puts on his nice act; Nancy tells Booth everything. "Good morning, Nancy. Great to see you. I'm sure looking forward to these muffins Kyle made this morning."

Nancy grunts and turns on her heel. She takes the separate plate I made, knowing Joey wouldn't be down to eat with everyone. With her back to us, she says, "Kyle, Bruce needs the grocery list after breakfast. Drop it off in the security office as soon as it's done. Eddie, you have an appointment with the doctor in an hour. Mary, you need to do your chores this morning."

"Sorry again about breakfast, guys. I'm gonna get started on the grocery list. I'll make a dessert for you tonight. Chocolate cake, maybe."

"It better be fucking good, K. This muffin shit's for the birds."

From behind the pile of canned vegetables in the cabinet, I pull out the half-empty jar of instant coffee and make myself a cup. It tastes awful, even with double the sugar and milk. Wincing, I take another sip and start my list. Once it's complete, I go to the security room. Bruce is sitting at the desk watching the monitors.

"Here you go, Bruce. This should get us through the week. Well, barring any other unforeseen catastrophes."

"Yeah, sorry about this morning, Eddie was causing trouble upstairs. Me and Nancy went to deal with him, and I didn't know that Booth kept you so long. I turned everything off, but I guess that wasn't enough. I'll say something to the doc later. You never know when something's gonna go wrong around here."

"No worries. Just let me know when the groceries get here, please. What do you think? A couple of hours or so?"

"Yep." Bruce turns back to the monitors, my signal to leave.

I go back to the kitchen and make four sack lunches, write a name on each with a green Sharpie, and put them in the fridge. Once I'm done, my day is wide open, which is not good.

Forced busyness is the best method for keeping my depression on the straight and narrow. Booth knows it and still schedules these open days for everyone. He does it either out of masochism or as his own wellness check. There's no better litmus test for mental illness than hours on end with nothing to do, I guess. My depression might decide today is the day to sleep for twenty-three hours. Joey's OCD might pick five hours of making his bed. Mary's PTSD could pick a panic attack. Eddie's psychosis is like a twisted wheel of fortune, and the dominant voice in his head will dictate his activity.

I make brioche dough for rolls to go with dinner. Bread is a project that will give me focus for the day. I make a double batch so I can surprise Mary with cinnamon rolls later this week. The cinnamon rolls work against my talk with Booth this morning, though. I'll have to get down to the kitchen an hour and a half earlier to let them rest and rise.

Maybe it's counterproductive, but I'd rather make Mary happy than Booth.

The day nurse, Lori, brings in my meds and gets the dish soap out of the locked cabinet. She watches me take the pills while one side of the sink fills with water and suds. Doing the dishes is a hassle, since they dispense cleaning supplies under supervision and set the water heater to warm, not hot. After all, a patient could drink cleaning supplies or scald their hands under hot water.

"Lori, I think I'm going to go out today."

"Okay. You sure?"

"Yeah."

"Sign out with Bruce whenever you're ready."

"Okay. I need to take a shower first."

As soon as I'm back in my room, I pull jeans and a cut-up sweatshirt out of the army surplus rucksack I haven't bothered to unpack, then go into the hall. Lori is walking by.

"Lori, could I have an Ativan? A half a pill, or even a quarter? I'm nervous or excited or anxious. I can't decide which. Maybe it's all three, but I'm getting fidgety. A smidge to take the edge off?"

"You can have the Ativan, but Booth doesn't allow partial doses. Do you want me to get it?"

Of course Booth would find a way to make this harder than it needs to be, too. "No, I don't want to be a zombie. If I take the whole dose, I'll fall asleep at the table facedown in a Danish. Hopefully, the shower will help. God, I hate this. First thing I'm going to do when Booth lets me out of here is take a shower as hot as I can stand and shave my legs."

"Kyle, you know you can shave your legs here, right?"

"No, Lori, I can shave my legs *with supervision.* No offense, but I'm not letting you watch me shower."

"Well, getting out today is a step in the right direction, anyway. Keep with the program, follow the doctor's instructions, and you'll be home in no time." She offers a smile, warm and tired.

I shower in the lukewarm water and wash my hair with raspberry-scented baby shampoo. I wasn't joking about the hot shower. I daydream about it while I'm in this crappy lukewarm water. The distraction calms me down. I dry off and wrap myself in a towel. My jeans are scratchy when I put them on, and my sweatshirt is heavy against my skin after T-shirts and flannel pants for weeks. The fact that I'm so uncomfortable in what were once my everyday clothes ratchets my anxiety right back up. I stop and take a few deep breaths: in through the nose, out through the mouth, making fists in time with my breaths. The fists are not part of the normal deep breathing technique, but they're my own stress reliever. Whatever works. I'm sure Dr. Booth wouldn't approve, which sort of makes me like it more.

In the past few weeks, I've noticed most of us crazy people have stress tics. I clench and unclench my fists, Joey fiddles with his hair, and Mary plays with the tissues in her pocket until they're confetti. There was a guy in the psych ward who snapped his fingers and drove everybody nuts.

Five inhale-exhales later and I'm calm enough to keep going. I run a comb through my hair, put on more lip gloss, and slip on my turquoise Vans before heading downstairs to get my wallet from Bruce. It's locked in the security office to keep it from being stolen. No locks on our rooms means nothing's secure.

"Kyle, I was about to call you. The groceries will be here about one o'clock."

"Okay, thanks. I'll put them away when they get here. Can you get my wallet for me? I'm gonna go out for a while."

"Sure. I'll need you to sign out, too," he says as he pulls a clipboard from under a pile of papers, then slides it across the desk to me. "Remember—no more than two hours. Don't lose privileges on your first trip out. I'd hate to have to report anything."

"Don't worry, Bruce. I'll be good."

CHAPTER TWO

"Come on, Kyle. You can do this," I whisper while standing in the entryway doing my breathing-clenching thing again, working up the courage to go out onto the sidewalk. After a ten-count, I pull open the door and throw myself outside. It's nearly winter, and the air is sharp enough that it's jarring.

The noise on Division hits me first—the cars rumbling and honking, a police car siren. The city smell is second: exhaust, the vent shaft from the train tunnel, trash in the alley. Third is the heat; the sun is out and shining over my right shoulder. The windows at Hope House are north facing, and this is the first direct sunlight I've gotten in weeks. I turn toward it like a flower, pointing my face up and closing my eyes. My moment doesn't last long; a briefcase hits my thigh, buckling my knees and putting an end to my reverie.

"I can do this. I know how to do this," I chant, earning the stink eye from a passerby because I'm talking to myself.

I give her a shrug and a smirk, then stand straight, roll my shoulders back, and step to the curb. A break in the traffic allows me to jaywalk to The Coffee Shop. I lay my hand against the brass push plate and get through the door before I lose my nerve. The store's extraordinary aroma stops me dead as soon as I'm in the open doorway. My brain is assaulted with, well, coffee. The air is heavy with the nutty, floral smell of freshly roasted and ground beans.

Allowing my senses to acclimate, I look around. The interior is not what I expected, from what little I could see from my windowsill vantage point. The shop is more laboratory than café. The walnut bar, booths, and vintage light bulbs add warmth, but every other surface is austere white or steel. The menu is a handful of words and numbers on the wall. There are no pump bottles of flavoring, no pink, blue, or yellow sweeteners on the counter. There are five booths, a vintage espresso maker, coffee grinder, and bowls waiting for sugar and cream.

"In or out! Don't stand there with the door open!"

It's the never-smiling guy. It takes the merest hiccup of a moment to get moving again, but I don't want to be locked into his angry gaze any longer. I walk the rest of the way into the shop and wait until my mind calms. I take four steps to the counter to place my order.

"Hey. What can we get for you?" The always-smiling guy is at the end of the counter waiting for me. My pause at the door wasn't a severe transgression for him, it seems. Only for Mr. Serious.

"Give me a second. I haven't been here before. The coffee smells amazing."

"Ah, the devil's drink. It's our evil potion to lure in the beautiful ladies." He gives me a wink and a smirk I'm sure works all sorts

13

of magic for him. He nods his head to the right. "Jackson over here is our very own potions master."

There's a huff from Jackson, but Smiling Guy ignores it and keeps talking. "Take a second to look over the menu. What you see is what you get. No bells and whistles. I can answer any questions."

I scan the eight lines on the wall, taken aback by their starkness and simplicity. Eight items. "That's the whole menu?"

"Yep. Like I said, no bells and whistles. We have whole milk and sugar. No flavors. No cream. No soy. Just coffee from a family farm in Costa Rica. We roast it here, grind it fresh, and serve it the way it should be. We are what the name says—a coffee shop. No more, no less."

The men both stand up straighter and wear expressions of pride, rather than the happy and grumpy faces I'd seen up to this point. I have to smile because I recognize the expression; it's the same one I have when I talk about my baking.

"I'll have a flat white."

"For here or to go?"

"Here." I hand over a ten, and he gives me my change.

"Grab a seat. I'll bring it to you as soon as it's ready."

Choosing the booth that offers the best perspective for seeing what's happening in the store and out on the street, I watch in a sort of trance as Jackson makes my drink. You can see the passion for what he's doing on his face, even in the simplest of gestures. He pulls out a scoop of beans and pours them into the grinder. There's a short blast of noise as the machine pulverizes them, then the ground coffee pours out into a metal cup sitting on a scale. He tips the grind into the espresso machine's filter, then takes a metal tamp and presses down. He places a white cup on the base of the espresso machine and turns a couple of knobs. After a moment, he slowly raises the machine's lever, holds it there for a few seconds, lowers it with force, and the espresso pours out.

Each movement has the practiced motion of a violinist pulling a bow. I don't look away from the performance until the cup hits the saucer; the clink breaks my concentration. I look up at his face. He's staring at me, and the proof he's done this thousands of times is there as he grabs a steel pitcher and steams the milk without averting his eyes—they're the same dark brown of the espresso he's made, and ferocious.

I have to look away; his intensity makes studying the marbling of the white stone floor a necessity. I'm searching for patterns and shapes in the veining when weathered brown boots walk up to my table.

"Here you go. There's a spoon and sugar. If you need anything else, give a shout. My name's Jamie." Smiling Guy's blue eyes are kind and crinkle at the edges when he smiles.

"Thanks, Jamie."

He nods and walks back to the counter.

Surprise hits again when I see what he's brought to my table. There's a white cloth napkin folded into an envelope with an antique silver spoon and tongs tucked inside. The tongs are partner to a tiny ceramic dish stacked with sugar cubes. These two fellows are flipping my expectations on their head. I'm beginning to think the name of the store is not only a reminder of the purity of their product but also an inside joke for an implied casualness that doesn't exist in their space.

Then there's my drink. A flat white isn't complicated. This one, though, is a production. The cup is one-third filled with espresso, but it's not like any espresso I've ever seen. It's topped with a layer of creamy foam the color of nearly-burnt caramel and has left a thick coating inside the glass cup where Jamie jostled the liquid as he carried it to the table. Next to the cup is a white pitcher of steamed milk to add in. Other places pour the milk into the espresso for you. The Coffee Shop, though, left me with the experience of combining the two myself.

I pick up the pitcher and tip the milk into my cup. This is the best part of taking milk in your coffee—watching them combine, light and dark, creating tiny tourbillons and eddies. These guys must appreciate it as much as I do, since they've given me a glass cup rather than the standard white ceramic. I watch with reverence, then turn my attention to the bustle on Division.

There's an irony in my excursion this morning. Here I am sitting, looking out the window, and watching people and cars pass. It's a window and a handful of people, same as the house. I frown, wondering if Lori's praise for going out is deserved. Self-doubt is part of the disease. I know this but still sit and let the negative thought grow and swirl in my head, the movement outside the window blurring with my unblinking stare.

"Are you going to drink it or sit there staring out the window? You won't be able to appreciate it properly if it falls below one hundred degrees."

Jackson is at my table now. I won't let myself look at his face, even though he would be terrifically handsome if he weren't so pissed off. I turn my head toward him and focus on the collar of his shirt.

"Sorry. I was lost in thought. I am absolutely going to drink it. This is my first real coffee in weeks." I grin, focusing on the cropped hair above his right ear. If my gaze is close enough to the other person's eyes, I can get away with not making eye contact without it being off-putting.

"Don't let it go to waste. A lot of work goes into those two cups."

I take a slurpy sip, making sure the drink isn't going to burn my tongue, and close my eyes to the assault of flavors. I hum as the syrup-thick espresso coats my taste buds with an unexpected sweetness. I suddenly get why wine fanatics do so much sniffing and swirling at a tasting. This drink is more like a fine wine than any other espresso that I've ordered. "Oh, man. It's the most spectacular cup of coffee I've ever had. I won't let a drop of this go to waste." I reach up and touch my fingers to my lips. "How did you do this? It's amazing."

He huffs out a half-laugh. I take a chance, shifting my eyes to the left, to see if the laugh means his anger has dissipated. My compliment must have done the trick: he's not quite smiling, but the start of an arrogant smirk is dancing around his expression.

Without another word, he turns and walks into the back room. I'm left dumbfounded by the encounter, but the lingering taste brings my attention back to the deliciousness in my cup. I force myself to not gulp it down but drink at what I think is a reasonable pace until the cup has the thinnest coating of brown inside. Frowning, I wonder if I could swipe my finger through the cup to wipe it clean. Or could I lick it clean?

"That would be okay, right?"

"You better be careful talking to yourself; someone might think you're crazy," Jamie teases. He's at the next booth, wiping the tabletop with a towel.

My cheeks heat with embarrassment. "Only if you answer yourself, which I do. So maybe I'm not the best example."

"No worries. I'm messing with you. We all do it." Jamie's beaming.

He's about to turn on the flirt, and I'm not ready to deal with that, so I change the subject. "So, you guys don't have food, right? Not to be rude, and not that this is like any other coffee shop, but it's strange."

"You flatter me. We aren't like anyone else, and it's very intentional. There's some talk about adding food, but Jackson's dead-set against it. Doesn't want to distract from the coffee."

"But food could be great. The right person could make it complement the coffee. Think about it like wine pairings."

"If you know anyone to recommend, I'm all ears. I'm not going to give up on something just because Jackson says no a couple of times. If I did that, he'd still be holed up in the chemistry lab. Well, this is basically another chemistry lab. But at least in this one he gets to hang out with me."

"I'm sure that's a great improvement for him," I add, snarkily, wishing I had the guts to tell him I'm the perfect person. The distinct awfulness of being in Hope House punches me in the gut. "I'll let you know if I find anyone. Hey, I gotta get going. But thanks for the coffee."

"My pleasure. See you soon."

I speed walk out of the café and onto the sidewalk, then jog across the street to Hope House.

"Where's the fire, Kyle? You okay?" Bruce asks as he passes me the sign-in sheet.

"I'm good. Just have an idea and need to get it down in my journal before I forget." I tap my temple with my index finger. "You know how glitchy this thing gets."

CHAPTER THREE

I run up the stairs and am out of breath by the time I get back to my room. Crossing the street today is the only exercise I've gotten in weeks, and right now is the best I've felt in months. I grab the journal from my bedside table and hop into my spot on the windowsill. I pause to catch my breath, looking back across the street. Jackson is on the sidewalk outside The Coffee Shop, a phone held to his ear, pacing, with his free hand gesticulating. His angry face is back.

When I look away and close my eyes, I'm bombarded by images of desserts: hazelnut macarons, vanilla shortbread dusted with coarse sugar, lemon tea cakes with puckery-tart glaze, mini cinnamon buns, Cuban *torticas* with a thumbprint of dulce de leche. I open my eyes and start writing down ideas, half words and half scribble-sketches.

There's a tap on the door frame. Joey is standing there, and I smile. He waves.

"Hey, Joey. I missed you at breakfast this morning, and you missed the excitement."

He shrugs and looks down at the floor.

"Still no talking, huh?"

He flicks his eyes up at me in acknowledgment.

"You can always write me a note."

He shrugs.

Joey breaks my heart. They won't keep him in the hospital because he's not dangerous, and he can't stay at home because his parents don't know what to do with him. So he's stuck in the limbo of the house until he has a breakthrough, good or bad. His OCD is telling him that he can't talk, and the voices are persuasive. Booth's pushing exposure therapy on him, which would mean putting Joey in a room with someone he loves and forcing him to do everything the voices are telling him he shouldn't. In theory, seeing that the voices aren't correct will make him better. But the emotional strength required is immense, and Joey just doesn't have it.

I close my journal and walk over to him. "Can I give you a hug today?" Sometimes touching is off-limits.

He nods and looks at me with grateful eyes.

I reach out, wrap my arms around him, and squeeze with everything I've got. He squeezes back and doesn't ease up for a good thirty seconds.

"Better?"

A nod and shrug.

"I need to get downstairs to the kitchen. The groceries should be here soon, and I have to get cooking to make up for breakfast. I'm sure you heard what happened. Mary said Eddie was making a lot of noise."

Nod.

"You wanna come sit with me while I work? I'll let you be my taste tester if you want."

Nod.

"Let's go." I grab his hand and keep holding on as we walk to the kitchen.

I've decided to make flourless chocolate cake tonight. It'll be the perfect apology dessert because, well, it's chocolate and also a bittersweet counterpart to the espresso I just had across the street. The cake has to come after the bread, though. The yeast demands attention. I have to let the dough come to room temperature before making it into rolls.

Joey hops onto the counter. He's watching me with more interest than usual, so my excitement must show. He wrinkles his brow and tilts his head to ask me what's up.

"I've got an idea brewing, and I'm excited for the first time in so long. I forgot how good this feels." Truth is, it's been more than months since I've felt this good; it's been years.

Joey smiles.

"You want some paper? I've got some in here for making the grocery list. You can write me notes instead of making faces at me all afternoon." I get the paper and a pen without checking to see if he tells me yes.

He scribbles *thanks* on the paper as soon as he gets it.

"Did Booth take your pens and pencils away again? You had them yesterday?"

He writes, *yep. punishment for skipping breakfast. says im not trying enough.*

I frown and pat his thigh before grabbing the things I need to make my cakes out of the fridge. "I'm sorry. Too bad Booth won't spend time with you to see how hard this is. Anyone could see how much you hate this."

He holds up the paper. *hes pushing aversion again.*

"Aw, man. I know you don't want to do it. Maybe it would work, though?"

He shrugs and his eyes mist.

"I'd do it with you in a heartbeat. It might be easier with me instead of your family."

He shakes his head furiously. *NO!!!* He flips the paper over to the other side. *U R my best friend here.*

"Don't get upset. I'm not gonna make you do anything you don't want to. Just want to be sure you know I'm willing."

He nods.

"Did you hear I went out today?"

Headshake.

"I did. I went to The Coffee Shop, the place across the street, and it was, well, interesting." I tell him about asshole Jackson, flirty Jamie, the amazing espresso, the oddness of the place, and anything else I can think of to fill the silence. Joey's no-talking is a good thing for me. My depression has always amplified my tendency to isolate; Joey counts on me to talk.

I'm folding batter and egg whites together when I hear Joey writing again. I look up when the pen stops scratching.

R they cute?

"Are you serious?"

He returns an emphatic nod and an almost-full smile.

"Jamie was cute and, sorry, but definitely straight. He went into full-on flirt mode as soon as he saw me, but I'm sure that's his default setting. Not sure about the other one. He was an asshole from the second I opened the door, so I tried to keep my distance. He was a pro at making espresso, and I'll be back for that, but I don't see any future heart-to-hearts with him."

Joey is staring at me, tapping his pen on the word "cute" over and over and over again.

"I'm getting to it, calm down! Cute's not the right word for him, but it's hard to get past the angry to see the handsome. I'm sure there are plenty of girls out there who have a thing for guys who act like dicks who'd lose their minds over him."

Joey gives me another shrug, and I go back to folding egg whites.

"So, I have a crazy idea . . ."

crazy? really? He raises his eyebrows and grins.

"Yes, really, smartass. The Coffee Shop doesn't have any food, and I thought that was weird, so I asked that guy Jamie about it. He said asshole Jackson doesn't want food. Thinks it'll interfere with his coffee. Jamie, though, thinks they need it and maybe just need the right person to make it for them."

Joey gestures for me to keep going when I pause to take a breath.

"What if I'm the right person?"

Scribble. *don't U have a job already?*

"Yeah, but what if everything's different when I get out of here? I'm not sure I can go back to my life as it was with everybody knowing what happened. They already worried about me on my bad days. Now it would be constant. Maybe I need a fresh start? Make a clean break. New baking. New apartment. I don't know. I love the bakery and the people I work for, but I couldn't take them constantly worrying over me. They'll do it because they care, but I don't need a reminder every day, you know?"

23

Nod.

"I'm excited to have something to do besides sit around and think about myself. Something else to focus on, even if Jamie and Jackson didn't ask me to do it. Maybe I can surprise them?"

Nod.

"So, to make up for the shitty breakfast, I was thinking I could make this chocolate cake. Nobody can be mad if they're eating chocolate, right? And I thought when I made a cake for you guys, I could also make little cakes for the guys across the street. Is that too crazy?"

Joey's looking at me like I have two heads.

"Okay. I know it's crazy, but even if nothing comes of it, it'll be good for me. I need to get up and do something."

Joey hops off the counter, nods, and gives me a hug that tells me he approves. He turns back to his paper and writes. *im gonna go back upstairs. C U @ dinner?*

"I hope so. It's gonna be a good one, I think."

He hands me the pen and heads back to his room.

I put the cakes in the oven and run upstairs to grab my journal. The Coffee Shop's just closed for the day. Jackson opens the door and walks out, locking it behind him. He doesn't turn around immediately but presses his fingertips to the door's push plate. It looks like he's passing it a kiss. The sweet gesture makes me smile, and I head downstairs.

Back in the kitchen, I run my eyes over the two sloppy pages I filled earlier, then turn the page and draw a diagram-y sketch detailing components. And so I get to work on my first dessert for The Coffee Shop.

* * *

Two hours later, I'm furiously mashing potatoes when Mary pokes her head around the corner. I can set a clock by it: five minutes before breakfast and dinner, Mary will always come to see if she can help. I let her get the drinks, same as breakfast.

Everything is ready, and I hope the food will be good enough to get Eddie off my back. Mary and Joey understand the occasional misstep, but Eddie isn't sympathetic to anything. He's an awful combination of psychotic and drug user. Eddie is only worried about Eddie, and he could give two shits about anyone else. In fact, there's always the added kick he gets from messing with people. It makes him laugh. Who cares if the other guy isn't laughing?

"Eddie, be on your best behavior this evening," Lori says as I walk into the dining room with the bowl of mashed potatoes. "Kyle's put a lot of effort into the meal."

I ask, "Hey, Lori, could you come in the kitchen real quick while I get the rest of the food?"

"Sure, Kyle." She follows me into the kitchen.

"I have a favor to ask."

"What kind of favor?" She scrunches up her nose; she's leery.

"Nothing illegal or illicit. I was just wondering if I could get you to deliver some treats for me? It's for the guys that run the coffee place across the street. Maybe you could leave them in the entryway for them?"

Lori grunts. "I'm not sure Booth would like it. Where's what you want me to take? You need to get dinner out there before Eddie gets worked up."

"Here." I hand her a brown paper lunch sack with Jackson's name written on the outside. "Thanks a million, Lori. I'd do it myself if I could."

"I didn't say I'd do it." But she gives me a wry smile that lets me know she will. "Don't tell the others. I don't want them thinking I'll run all over town for them."

"See you tomorrow, Lori. And thank you." I pick up the tray with the meatloaf, hoping my peace offering will do the trick.

"What's up, Special K? I'm fucking starving," Eddie yells as I push through the door.

"Hey, Ed. I hope it's okay. Save room for dessert."

"Quit talking about it and dish me out some food. Didn't you hear me say I'm starving?"

"Get it yourself, Edward. She cooked. It's not Kyle's job to serve you," Mary says.

Eddie starts to protest, but Nancy comes through the door, so he zips it and scoops out a pile of mashed potatoes, followed by meatloaf and three rolls. Now that he's clean, he must be making up for all those lost calories he didn't need when he was high; he eats enough for three men.

"Good evening, everyone. I trust you had a productive day and we will have a nice, quiet night." She's looking at Eddie for the last part.

"Sure thing, Nance. After I eat this, I'm gonna go flop myself down in front of the TV, find a good movie, and fall asleep with a big, full belly."

"And, since Edward has such fantastic plans for the living room, I will assume the rest of us will retire to our rooms. I have a letter to my sister to finish," Mary adds. "Kyle, the potatoes are delicious. Will you tell me your secret? I know you chefs don't like to divulge."

"Butter, Mary. Lots and lots of butter. That's always the secret."

Nancy walks down the hall. As soon as she's out of sight, a tiny ball of paper napkin goes flying across the table and hits Joey in the head.

"Leave him alone, Eddie," I snap. "And don't throw things. That's just gonna make more of a mess for me to clean up."

"What? Still not talking, Joe? You can talk to your old pal Eddie. Your little mind trick won't work on me. Nothing can kill me, dontcha know."

"Stop it, Edward. Please let everyone enjoy their food," Mary pleads.

"I gotta have something to do. It's fun fuckin' with you guys. I swear to God, none of you can take a fuckin' joke. Do any of you even know how to have a good time? That's all I'm doin' here. This place is a fucking drag."

"Then shut up and finish your food so you can go watch your stupid movie or look for your mom on tonight's episode of *Cops*," I snap.

"Fuck you, K."

He shuts up after that, though, and redirects his meanness at me instead of Joey with an elbow in the ribs every time he picks up a forkful of food. I take it in silence. I'm taking my last bite of meatloaf as another ball of napkin goes flying, but this one is from Joey. It hits Eddie square in the forehead, and Joey's grinning with pride.

"What the fuck, Joe? I quit, didn't I?"

Joey points between Eddie and me.

"Yeah," I say, "he was elbowing me, but it's no biggie. You don't need to start something with him, okay? I'm gonna go get dessert. I'll be right back."

I hustle into the kitchen to grab the plate with the chocolate cakes. There's a silent standoff happening between Eddie and Joey when I get back into the dining room. Mary worries and tears apart her napkin. This could turn bad fast.

"So, guys, I have my version of Ding Dongs. Let me know what you think, okay?"

"Little cakes?" Eddie sneers. "I figured for dessert I would at least get a whole cake or pie. Not some fucking Ding Dongs."

"Edward," Mary scolds. "Kyle, these are lovely. I can't wait to try one."

"Thanks. And, actually, they are cakes, Ed. Just small ones. So cool it or I can make sure you don't get any." I set the cakes in the middle of the table, and they each take one.

Joey gives me two thumbs up. He's got a huge grin.

"Pretty fuckin' good for a tiny cake. Give me a good old white cake from the grocery store and I'd be a happy man. This is too fancy-shmancy for me, but I'll still have a few more. I'll take 'em with me to the living room. Leave you boring-ass fucks to do whatever boring-ass shit you do. See you at breakfast. Try not to fuck it up tomorrow, K."

I roll my eyes and breathe a sigh of relief. Eddie picks up three more cakes and leaves to go watch TV.

We made it through another dinner unscathed. And today, that feels like accomplishment enough.

CHAPTER FOUR

Contrary to Booth's instructions, I didn't change my sleep pattern and went to bed as soon as I did the dinner dishes because I wanted to be awake when Jamie and Jackson got to the shop. I want to see Jackson come out of his entryway with my brown paper bag, hope to see their reactions.

I'm trying to be smart about this and not let Nancy know I'm awake already. Every fourteen minutes, I get back under the covers and lie still until her shadow passes the window in my door and moves on to Joey's room. As soon as the coast is clear, I hop back into position. I'm twitchy and on edge to the point that I remind myself of Eddie. It's good, even if it's so out of the ordinary, to be excited about something.

Nancy's coming down the hall; time to feign sleep. I pull the covers up so that only the top of my head sticks out and slow my breathing before she gets to the window. She pauses, checking for signs of life, and moves on. As I get back to my perch, Jamie has made it to the shop's front door, and Jackson is walking down the sidewalk with a baffled expression and my paper bag in his hand. Jamie takes a couple of steps forward, snatching the bag from Jackson as he hurries to the shop door and turns on the bulbs. As soon as the lights are on, Jamie pulls out the individually wrapped cakes. He lines them up on the bar top, and I laugh because, from this far away, they look like hockey pucks lined up for a shootout. I'm absorbed in piecing together what's going on when Nancy speaks. I nearly jump out of my skin.

"Good morning, Kyle. You slept a little later this morning. It will please Dr. Booth that you're making progress on his plan. Let me know if you need anything. The others, of course, are still asleep."

"Sure thing, Nancy. I'll be down to start breakfast in about thirty."

She nods and continues her checks.

In the few seconds that have passed, my cakes have moved from the bar, and the guys have started their morning routine. Maybe I can glean something when I go over later. This morning, I'm planning a do-over of yesterday's failed breakfast, but with blueberry muffins. It'll be quick and an easy cleanup. It's also a crowd-pleaser. Who doesn't like blueberry muffins and bacon?

Lori's waiting in the hall outside my room when I come upstairs after breakfast. "I delivered that bag for you. I hope he got it. I felt a little weird leaving it in the entryway."

"Yeah, he did. I saw him walk into the shop with it first thing this morning. Thanks again, Lori. I owe you one."

"No problem. I don't mind doing stuff to make your life easier so long as it's not going to get me into trouble. Let's keep it between us, though, okay?"

I hold up three fingers. "Scout's honor, Lori. I'm gonna shower real quick and head over to The Coffee Shop again this morning. The flat white yesterday hit the spot."

I shower double-quick; my excitement is even better motivation than the tepid water. I get dressed—black cargo pants and a red T-shirt—then trot downstairs to sign out.

"Hey, Bruce. How's it hangin'?"

"Good, Kyle. Someone's in a good mood this morning."

"Doing pretty good today! Can I get my wallet and sign out? I'm going across the street, same as yesterday."

"Sure thing. Don't forget you have an appointment with Booth at eleven."

"It's not gonna take me two hours to drink a cup of coffee." I scribble my name on the sheet, put my wallet in my pocket, and hurry to the front door.

Like yesterday, I pause to do three inhales and exhales in the entryway of Hope House, hoping to maintain the calm long enough to get across Division and through the door of The Coffee Shop. I watch the traffic, timing my exit onto the sidewalk so that the jaywalking can happen immediately. In the shop, I look up at the bar and am met with Jamie's and Jackson's faces, respectively happy and mad.

Before leaving Hope House, I was excited to find out what they thought about the cakes, maybe even conjure up the courage to introduce myself as the baker. But now that I'm standing in front of them, all my enthusiasm has vanished. Curling up in a ball on the floor sounds like a better option.

Before I can dissolve fully into my panic, Jamie says, "Welcome back!" He's smiling at his end of the bar, and it eases my nerves a bit.

I ready myself for the flirt to begin.

"You're looking lovely today . . . Wait, I didn't catch your name yesterday. Did I forget? No, there's no way I forgot. I must have been off my game." He holds a melodramatic hand to his heart during the speech. I glance at Jackson, and he's glaring daggers.

"No, you didn't ask." I chuckle a little.

"Well, are you going to tell me? I pride myself on knowing our regulars on a first-name basis, and I know we're going to see more of you."

"We'll see. I've decided that, at least for now, I'm going to work my way through the menu. So, tell me, what is a *café chorreado*?"

"It's a traditional Costa Rican coffee. In America, you'd call it a pour over. We brought our *chorreador* back from the farm that grows our beans. Jackson even designed and fabricated a filter for it. Didn't figure the health department would look too kindly on us using a sock in it like they did down there."

"No, probably not." I grin.

"It's the inspiration for this place, though—a wooden stand with a sock."

"I'll go with that, then. Maybe it'll inspire me, too."

"You can have it traditional style, which is one pour through, or robust. That's two pours and not for the faint of heart."

"I'll go traditional today and work my way up to the robust."

"I'll bring it over to you, same as yesterday . . . Wait, you still haven't told me your name."

"No, you're right. I haven't." I turn and go over to the same seat as yesterday.

They're both behind the bar preparing my order, but there's been a change. Jamie's smile is not as bright. I feel bad about blowing him off. For about a second. Jackson has a smug smirk. I suspect it's because of my encounter with Jamie; he probably enjoys seeing his buddy get shot down.

I pull out my journal to start on my "homework assignment" from the doctor from my appointment last week. I'm supposed to make a list of things I'd like to have in my life after I'm released, and it's been driving me nuts. Honestly, I'm having trouble picturing my life after Hope House, not sure what it should look like because I don't think I can go back to everything as it was. Or that I even should. Something about that life wasn't working if my depression got bad enough for me to slit my wrist.

But how do you picture a life you've never had before?

"Getting your daydreaming out of the way before your coffee today?" Jackson asks with unexpected joviality.

"I must have learned my lesson. Don't want my drink falling below your optimal temp. You know what you're talking about."

The compliment lifts the right side of his mouth in a half smile. His espresso-brown eyes sparkle. "Thanks."

"It's really my pleasure. I've been on nothing but instant coffee for three weeks, and hospital coffee before that. You can't imagine what a treat this is."

"Oh, man," he laughs. "I'm glad I could be of service. Come on, try today's drink. We don't get a lot of orders for it since not many folks know what it is. But it's definitely the one closest to my heart. I'd like to know what you think."

For the first time since he walked over, I look down at my drink. The layout is much the same as yesterday—sugar cubes, steamed milk, a cloth napkin, silver tongs, and a spoon. The liquid in my cup is not as syrupy thick as the espresso, but it's nearly midnight black. The aroma is twice as intoxicating, lighter in texture than yesterday's espresso but simultaneously darker somehow. I hold the cup under my nose and breathe deep, then take the fist sip, letting the coffee touch all of my taste buds before I swallow. It overwhelms my senses. I read somewhere that coffee has one of the most complex mixtures of flavor compounds in nature, and right now I believe it. There's sour and sweet and bitter and, I think, salty. My mind scrambles to hold on to any one flavor, but it's spinning.

"Whoa," I say. It's all I can manage.

"Yeah?" Jackson asks.

"Yeah." I look back up at him. He's grinning when he turns around and walks back to the bar.

I'm halfway through the cup before I turn my attention back to the blank journal page. The Coffee Shop has done the trick again; inspiration hits and I'm finally able to start the list.

1. Baking new desserts
2. Good, calm place to hang out and get new ideas
3. New apartment
4. Friends

The shop's door is thrown wide, and a woman walks in. Her presence is magnetic, demanding the room's attention. She looks like a Vargas pinup girl covered with tattoos. "How's it going, boys?"

"Hey, Fiona," they answer in unison.

She walks behind the counter and takes a spot behind the register. "Anything new I need to know about?"

"We got new beans yesterday," Jamie answers. "Best crop yet. I'm sure Jackson'll be happy to share with you."

"Sweet. I could use some. I was at the shop until eleven and then the band played a set. We didn't go on until midnight. I'm surprised I didn't see you last night, Jamie."

"Nope." He shakes his head. "I'm saving my party for the weekends, trying to be a grown-up. I was sick of Jackson riding my ass all the time for being hungover."

Jackson lifts an eyebrow at him but says nothing, turns, and walks into the back.

"You missed it, man. It was a killer set. Come out next Sunday."

"Maybe. We'll see." He's placating her. I recognize the tone of voice and lack of eye contact. "Oh, check it out, Fi. We have a potential new regular." Jamie tilts his head in my direction.

I whip my head around and look down at my journal. I can't take looking at them while they're talking about me or get caught eavesdropping.

"The girl over there in the far booth. This is her second day in a row."

"Yeah, so is she here for the merchandise or as a member of your admiration society?"

"The merchandise. She's immune to my charms so far. Won't even tell me her name."

"Really? Those of us with a Jamie immunity are a rare breed."

"Ha. Anyway, I gotta finish with the books. Our silent partner's coming in soon." He makes quote marks with his hands when he says "silent." "You got the counter?"

"Aw, fuck. He's coming today? You know he hates me."

"Don't think that makes you special. He hates everyone."

"True."

Jamie goes through the same door Jackson did a minute ago.

Fiona starts wiping down the bar, then walks toward my booth. "Hey, I'm Fiona." She extends a hand.

I'm put off by her forwardness but play along. I just wrote that I want friends, right? "Kyle." I shake her hand.

"So, what brought you to The Coffee Shop, if not your membership in the Jamie Admiration Society? There's also a group of weirdos who come in to get Jackson to be rude to them. You're not one of those, are you?"

"What? No. I needed a decent cup of coffee and live across the street right now."

"The coffee's really good, right?"

"*Amazing.*" Without thinking, I push up my sleeves to my elbows.

Fiona's eyes focus on my scars for a second, though she tries to hide it.

I scramble to pull my sleeves back down and look at the floor.

"I'll let you get back to what you were working on. You okay?"

I nod. "Uh, yeah. I'm good."

She moves to the next booth and the next, wiping down the tables.

I go back to my list. I contemplate adding "get a new job" to the list but can't bring myself to write it down. That step feels too hugely upending. I know that Booth wanted more than this, but I really can't think of anything else. There's nothing to change when there's nothing there. My life is . . . disturbingly empty. I take a few more sips of my coffee, then gulp down the last bit. I'm putting the journal back into my bag when the door opens again.

"Hello, Mr. Turner," Fiona says.

I pull my bag over my head and across my body and turn.

The man is surveying the shop with disdain. I don't know that I'd ever actually seen someone look down their nose at something until now. "Ms. Suarez."

Fiona stops wiping. "Yes, sir?"

"Get behind the counter."

"Excuse me?"

"Get behind the counter and stay there."

"I'm just—"

"I can see what you are doing and I don't care. Get back behind the bar."

Fiona is standing there staring at him, her mouth slightly agape. Just as she moves, I assume to obey his orders, Jackson comes out of the back.

"What's going on out here?" Angry face is back.

Fiona opens and closes her mouth, but no sound comes out.

I want to step in and defend her, but apparently I'm just as frozen and soundless.

"Just setting expectations, son." Mr. Turner smirks.

Jackson turns his head and looks at Fiona. "It's okay. Keep doing what you were doing. I trust you."

Not knowing anything about these people, I feel the million unsaid words and feelings behind the sentences.

Fiona nods, then scurries to my table, the farthest from Mr. Turner. She rolls her eyes at me, then asks, "May I clear your table, ma'am?"

I nod, still soundless, and wrap my fists around the strap of my bag. I've got it in a death grip.

"Please come see us again," she says, both to appease the elder Turner and, just as obviously, asking me to forgive the confrontation I witnessed.

I nod again and walk to the door. Mr. Turner inclines his head at me as I pass, and I find myself running back across the street to Hope House for my appointment with Dr. Booth.

It's not until I get back to my room that I realize I never did find out what they thought about my cakes.

CHAPTER FIVE

I make it to Booth's office with a minute to spare and wait outside the closed door for my appointment. My Coffee Shop visit was stressful but exciting, and I'm bouncing on the balls of my feet with pent-up energy.

Right on schedule, Booth says, "Kyle, you may come in." He's behind his ginormous desk, my file open in front of him.

"Morning, Dr. Booth."

"Good morning, Kyle. How are you feeling today?"

"Good." I pause, realizing that single word doesn't do my mood justice. "Actually, I think the best I've felt in a while."

"Well, that's quite the dramatic change from yesterday." He doesn't look up from the folder. "What brought on the improvement?"

"I'm sure you know that I used my off-site privilege for the first time. It's helped, getting out." My voice is too high and fast. My toe taps on the beige carpet. I'm being too . . . much.

"Hm. So, what did you do that was so . . . helpful?"

"I went across the street and got a cup of coffee. I went again today."

He's studying me.

I need to dial back my excitement a little. Or maybe a lot. I certainly can't tell Dr. Booth about my desserts for The Coffee Shop. He'll remind me how harmful it can be to get my hopes up. How it will be a setback to my recovery if things don't work out as they have in my head. He's already skeptical about my good mood—I can see it in the way he's eyeing me—so I have to cool it for my own benefit.

"I guess I'm not used to the caffeine," I say quickly, trying to explain the jitters. "I haven't really been drinking the instant coffee here because . . . well, it's terrible. And now I'm drinking espresso and . . ."

His eyes are moving over me, looking for anything sketchy or suspicious, clues of illicit, illegal, or just plain frowned-upon behavior. There's a furrow between his brows. It looks like bad news; I brace myself.

"Is there anything else about your excursion you'd like to share, Kyle?"

"Anything else? No, not really. I talked to one of the guys who works there about restaurant stuff."

"And what else happened since we spoke? Nancy reported that your sleep pattern was better last night. I applaud you for following my direction. Maintaining the prescribed sleep schedule is, as you know, beneficial. Overexposure to darkness is detrimental to a patient with your condition."

"Yes, sir. I slept well last night. Thank you for your recommendation." The urge to grit my teeth is overwhelming.

I get that smug look from him, the one he gets when a patient pays him a compliment. He's easy to play. What I wouldn't give to be a fly on the wall during one of Eddie's sessions with him. Eddie would play this guy like a fiddle for the full forty-five minutes and love every second of it. With all his omniscience, does Booth actually know anything about Eddie from their one-on-one encounters?

"I'm pleased your cup of coffee has had such a restorative effect. So, tell me, Kyle, have you completed your homework assignment?"

"That's what I've been working on across the street, actually. I wanted to put some time into it," I lie. He doesn't need to know that I spent about five minutes on his list.

"We need to go through and discuss each item. Please read it."

"Sure. The first thing is that I'd like to make new desserts."

"That's an excellent beginning, and a perfect excuse to bring up another issue I would like to talk about during our time today."

"Okay . . ."

"Please continue. What is the next item?"

"Do you want to talk about the issue, or . . . ?"

"That can wait until the end, Kyle. Continue."

"Find a place to hang out and get new ideas."

He nods but stays silent.

I keep going: "A new apartment."

"Excellent. That's three. Continue."

"Find some new friends. People outside of work. That's . . . those are all of the things."

"Good. Your goals are reasonable and we will work toward them. This is a perfect place to pause and discuss." He assumes the Caring Pose. "I spoke with your employer earlier this morning."

"With Rebeca?" I scoot forward in my seat. I miss her. She's not just my boss but the closest thing I have to a friend outside of

Hope House, unless you count Stewart, the handsy drunk at the bar down the street from the bakery.

"Yes." He nods. "She called to ask how you are, and when you might be back at work."

"And?" The one thing that's driven me nuts about being stuck in Hope House is not knowing when I might get out, so I really can't wait for his answer.

"I told her I had no time frame at this point in your recovery, and that it would be in her best interests to fill the opening."

"*What?*" Hot-blooded panic courses through me. "With somebody else? Temporarily, right?"

"I'm afraid not. I will be in charge of securing any post-release employment for you. You can rely on me to find the most suitable position."

"But—"

He holds up a hand to silence me. "Trust me, Kyle. I have your best interests at heart."

I ball my hands into fists, cutting into my palm, and fight the urge to slam them on his desk. I want to scream at him. Instead, I cry.

He scoots the box of tissue on his desk closer to me and looks at my chart. "Kyle, your life needs to be different when you leave here. In order to prevent any future depressive events, you need to institute changes. It is my job to put those changes in place for you."

"And not ask me first?"

"I don't need your permission, Miss Davies. I am responsible for your care." He checks his watch. "And our time is up. We will have to resume this next week."

He pauses, leaving room for me to speak, but I stay silent.

"You may go now."

I stand and run into the hall and upstairs. I stomp into my room, slam the door, and throw myself onto the bed. It feels like I'm throwing a temper tantrum, but honestly, that's what my mind wants to do right now, so why the hell not? A minute later, Joey knocks timidly.

"Not now, Joey. Give me a little while. I'll explain later."

He raps the doorframe to signal his okay. I listen to him walk back to his room and wait for his door to close before I let myself sob. Lori makes two wellness checks, then I feel a hand on my back.

"Are you okay, dear? You saw the doctor this morning, right? I'm going to assume this is his doing. Or did something go wrong while you were out?" It's Mary. Lori must have fetched her. Mary's in her comfort zone when she goes into "mom mode" and gets to take care of us. She hands me one of the tissues from her pocket.

"No, I'm not okay. And, yes, it was Booth." I use Mary's tissue to blow my nose, then squeeze it into a ball in my fist. "Of course it's him. I've never had anyone push my buttons like that."

"He does tend to use a heavy hand. Do you want to tell me what happened to get you so upset?"

"I'd say heavy hand is an understatement with the shit he just laid on me. Rebeca, my boss at the bakery, called to ask how I'm doing. He told her not to anticipate my return anytime soon. Told her to replace me, since he would be recommending new employment for me anyway, and he thinks returning to that environment could be detrimental to my recovery. Just told her all of this without even talking to me about it, assuming he's right."

I can feel Mary hesitating. "Are you sure it's not the right decision to make, though?" she asks delicately. "To go work somewhere else when you leave?"

"It might be. I don't know. It's not about that, Mary, it's that he didn't let me make my own decision. And *he* told Rebeca, instead of letting me do it. I would have explained it to her so she doesn't feel guilty. So she'd know that her bakery didn't have anything to do with me trying to kill myself. How can he tell me to be accountable for my decisions and then not let me make them?" I sigh in a great, wracking sob. "The hardest part about the whole thing is that he's right. It is the best decision for me, and it's gonna hurt like a son of a bitch to tell that man he's right."

Mary chuckles. "Ego is not a problem for the good doctor. Maybe you can figure out another way to approach it? A way to show that you made the decision and not him."

"Maybe." I dab my eyes dry with the tissue. "Thanks for listening, Mary."

"Anytime, dear. Anytime. So, what's the plan for dinner this evening?" she asks, clearly changing the subject to distract me.

"Chili and cornbread muffins. If I want the chili to be any good, I need to get down there. It's better the longer it cooks."

"Not too spicy, I hope. Chili peppers and I agree with each other less and less the older I get."

I laugh. "No, not too spicy. I added a bottle of hot sauce to the grocery list this week for Eddie. He's gonna be the one who likes it so hot the capsaicin numbs his taste buds."

"Well, of course he is. That man can't do anything by measures. I'll be there at the usual time to help."

Once I've calmed down and the tears have stopped, I head downstairs.

* * *

I had no idea that cornbread would turn into the best tool yet for distracting Eddie. He doesn't pick on Joey tonight, but me, because I put sugar in the cornbread. And corn.

"K, everybody knows you don't put sugar in cornbread. Or chunks of corn. Cornbread is the food of the poor man. This is rich folk cornbread. This is some trippy shit, a baker that don't know how to make cornbread."

"Eddie, I know how to make cornbread. This is just a different kind of cornbread."

"Like I said, cornbread for rich fuckers. Next time just give me some crackers if you can't make real cornbread. My granny would roll over in her grave if she knew I ate sweet cornbread. Also, it ain't cornbread unless you make it in a skillet. A cast-iron one."

"I *do* know that, but, Eddie, there isn't a cast-iron skillet in the kitchen here, and muffins are easier to serve. The staff here wouldn't like me bringing a smoking hot pan straight from the oven to the table."

"I call it bullshit, K. Now pass me that hot sauce. I'm gonna finish this shit so I can get to watching TV and call my old lady."

I was going to call Rebeca, but that can't happen if Eddie's on the phone with his "old lady." Their conversations are never brief. In fact, they're so loud and vulgar that security usually has to head him off before he turns violent. On my second night here, Eddie was sedated and restrained, the aftermath of a phone call. He punched a hole in the drywall and threw one of the lamps in the living room.

I debate going to the security office but don't want to have this conversation in front of the staff; I don't want to bad-mouth the great doctor and have it get back to him. That's a guaranteed loss of privileges. Possibly loss of off-site, too. Losing my chance to go across the street isn't an option. It's the only thing making me feel better right now. I head up to my room to go to sleep.

* * *

It was a busy day. My hair was dusted with flour and the kitchen was swarming because I was overbooked and behind schedule. Outside there was an epic storm—the wind rattled the back door to the kitchen, the raindrops pelted the metal door. I was boxing a birthday cake with another cake in the oven. As I carried the first cake to the customer, the lights flickered once, twice. I said a silent prayer, took two more steps. The lights went out. The three customers in the bakery and Rebeca pulled out their phones for light. The customers put on jackets, opened umbrellas, gathered their purchases, hustled out into the storm.

"Rebeca, the cakes are in the oven! What am I going to do? She's coming at six to pick it up!"

"Nothing you can do. We have to hope they get the lights back on. If they don't, we'll figure it out. We can assemble something from the cupcakes in the case."

"She doesn't want cupcakes, Rebeca. She wants this gigantic cake I promised her. She's gonna be fucking pissed."

The father came to pick up the cake. He paced the store, on the phone with the mother. I heard shrieking through the phone. I hid in the back, in the darkness, letting Rebeca take the abuse. I snuck out the back door.

* * *

The next morning at The Coffee Shop, Jackson and Jamie are tense, and I'm not in the mood to make happy conversation. Yesterday's session with Booth put me in a funk and the dream added to my unease. I brought them cinnamon rolls, using the treat as an extra motivation to get myself out the house, but now that I'm here I can't bring myself to hand Jamie the bag.

Jackson is cold, stone-faced, and terrifying. He doesn't speak.

"Welcome back," Jamie says, but his tone is flat, turned down.

"Hey," I whisper. "I'll have a cappuccino." I hand him my ten and don't wait for change before going over to my booth.

I focus on the outside today—the traffic and clouds sweeping by. It looks like rain. Or maybe snow. The gray sky pales the world, dimming the vibrancy of the street.

The chink of my order hitting the table turns my head.

"Enjoy." Jackson's brought my drink. As soon as everything is in place, he walks back behind the counter.

The store is quiet. My table is the only one occupied. The guys don't talk to each other, and the tension between them is palpable.

On my way out, I see one of their vintage saucers on the back counter with one of my chocolate cakes in the middle. There are utensils on the plate. It was either eaten continental style—a knife in the left hand, fork in the right—or it was dissected. Both options make me want to smile, but smiling feels wrong. The fastidious consumption of my tiny cake is Jackson's doing, I know it. I wonder if Jamie convinced him, or his father bullied him into trying one, but run out the door before I can think too hard about it.

CHAPTER SIX

On Sunday morning, I make biscuits to go with our eggs and bacon. Joey doesn't come down. He's getting worse, and I'm worried about him. I know Booth is pushing harder and harder for the aversion therapy since Nancy has asked about my willingness to participate, twice in the past two days. Joey's mom was crying when she left two days ago, and he's only come out of his room for dinner once since then.

After breakfast, I have a meeting with Booth. I've never seen him here on a weekend, which has my anxiety ramped up. Two unscheduled sessions in one week can't be a good thing. I knock on his door.

"Come in."

I have to stifle a snort of laughter as soon as I see him. Booth's work clothes are pompous at best, but his casual clothes are ridiculous—lavender polo shirt with a white sweater tied around his shoulders. He looks like the preppy guy's dad in an eighties movie.

"Thank you for coming, Kyle."

I didn't know it was optional but keep the snark inside and say, "Sure."

He leans back in his chair, a file open on his lap. It's not mine: it's thicker, more tattered. "I asked you here this morning to discuss Joey."

I nod. The mention of Joey brings a lump to my throat. I couldn't speak if I tried.

"Nancy confirmed your willingness to participate in aversion therapy."

It's not a question, but I nod again.

"I'd like to begin next week."

I swallow. "Is Joey okay with that? He told me he didn't want to do it."

Booth sits up like I surprised him and has to catch Joey's file before it slides onto the floor. "He told you? Has he spoken to you, Kyle?"

"No." I shake my head. "Sorry. He wrote it down. He hasn't said anything out loud in a couple of weeks."

"How did he write it down? His pens were confiscated," he says, his voice a little louder than before.

I look down at my lap. "I let him use one of mine while he was in the kitchen with me last week." To keep from making it any worse for myself, I add, "But he gave it back before he left. I didn't let him keep it." I would have if he'd asked, though.

"I plan to begin Joey's new therapy next week."

"Are you sure? I don't think he's ready." I push to the edge of my seat and put my hands on the edge of his desk.

"Yes, Miss Davies, I am quite sure." Booth looks over the top of his glasses in warning, his eyebrows drawn together.

I gulp and push away from his desk. Somehow, in the past few days, I managed to forget how to speak to Booth, how to massage his ego. "Sorry," I say into my lap. I close my eyes and breathe.

"I will require your participation, for at least the first session."

I knew Booth would probably ask me to do it, but I'm still surprised. "Joey said he didn't want me to do it, Dr. Booth. When we talked about it the other day, he got *really* upset."

"This is the most prudent course of action," Booth says sharply. His point is taken: he doesn't need to explain anything to the likes of me. Then, briefly, he softens. Or more melts, like margarine that's been left out on the counter. "We are all trying to help him, Miss Davies."

And so I nod, although his unexpected reassurance hits me like a gut punch. For some reason, even though I don't always trust Booth's treatment for me, I'm pretty sure he's actually doing what he thinks is best. "What will I need to do?"

"As we move through the session, Joey will be doing most of the work."

"Okay."

"I have one concern."

I raise my eyebrows at him and bite my tongue to keep from asking him how he only has *one* concern.

"I am thrilled with your progress this week. It has been impressive. But Joey's treatment will be difficult."

"I'll be okay."

"Kyle, how long have you shown symptoms of depression?"

I scratch at my neck, suddenly tight. "I don't know. Since I was eleven or twelve."

"And you never sought treatment before your suicide attempt?"

My hands claw at my thighs, looking for a loose thread or a hole in my jeans, anything to occupy them. "No," I choke out. I hate talking about my inaction, my denial. I was always sadder than everyone else and had good reasons—abandoned by my mom, no dad. I always thought I was a loner because I had to be, not because of something wrong with me. Turns out I was wrong, though I'm not comfortable admitting it yet.

"Why?"

I shrug. "I don't know. I guess I didn't realize I was that much worse than anybody else."

"Hm." He places Joey's file on the desk and picks up a fountain pen, clicking the cap off and on. "I need to know that I can trust you, Kyle. That you'll ask for help if it gets to be too much."

"I will," I tell him in my sincerest voice, even if I don't entirely mean it. I haven't rewired that part of my brain yet, the one that lets me ask for help. Once I leave Hope House, I'll be back to having no one to ask.

"The nurses and I will discuss your progress again next week. If we find it satisfactory, then we will move forward with the plan for Joey."

"Okay." I exhale, not realizing I'd been mostly holding my breath since Booth brought up my depression.

"See you Tuesday at our group therapy. Good luck."

I smirk at him, walk into the hallway, and wonder why he's wishing me luck. He's still clicking his pen cap as I walk into the kitchen to make cookies.

* * *

Two and a half hours later and I'm walking toward the security office with a dozen *torticas*, these Cuban sugar cookies. Each cookie has a little thumbprint of *cajeta* in the middle, and they're almost too adorable to eat. I'm not entirely sure what I'm going to do with them—if I'll leave them on Jackson's doorstep or chicken out and keep them like I did with the cinnamon rolls.

"I'm running to the grocery store, getting stuff for more desserts. Shouldn't be long," I tell the security guard. He's one of the weekenders; I don't know his name.

"Okay. Sign in when you get back." He doesn't look up.

I'm out of the building and headed to the gourmet store. It's funny that a little more than a week ago, I was scared to the point of panic over leaving Hope House and now can't get out of there fast enough. I don't need my breathing technique anymore—just out the door.

Two pounds of hazelnuts and twenty dollars later, I'm almost back to the house when I spot Jackson on the sidewalk, waiting to cross Division.

"Jack—" I start to call out. I stop myself before I go too far. I've never talked to him about anything other than his coffee, and he's never seemed all too keen on talking to me. He probably doesn't want to talk to a customer on his day off. I hate it when people from the bakery try to talk to me at the grocery store.

His expression morphs from confused to angry and most of the way back to confused again when he sees me frozen on the sidewalk ten feet away. "Oh, hey, Kyle. It is Kyle, right?"

I nod.

"What are you doing here? You know the shop's closed, right?"

"I know. Sorry to disturb you," I stutter. "I live right here, across the street from the shop, and just wanted to say hello."

I haven't stood this close to him before, and it's overwhelming. He's at least a half foot taller than me, enough that he feels towering with my anxiety kicking in. He's not in his usual jeans and button-down shirt, but what are probably workout clothes. I take a deep breath, a covert effort to calm myself, but it doesn't help; my sense of smell does a happy dance at the combination of coffee and san-dalwood coming off him. Does he sweat coffee?

"No, you're not disturbing me." His expression softens. "I'm just heading home from the park. What have you been up to today since there's no coffee?"

"Just ran to the store." I hold up the bag of hazelnuts. "Had to get some last-minute supplies for dinner for my housemates."

"Do you cook for your roommates often?"

"I'm living at Hope House right now and have kitchen duty, so I cook all the meals for the residents." I look at my shoes but peek up through my hair to check his reaction.

"Sorry. I didn't know." Jackson shoves his hands into his pock-ets, looking sheepish. His reaction tells me he knows what Hope House is.

"Nothing to be sorry about."

"So, is it okay living there?"

"Yes and no. Two of the residents are great and one isn't. Same with the staff. Same as everywhere." I shrug. "What park did you go to?"

"Humboldt. I like to sit by the boathouse, enjoy the quiet. Feel like I'm out of the city for a minute."

"Why don't you go to the beach at Lake Michigan instead? If you're looking across, you can't see anything but water. The lake at Humboldt's tiny. There's city on all sides."

Jackson shrugs. "There's something about the boathouse early in the morning. I've been there all day. For the first hour and a half, there was this layer of fog sitting on the water. It was so still and quiet."

"Sounds lovely. Quiet's hard to find sometimes." Grinning, I look up at him.

"It is." He shuffles his feet, fidgeting. Our topic is running out of steam, but even this smallest of small talk is nice. It makes me feel normal. I'm so used to everything at Hope House, which is . . . well, decidedly not.

"I need to get going. Gotta get dinner done on time, or the not-so-okay housemate will get even more not-okay. I just wanted to say hello. See you tomorrow."

"I'm glad you did. I don't want to overstep, but if you need anything . . ." He trails off.

"No, I'm okay. Just let me be the quiet girl who comes into the shop every day. That's what I need right now." I look straight into those espresso-brown eyes, pleading. The confusion lingers there, but also maybe happiness, maybe worry. Most important, though, I don't see pity.

"Of course. Just know I'm right across the street."

"Okay, thanks."

Finally, just before I turn away, he gives me a smile in return. It's the first full smile I've seen from him, and I want more. "It was good to see you, Kyle."

I've become giddy. I turn to walk away, and then stop. "Hey, Jackson?"

He's still facing me. "Yeah?"

I dig in my bag. "I actually made some cookies this morning. Want some?" I shove the parcel in his direction.

"Um. Sure." He's surprised by my offer, like he doesn't know what to do with the gift.

"Enjoy." I trot into the house, run upstairs, and throw myself onto the bed. I can't believe I had the nerve to give him the cookies. Now I wonder if I just made things better or worse.

* * *

I finish dinner with five minutes to spare, and I'm pouring milk when Mary comes in. "You sure are on top of it this evening. Anything to thank for your acceleration today? Joey, perhaps?"

"No, I haven't seen him," I answer, frowning. The constant stream of thoughts about my conversation with Jackson is suddenly diverted. I hadn't thought about Joey or Booth since coming back inside. "I can give most of the credit to a successful cookie baking venture. Would you like a sample before dinner?"

"I'll never turn down a cookie. They're my weakness. Well, one of them anyway." Mary's eyebrows draw together at the thought and her voice turns sad, but she smiles when she eats a tiny cookie in one bite. As soon as she can manage she says, "These are delicious."

Just then, Eddie's heavy footfalls echo down the hall.

"Let's get this party started. Do you know if Joey's coming down for dinner?" I ask Mary.

"I haven't heard anything. Maybe he'll come down if he smelled these cookies baking." Mary carries the cups into the dining room but stops on a dime to keep from getting run over by Eddie. "Why such a hurry, Edward?"

Sue, the on-duty nurse, hustles in behind him. "Eddie, you need to stop and answer my question. Don't make me get security."

I've never actually seen Eddie worked up like this before with a member of the staff. Usually his outbursts toward the staff happen in his room, not out in the open like this. He's red-faced, and I can see his pulse in the vein on his neck. Spit flies as he yells. Mary and I stand in shock, our backs pressed to the wall. It's one thing to hear it from down the hall and quite another to be in the room with his outburst; it's scary.

"Why not, Sue? It's not like those short-termers that come in here one Sunday night a month are gonna do shit to me. They know better than to fuck with me, 'cause I ain't afraid of 'em. So, yeah, Sue, get security. I ain't afraid of you either, and I sure as shit ain't answering your fucking question."

"Kyle, please go to security and fetch the officer on duty."

"Yeah, sure, Sue." I scurry out the door, looking over my shoulder at Mary as I go.

"I've been watching on the cameras. She need some help?" the guard asks as soon as I walk into the office. True to Eddie's word, it's a short-termer. I don't have any idea what his name is or why he's still sitting here. Maybe it's his first shift, and he doesn't know about Eddie yet.

"Uh, yeah. She sent me down here. You need to get Mary out of there," I tell him.

"Don't worry about it. I'll get this under control in no time," he says, heading down the hall. He hitches up his pants as he goes. It does not instill confidence.

On the monitors, I see Mary standing against the wall. Only ten feet from the dining room, I can still hear them. Shit, I could probably hear Eddie from across the street.

"Just calm down, buddy," the guard says. "Nothing's worth getting this excited over."

There's a noise over my shoulder, and I see Joey peeking around the corner. I'm about to give him an "it's not okay" signal when Eddie interrupts the guard's inept attempt at persuasion. Something crashes in the dining room.

"Fuck you, you fat fuck! Sue here thinks what I do is her business, and it's not! You part-timers only have to make sure we don't off ourselves or each other. That's it! *Finito!* If you think we need you for more than that, you are sadly mistaken, buddy!" Eddie spits out the last word with so much bitterness I flinch.

Joey runs back upstairs. A door closes, so he's probably retreated to the safety of his room.

I'm watching this whole thing unfold on the security camera. Mary hasn't moved, still holding the cups of milk in her hands. Eddie has, though. The crash must have been Eddie's chair, now lying on its side in the corner. Why aren't Sue or this guard getting Mary out of there? She doesn't deserve to be in Eddie's line of fire.

"Eddie, I need to know what you were doing in the hall. I might be part-time, but I'm not stupid. I know you were doing something, and I need to know what it was."

"Fuck you, too, Sue! I still ain't tellin' you shit! You ain't got the decency to believe me when I tell you it was nothin'." Eddie pulls a chair over, an improvised blockade between him and the staff.

"Eddie, why don't we go down to the office and have a little talk? I won't make you tell me anything you don't want to," the guard tries to say.

"I repeat: fuck you, fatso! I ain't going nowhere. I'm gonna sit here and eat my dinner, and then I'm gonna watch TV, same as every other night. You two can just fuck right off and leave me to dine in peace." Eddie grabs the blockade chair, sits down, and takes his place at the table. He puts a pile of spaghetti on his plate like nothing's happening.

"Eddie . . ." Sue warns.

The guard scoots a foot closer.

In response, Eddie jumps up, kicking the chair and sending it clattering and banging into the first. He turns to Mary and knocks the cups out of her hands, spraying her with milk. The guard moves closer now and pulls out what looks like a gun, pointing it at Eddie. Mary screams.

I want to run down the hall and help her, but my sense of self-preservation prevents it. I'm frozen in place.

"Man, don't make me use this. You need to calm down and come with us," the guard says.

Eddie's exits are blocked now—Sue and the guard on one side and Mary on the other. Taking the path of least resistance, Eddie throws an elbow into Mary's sternum, knocking her into the wall so hard, I see her head rebound off it. She falls to the ground, immediately followed by Eddie. I yelp and run to the dining room, my concern overriding my fear.

The scene when I get back to the dining room is surreal and scary. What looked like a gun on the monitor was a Taser, and Eddie went down because he got hit by the probes, one in each pectoral. I stifle a giggle because, well, Eddie was wrong: this security guard did do shit to him. My brain is all over the place with adrenaline.

Sue is crouching over Mary, checking vital signs.

"Is Mary okay? Can I help?" I ask.

"She'll be fine. I don't think Eddie pushed her hard enough to do any real damage. She panicked as soon as I sent you out of the room and hyperventilated when the Taser came out. I'm afraid this is my fault. I assumed Eddie would be less likely to be violent toward Mary than you."

"Well, you were wrong. We're all expendable when we get in his way. You know that now."

"I'll know when it happens again," Sue replies.

Eddie's been restrained by the guard and has gone ragdoll limp. The rest of the night will be quiet. I go to reheat the spaghetti I cooked.

Maybe Joey will let me in if I bring dinner.

CHAPTER SEVEN

With a plate of spaghetti and cookies in hand, I tap on Joey's door. He opens it with his head down, then blanches when he looks up and sees me. I'm sure he assumed it was one of the nurses.

"Hey, Joe," I say, ignoring the fact that he doesn't want to talk to me. "Can I come in? Eddie lost it during dinner. You heard part of it, I know. Sue is dealing with that, so I thought I'd bring your food up." I reach into my pocket. "Here. I brought a pen so you can write."

Joey snatches the pen, then nods, letting me know I can stay. He takes his dinner, carries it over to the windowsill, and digs in.

"Hungry?"

Nod.

"Did you get the lunch I made for you?"

Headshake.

"Man, I didn't know you hadn't eaten all day. I would have brought it to you."

Shrug.

"Well, eat up. It's not much, but it'll keep you from starving. I was running late; I went out this afternoon."

He pauses his shoveling to give me an okay sign, then tilts his head to the right—a questioning look to ask what I was doing.

"I went to the store to buy hazelnuts for more cookies, then bumped into Jackson from The Coffee Shop while I was out."

Joey grabs a sketchbook from his bedside table and writes. *i saw u talking 2 him.* He points to the sidewalk.

"Yeah?"

Nod. *and?*

"And nothing. I don't think he was happy to talk to me."

Headshake.

"What do you mean, no?"

He writes, then holds up the page for me to read. *he likes u. he smiled @ u. he NEVER smiles.*

"Dude, you are crazier than I thought. He doesn't like me, he just smiled because I smiled at him. I'd also just weirded him out by telling him where I live."

Headshake and scribbles. *he smiled because he likes u.*

"Okay, whatever. I'll let you keep thinking that. How do you even know he never smiles? Have you been stalking him?" I hope Joey doesn't point out I'm doing that exact thing, but maybe he doesn't know since most of my stalking happens while he's still asleep.

He blushes and shrugs.

"Oh, man! You have been?" I laugh at how adorable he is. Then it hits me, though, how much Joey probably wishes he could go to the shop with me instead of watching from his window. Maybe one day we can . . . I try changing the subject. "So, do you know what

Eddie was up to that had Sue asking questions? He flipped because he didn't want to answer her."

Nod.

"Spill, Joe."

it's no biggie. he was saying some stuff to me

"What kind of stuff?"

Shrug.

"Don't blow me off," I warn.

Headshake.

"This is bullshit! Don't let that asshole get into your head."

Joey holds a finger to his lips to quiet me.

Taking a deep breath to calm myself, I continue, "Joey, do not let Eddie fuck with you. Things are hard enough right now with Booth. You know we're starting aversion this week, right?"

Headshake. He starts to cry and jumps from the windowsill, his empty plate clattering on the linoleum, then throws the pen at me.

I stand and pick up the plate and fork, ignoring the mess of sauce and crumbs left behind. As soon as I'm upright, he shoves me toward the door.

"Joey, what are you doing?"

He shoves me again, and the crying's gotten worse. He's squeaking with the effort of breathing through the sobs. He throws a hand out and points at the door, then mouths the word "out."

I crash into Sue as soon as I reach the hallway. Joey slams the door behind me.

"Kyle, is everything okay?"

"It's fine," I reply and huff out a frustrated breath. "It's been a bad night. How is Mary? Is she okay?"

"She'll be fine. It was just a panic attack. She's sleeping now. Do you need anything? An Ativan?"

"No, I don't need any meds. I'm gonna clean up from dinner, then head to bed."

"Just let me know if you change your mind. I'll be even closer than usual tonight."

By the time the kitchen is clean, I've calmed down from Eddie's blowup. I'm still fuming about Joey, though. I knew he didn't want to do the aversion with me, but I didn't expect that kind of reaction. I need a plan, but I have no idea what it would be since Joey's definitely not talking to me anymore. I sit on my windowsill for a long time, trying to settle my thoughts so I can get some sleep.

*   *   *

I adopted a kitten, a mangy stray with the scrawniest little tail, when I was eight. I named her Muffin, because her fur was the color of the ones in the bakery window on my way to school. Mom "didn't need another damn mouth to feed," so Muffin had to live outside, but Mom also didn't care where I was, so I spent all of my time outside with her. I brought my milk carton home from my school lunch to feed her. I planned to steal some money from Mom's purse to buy real food for her, too. Muffin would curl up on my lap and purr.

And then Mom found out. "Get in the damn house. I told you to quit messing with that mangy cat."

Muffin wasn't there the next day. Or the next.

When I asked Mom, she said, "Forget about that thing. It won't be back."

*   *   *

I wake up crying. Everything I've ever loved has gone away.

* * *

Monday dawns clear and cold. The sun reflects off the windows on Division and rises over Goose Island. I press my cheek to the frigid glass for a full two hours, hoping Booth won't bother too much over the schedule deviation with all the chaos from yesterday.

Sue sticks her head inside the door. "Kyle, no need for a big breakfast this morning. Eddie and Mary are still asleep and should be for some time. It's just you and Joey this morning."

"Thanks, Sue. I'll probably just pull some toast and fruit for us, then. Joey loves strawberries. Maybe that'll get his day off to a good start. Give me fifteen minutes, and I'll have it ready to go. After that, I'm gonna head out for a while. I need to get out of here."

"Sounds like a good idea."

Thirty minutes later, I'm pushing through The Coffee Shop's oak door and freezing. It wasn't this cold when someone, probably Rebeca—because who else is there?—packed my bag. Whoever it was clearly had a list of rules: there are no drawstrings or shoelaces or scarves. The warmer temperatures also meant they didn't pack my coat.

I'm in line behind a woman in a Moncler parka that cost more money than my entire wardrobe. My teeth are chattering, and my exposed skin is covered with painful prickles from the cold. I hold my hands to my face, partly so I can blow on them to warm up, but also so I can cover the grin that's spreading because of Moncler's conversation at the counter.

"What do you mean I can't get an iced coffee? Every coffee place in the city has iced coffee."

"I'm sorry, miss, but we're not like every coffee place in the city. We're very traditional here." Jamie turns on the megawatt smile, hoping to woo her with charm and dimples.

"Well, surely you can make an exception?"

I muffle a snort because I'm pretty sure that last bit will bring Jackson into the conversation, and even though I can't see her, I'm sure she's fluttering her eyelashes at them.

Sure enough, Jackson pipes up, holding a hand up to silence Jamie.

"Actually, we can't. We get our coffee beans from a single farm in Costa Rica. They are all ground here, in one grinder, by one person. We have a number of options to choose from. I'm afraid none of them are iced, since we don't have an ice maker on the premises. Ice dilutes and reduces the quality of the coffee, and too much time and care go into the beans to intentionally degrade the brew."

"But I want an iced coffee," she whines.

Jackson continues, "We also have the front door. And if you even think about buying our coffee and dropping your own ice in, I will know."

I snort into my hands and hope she doesn't hear it. The handful of customers watch the exchange with amusement. I wonder if any of these people are the ones Fiona mentioned—the people who come here and try to get Jackson to yell at them, even though he didn't yell at this woman. As a matter of fact, he didn't even raise his voice.

Moncler stomps her foot and huffs but sees Jackson's fiery expression and decides to cut her losses. She uses the front door. Since I started coming to The Coffee Shop, I've seen this happen one other time but no loud voices or foot stomping by that customer.

"She doesn't know what she's missing. But then, she did spend two thousand dollars on that coat, so she probably doesn't care."

"Who spends two thousand dollars on a coat? That's ridiculous," Jamie says.

Jackson nods and adds, "My stepmom has one of those coats. I recognized the logo." His furrowed brow relaxes when he turns to me. "What are you trying today?"

"Dealer's choice? Make me your favorite." I hand Jamie a five-dollar bill.

"Sure," he replies, turning away and going to work. "Jamie will bring it to you."

I take my seat, looking across the street at Hope House. Joey's sitting in his window, and I wave. He doesn't return the gesture. The other bedroom windows are dark, and I wonder if Mary really is okay. I'll have to wait until she's awake to find out. The nurses aren't allowed to give me details.

"Here's your dealer's choice. No accessories today." Jamie sits a cup and saucer in front of me. There's no vintage silver, no cloth napkin.

"You gonna tell me what it is?"

"He didn't tell *me*." Jamie shrugs and tips his head toward the counter. "I hope you like it."

"I don't doubt that I'll like it no matter what it is. Thanks, Jamie."

I take my first sip and look up at Jackson, surprised. He's watching for my reaction. It's exactly the same flat white as I had on my first visit—not brought up to full temp, like it's been sitting on the table for a few minutes. There's a little sugar. I'm guessing it's one cube, the same as I added, and the same amount of milk poured in. Jackson nods at me, a twitch of his head, and goes into the back room.

I turn to the window, watching the traffic. How do I deal with Joey? What do I make of the drink Jackson just made for me? What do I need to do to get out of Hope House and move on with some kind of life? I sit for a while, my cup empty, trying to process everything that's happening.

When I scoot across the seat to leave, the dusty blue sweater Jackson was wearing when I got here is lying on the bench next to me. He's still in the back, so I look at Jamie, questioning. Where did it come from?

He waves his hand at me and mouths "take it," so I slip the sweater on, smelling the coffee that has seeped into its pores and its softness against my skin.

CHAPTER EIGHT

I make it to the Tuesday morning group five minutes before it's scheduled to start and grab my preferred seat: the one farthest from Dr. Booth. Bruce is here, leaning against the wall just inside the door with his arms crossed. Mary shuffles in a couple of minutes later, groggy.

"You okay, Mary? I've been worried about you."

She shakes her head. "Not my best. I've been having nightmares. Flashbacks to the night Bill was shot. I'm afraid I'm going to be looking at nights like this for a while. That Taser scared the daylights out of me."

"I knew it would as soon as I saw it on the camera. I wish Sue would've sent you to the office instead of me. That Taser wouldn't have bothered me a bit. She didn't think of that possibility, and she apologized for it."

"She apologized to me, too, when she came in after one of my terrors. It's not her fault. She's only here two nights a week. It would be silly to expect her to remember everything about us. And she couldn't have known it would come to that."

"I know. But I still wish it would have been different."

Joey and Dr. Booth come in together. Joey takes the seat to my right, leaving an empty chair between him and the doctor, and pulls his knees up to his chest. He gives Mary a sad grin before turning and scowling at me. Guess he's still mad, then. Dr. Booth sits, then shuffles a few papers together before sliding them back into the black leather portfolio on his lap. He scans the room over the top of his glasses to make sure we're all in attendance.

"We can begin, then. I'm sure Eddie will join us in a moment. You're all aware of how I feel about punctuality."

We nod in unison. *Don't be late* is oft repeated at Hope House.

"I would like to begin by asking everyone to name their favorite thing today."

Eddie barrels into the room and throws himself into the chair on the doctor's right, sending it skidding back a foot on the linoleum.

"Eddie, since you're late, I'll let you start us off. Your favorite thing today?"

"Cable TV," Eddie grunts.

Booth nods at Mary. "A letter from my sister that came this morning."

Booth's eyes move to me and he arches an eyebrow. I was going to say coffee, but change my mind at the last second, for whatever reason. I think I want to keep this one thing mine. "The window in my room."

I turn my head to look at Joey as soon as Booth moves his gaze.

Joey shakes his head emphatically; he's asking Booth to leave him alone, but it's never a good idea to not answer. This isn't good.

I shiver with anxiety and pull my hands into the sleeves of Jackson's sweater.

Booth is homed in now. "What is your favorite thing today, Joey? Surely there's something on your list. It doesn't have to be a good thing. It can be a painful or unhappy thing. You know there's no judgment here. Nothing will happen to you. We talked about it this morning. You agreed to participate."

Suddenly this group therapy session has become an aversion session. It's all kinds of fucked up to do this to Joey with all of us here. I turn to glare at Booth. I already don't like the guy, but this . . . I realize this makes me hate him. I curl my hands into fists inside the sweater's sleeves.

Joey gives another emphatic headshake.

"Joey, we're all waiting. You know, logically, that your speaking can't hurt us. Also, Mary and Kyle have both volunteered to be with you for this therapy. You have no more excuses. You need to answer my question, just like everyone else. I won't take no for an answer."

"Please, Dr. Booth. We don't need—" Mary starts, but stops when the doctor holds up a hand to silence her.

Joey's eyes well with tears and his fingernails dig into his forearms. I see four half-moons of blood form. His Converses are tapping a double bass on the edge of the seat.

"We're waiting," Booth pushes.

Joey's feet tap faster and louder. Mary sniffs, crying already. I'm looking back and forth between Joey and Booth, wanting to step in and help my friend. I'm afraid, though. I don't want to piss off Booth.

The pot reaches its boil and then, miraculously, boils over: Joey speaks; Mary and I gasp. "Dr. Booth, I really don't wanna talk today. I can't. I can't. I can't. Please. Please. Please." He's still shaking his head and stomping his feet.

I've got to try to help Joey. It's killing me watching him suffer. "Dr. Booth," I plead, crying now, too, "can you give him a minute? He really needs a minute."

Booth shakes his head and opens his mouth to respond but is overtaken by Eddie's near-shout. "Hey, Doc! I wanna talk about the shit my old lady pulled this week. I really gotta tell somebody about it, and who'm I gonna tell besides you fuckers?" He ignores Joey, Mary, and me falling apart on the other side of the circle. "Come on, lemme tell you what this bitch did. This is some real crazy shit, man. She had this whole shit-ton of coke she was supposed to offload . . ."

Eddie's manic-psychosis and coke-meth-twitchiness always take over in group.

Joey exhales a sigh, but he's clearly not okay. He starts sloppy crying and stutter-muttering under his breath.

I pull my fists farther into the sleeves of Jackson's sweater to stave off my anxiety, curling tighter into myself. To my left, Mary pulls a tissue from her cardigan pocket and starts making Kleenex confetti. She's sobbing. Booth sits forward in his seat, still focused on Joey. Eddie's rant is picking up momentum and increasing in volume, but Booth ignores him. I'm shaking so hard with fear and anger over what's going down that my teeth are chattering.

". . . and then the crazy bitch went and kicked in the door of his trailer. Stupid, right? I mean, you fuckers aren't even nuts enough to pull crazy shit like this. It's nuts. Bitch is crazy, right? She should be in here instead of me!"

Eddie shows no sign of slowing down, even as Joey's muttering amplifies. "I wasn't supposed to talk. Why did he make me talk? I wasn't supposed to talk. Why did he make me talk? I wasn't supposed to . . ."

". . . I mean, she had a knife, not a gun, and half the coke she was supposed to deliver . . ."

"Why? Why? Why?"

". . . dumb bitch wouldn't know her ass from her . . ."

There's a whoosh of air. Joey is out of his seat, and the empty chair between him and the doctor goes flying into the wall. The plastic knife that was on his breakfast tray is in his right hand. Dr. Booth rocks back in his chair, holding out his hands in defense.

"I wasn't supposed to talk!" Joey yells at the doctor, shaking the plastic knife at him. His face is bright red, wet with sweat and tears. "Why did you make me talk? Why did you make me talk? Why did you make me talk?"

"Joey, you don't want to do this. You don't want to go back to the hospital, do you?" Booth asks.

"You made me do this. You made me. You made me. I wasn't supposed to talk, and now you're all dead. I've killed you. I've killed you. I've killed you."

"You didn't kill us, Joey," Booth says. "Your mind can't kill us. You know that's not how it works."

Eddie's sitting next to the doctor with a huge, satisfied smirk on his face, like he's enjoying the show.

Joey jabs the knife in Booth's direction, then pulls it up to his own throat, pressing hard.

"Joey, don't do something you'll regret. It will be okay, Joey."

"Quit saying my name! It's too late!" He looks at me and blinks three times. "I killed you. I killed you. I killed you."

I mouth the word "no" and shake my head.

Bruce charges and tackles Joey, pinning him to the ground. Booth picks up the knife and puts it in his pocket. Then Bruce slings Joey over his shoulder like a sack of potatoes and carries him into the hall.

Joey's kicking the drywall and screaming, "You're all dead! I've killed you! I've killed you! I've killed you!"

Mary and I are staring at the doorway Joey just disappeared through, both sobbing.

Dr. Booth sighs, straightens his shirt, and says, "Eddie, you can finish your story now."

Mary and I turn back around to face the doctor, waiting for some acknowledgment of what happened, but his eyes are fixed squarely on Eddie and he's assumed the Caring Pose. Booth doesn't look at Mary or me for the rest of the session.

Numb and dumbstruck, I don't hear another word Eddie says. I don't hear what happened after his "old lady" kicked in the trailer door, bringing a knife to what I presume was a gunfight.

I don't hear the doors open and close down the hall as they take Joey back to the hospital.

CHAPTER NINE

As soon as Booth excuses us, I bolt to my room, slam the door, and wedge a note into the wellness check window that says "DO NOT ENTER!" The nurses don't have to obey my scribbled order, but they won't disregard it unless they have to. I can't remember the last time I was this angry. What the fuck was Booth thinking, pushing Joey like that? Now my friend is gone for who knows how long.

I climb onto the window seat and watch The Coffee Shop, tapping my toe on the sill. They don't have a set closing time. Jackson roasts beans each morning, and the store closes when they run out. I figure I've got an hour or two of sitting here before he comes out. He said "if you need anything" yesterday. It might have been polite conversation, but I intend to take him up on the offer. I do need something. I'm not sure what, but his is the only offer outside of this house currently available, and I can't be here anymore. Not right now. I pull myself almost all the way into his sweater—knees

74

up, arms in, chin tucked. I leave my eyes out so I can keep watch, but the rest of me soaks in the smell of coffee and sandalwood while I count the seconds.

Eighty-seven minutes later, Jamie flicks the door lock from the inside. I have ten minutes before Jamie leaves and another six before Jackson follows. I sign myself out, stand in the entryway, and wait. Thirteen minutes until he'll be on the sidewalk. True to pattern, Jamie leaves, walking west, and six minutes after that, Jackson's moving toward the door. I trip outside and weave between the cars on Division, not waiting for the light at the corner, and am at his back as he locks the shop. Now that I'm standing next to him, I'm scared witless.

Maybe this wasn't a good idea.

"Jackson," I whisper.

He turns around with that half-angry, half-surprised expression again, but he softens when he sees me. I didn't think about him not recognizing my sob-scratched voice, especially at whisper volume.

"Kyle? What are you doing here? Are you okay?" He scans me head to toe and back up again, looking for signs of injury. Before he can finish his assessment, I take a deep breath, throw myself at him, and wrap my arms around his waist.

Jackson stumbles back but manages to keep his balance. I've never been much of a hugger, and haven't let myself even think about the possibility of hugging anyone but Joey in longer than I can remember, but today has been a disaster. I'm pretty sure Jackson isn't thrilled since he's not returning the gesture, but he's also not pushing me away. I'll take what I can get.

"Clearly, you're not. But . . . isn't there someone else who could do a better job with this?"

"Maybe. But please let me do this. You said if I needed anything. Well, I need this. Just give me one minute. Okay?"

He doesn't reply. I feel the muscles in his back flex as he moves his arms, ghosting them around my torso. He's trying to find a position he finds acceptable, I think, but he's so uncomfortable. His chin whispers across the top of my head. He's just the right height to let his chin rest there, but that would require him to relax, and he's not doing that.

So I tell him to. "There is no wrong way to do this. Relax." Even though I'm anything but. "It doesn't matter where you put your arms or hands."

"This is why I know there's someone else better for this job. I'm screwing this up."

"Nope. No screw up. This is exactly what I need. Just hug me back."

His arms settle one by one, his hands sitting on my lower back. His chin finally rests on my head.

I sigh. "Don't move. This is perfect."

And it really is. It feels so nice to be held again, so . . . safe, to be taken care of in a way that's not calculating or medicinal. That's just human. I count to sixty, as promised. I figure he's counting, too, giving me the seconds I requested. No more, no less. At sixty-one, I loosen my grip and tiptoe back two steps. I can't look at him. I can't acknowledge how much he just gave me, how much I took. I turn away, looking at the sidewalk. "Thanks."

I start walking away.

"Woah, hold up. What's going on, Kyle? Why did you hug me? Did something happen?" he asks, jogging to catch up. "Will you stop and talk to me?"

"No." I shake my head. "I don't want to stop. I needed something, and a hug was the first thing I thought of."

We walk at a good clip for a few blocks; I'm too frustrated and angry to slow down. Jackson is quiet, but keeping pace with me.

Eventually, the quiet gets to be too much, so I say, "This morning I watched my best friend in the house lose his shit in the middle of group therapy. The doctor pushed him to it. Didn't listen when we asked him to stop. All he had to do was let it go, but he wouldn't. And they literally carried Joey back to the hospital kicking and screaming. This will set him back months, maybe years, all because the doctor wouldn't shut up."

"I wish there were something I could do to help," Jackson says. The words aren't unexpected, but there's a sincerity in his voice I find unexpectedly touching.

"You *are* helping."

At the crosswalk, I reach out and grab his left hand, wrap my fingers around his, and once again take in his confused expression. Jackson looks down at our hands and squeezes with a flex of his fingers, like he's testing something. The signal changes and we resume our walk, hands still clasped. I'm happy he doesn't let go. My brain is ping-ponging between anger and grief over Joey and gratitude for Jackson.

"Thanks again," I whisper as we go over the Chicago River.

"For what? Holding your hand?"

"Yep."

Squeezing, I pull us across the street right before we get to the second Goose Island bridge. At the midpoint of the river, I let go of Jackson's hand and stop. I stick my hands through the steel beams, leaning onto my forearms. He mirrors, leaning next to me, his hip brushing mine.

"I'm afraid we don't know all that much about each other," he begins, "but if we're going to be seen walking around town holding hands, that's something we'll have to change. I don't do things this . . ." His face scrunches up, as if he's searching for the right word. Finally, he finds it. "Willy-nilly."

I burst out laughing, and it feels incredible. "Willy-nilly? Seriously?"

"It's a technical term," Jackson tells me, his expression serious.

I laugh even harder.

"And even more proof that we don't know each other very well. I'm fond of using exact, technical terminology when describing things. It ensures precision."

I take a moment to collect myself.

"Indeed," I reply. "We do need to get to know each other better. I suspected there was a sense of humor buried underneath all that seriousness, but had no hard evidence until just now. Jackson, are you undercover funny?"

He barks a laugh at my question. "What exactly is 'undercover funny'?"

"You know, when someone is funny, but only in private situations. Publicly serious, secretly hilarious."

"I like that." He looks at me and smiles. "And you may be right. Now, tell me something about you. Where are you from?"

"Here in Chicago, born and raised. I've never been farther than the suburbs."

"Wow. Really? I'm from here, too, but can't imagine never having left. Is that a good thing? Never leaving?"

I shrug. "I'm not sure. I don't know any different. My mom left me to fend for myself as far back as I can remember and ditched me for good when I was ten."

"Your mom left when you were ten? That's awful. Where did you go when she left?"

"To live with my grandma."

"How was that?"

"Okay. She was old and not in the best of health. She died last year."

"I'm sorry." He looks at me with the same understanding expression as when I told him about Hope House. There's no pity in his gaze. "So, where's your mom now?"

"No idea. I haven't seen or heard from her since she left." I shrug. My mom's been absent for so long, I don't feel anything when I talk about her. My grandma, on the other hand, is a more tender subject. I can feel that sadness creeping up, so I change the subject. "You've obviously left Chicago. Where's your favorite place you've been?"

"Costa Rica, no question. It's where I found my coffee."

"Your coffee? What do you mean?"

"Our plantation. All of our beans come from Felix's family farm. Jamie and I are contributing to his legacy."

"How did that happen?"

"Jamie took me to Costa Rica on vacation, and we stumbled upon the farm. Felix gave us a tour, and I was just . . . enchanted. It was the most magical place. There's really no way to describe it, but my soul just felt this peace. So when Jamie came back to Chicago, I missed the flight back and stayed for two years. I lived on the land and learned everything Felix was willing to teach. When I finally came back, I convinced Jamie to open the shop with me."

He tells me about the rain forest, the mountains, the ocean, and the coffee. He talks, not pausing. It's exactly what I need—to stand here, looking at the water and skyscrapers, hearing about this fantastical place I can hardly imagine. I lean on the railing, shifting now and then so my hip brushes against his, and listen. We're in this one place long enough that the pinks and oranges of sunset bounce off the skyline.

The flashes of color bring me back to the now. I realize that I'm late getting back to Hope House. "Shit!"

Jackson jumps.

"I'm late. I have to get back. I'm going to be in so much trouble!"

"What? Back to your house? Do you want me to grab us a cab? It'll be faster."

"No, I don't have any money for a cab. I didn't bring my wallet." I start walking back toward Hope House. "I'm only allowed to be gone two hours a day. I have no idea how long I've been gone this afternoon, but if the sun is setting . . ."

"I can pay for the cab, Kyle," Jackson offers.

"I'd rather walk. I probably won't be allowed to go out after this, at least for a while. Overstaying my leave is a big deal."

"Can I help? Make a call? Let him know where you were?"

"I don't know that it would help. Probably not. I'm not sure the doctor would be swayed by the 'we lost track of time standing on a bridge' defense."

"I get that," Jackson says, "but I can be quite persuasive when necessary." He smiles his full smile that crinkles the corners of his eyes.

"I have no doubt that there's a good quantity of persuasiveness in you, Jackson. No doubt at all."

I stop halfway back to Hope House. This is crazy. Of course it's crazy. But, God, after everything that happened this morning . . . the idea of going back and lying in bed, alone, thinking of Joey . . . it sounds like hell. "I have an idea."

He stops and turns to face me. "Okay . . . ?"

"Just hear me out?" I raise my eyebrows.

He nods.

"So, I was thinking. If I'm already late, how much would it matter if I'm even later?"

"I don't know, Kyle. How much do *you* think it will matter?"

I shrug. "I'm honestly not sure. Booth will take away my off-site privileges, but I think he's going to do that anyway. I don't know how far I can push him, but I don't think a few hours is too much? Worst case, he sends me back to the hospital, says my behavior is harmful in some way."

Jackson nods and looks at the sidewalk, giving me the space to work through this on my own.

"So, here's my idea. You make that phone call, letting him know where I am, that I'm safe. Then, maybe we can go somewhere, have dinner or something . . ." I trail off, suddenly unsure about my now-not-so-brilliant idea.

He looks at me with an expression I find absolutely inscrutable. "I don't know."

"Look, I know this sounds like a horrible idea. But, also, I kind of think it's the most wonderful idea I've ever had. It's a chance to feel normal again, even if it's only for a couple of hours. Please, Jackson."

"Me calling Booth . . . are you sure that's a good idea? What if he asks about us? I don't know how to answer." His brows are drawn together, so serious and thoughtful.

I chew on my bottom lip. "I didn't think about that. I think you're safe telling him the truth: we're friends. You know, who indulge in some willy-nilly hand holding."

There's his smile again. This time, I beam back at him.

"Okay. I'll say yes for now, but if the doctor's not okay with any part of this, you go back to Hope House and accept whatever punishment he doles out."

I nod. "Agreed. Let's go. I'm hungry."

"Me, too," he says. "All I've had to eat today are some delicious cookies this weirdo made me."

I smile all the way to his apartment.

CHAPTER TEN

We get to his building and he leads me up the narrow staircase to his home above The Coffee Shop. It's both exactly what I expected and the complete opposite. It's a traditional loft, so there are no walls delineating the living room, kitchen, and bedroom. There are hardwood floors and one exposed brick wall; the plaster ones are brown, the color of tree bark. The kitchen has the same laboratory feel as the bar downstairs; stainless steel surfaces abound. The furniture is well-worn, and there are tidy stacks of books on the table and shelves.

And then we get to the part that's opposite my imaginings: the bedroom. The bed is a sensuous thing, a massive antique four-poster. I would need a running start to launch myself into it. There's a heap of fluffy pillows and a down comforter, all covered in deep rain-forest-green cotton.

"Here it is," Jackson says, waving an arm. "Make yourself at home. I'm going to call Hope House. You said your doctor's name is Booth, right?"

"Uh-huh."

I walk over to the couch and run my hand over the red velvet brocade pillow sitting at one end. I brush back and forth—with the nap, against the nap, with the nap. I study the bookshelf as his call goes through, reading the spines. There's a little bit of everything on the shelves, from architecture to zoology.

"Hello, sir. My name is Jackson Turner and I'd like to speak with Dr. Booth, please." He pauses for a response. "Yes, I'll hold. Thank you." He holds the phone away from his ear and whispers, "I should probably find out your last name. For the purposes of this phone call, you know."

"It's Davies."

He puts the phone back to his ear. "Oh, the doctor has left for the day?"

Of course Booth is already gone. Now my being late will piss him off even more. I'm sure he doesn't want to deal with Hope House when he's not there. The nervous knot in my gut twists at the thought.

"Could you contact him? I need to speak with him rather urgently. It's regarding the whereabouts of Miss Kyle Davies."

I roll my eyes. So formal.

"Yes, she's perfectly fine. In fact, she's been with me this afternoon. We went on a little excursion, and I'm afraid we lost track of time. I really need to speak with the doctor and ensure my dalliance won't affect Miss Davies's standing."

I walk over to the bed and knead the down blanket.

"Yes, I should be available for another hour or so. He can contact me at this number." He recites the digits and then, I assume, hangs up.

I have my back to him, unable to look. It's more vulnerable than I was expecting, hearing Jackson speak to someone from Hope House. Having these two areas of my life collide. I'm so focused on the feel of the down in my fists that I miss him walking up behind me until he rests a hand on my right shoulder.

I startle.

"Sorry, I didn't mean to frighten you. Are you okay?"

"Yeah. I'm fine. It's just been a long day."

"I know. I wish I could do something about your friend. It doesn't sound like a good situation."

"It's not. Though, honestly, the hospital may be the best place for him. His OCD was getting worse." I pull in a quavery breath. "He's just this young, sweet kid. The psych ward has to be a nightmare for him."

"I suspect I'm like most people and assume it's all very *One Flew Over the Cuckoo's Nest*."

I think about it before answering. Hope House actually isn't all that different from the movie version. Eddie is like McMurphy. Joey is the silent Chief; Nancy, our Nurse Ratched. "It's like that, but it isn't. That's definitely the fictional version of things. There are very different people with very different illnesses all trying to make it work."

"Can I ask why you're there? You don't have to tell me, but . . ."

His phone rings, sparing me.

"Ah, that'll be the good doctor. Let's see what he has to say." Jackson steps into the kitchen. I turn my focus back to fist-making.

"Hello? Yes, doctor. I'm so sorry to disturb your evening." Pause. "Yes, I understand that you're a busy man. I appreciate your getting back to me in a timely manner. I was calling to discuss

85

one of your patients, Miss Kyle Davies." Pause. "No, sir, nothing like that. I don't want to discuss her treatment but, rather, let you know that she has been in my company this afternoon. Is still in my company, actually." Pause. "Yes. I do understand that there are rules, but it is entirely my fault she has overstayed her time away from your facility this afternoon. I can assure you that I do not plan on making a habit of ignoring the regulations you have in place. I would, however, like to ensure that Miss Davies will not suffer any repercussions for my irresponsibility today." Pause. "Thank you for that, Dr. Booth. I have another favor to ask of you, a personal favor of sorts. I have a family function to attend this evening."

I freeze. Maybe he's making up an excuse that'll make sense to Booth. I hope so.

"I plan to have her back by midnight. I can escort her personally if it will offer any reassurance to you or your staff." Pause. "Yes." Pause. "Yes, sir. Thank you for your understanding." Pause. "I will be sure and mention you and your excellent facility to my father." Pause. "Yes." Pause.

I wonder what all the gaps in Jackson's conversation are about, all the pauses where Booth is talking. What's he saying about me? And how does he know who Jackson's father is? I knead the blanket harder.

"Yes. Thank you again for understanding." He must end the phone call, because he's standing behind me again. "You're in the clear until midnight. What would you like for dinner? I was thinking we could have something delivered. Chinese? Pizza?"

"Chinese would be awesome. I haven't gone this long without takeout my entire life."

He opens a drawer and hands me a menu. "Get anything you like. My treat."

I hand the menu back to him. "I'll eat pretty much anything. You can pick."

"You're sure?"

"Uh-huh." I nod.

He motions me to the couch while he orders, then joins me, sitting on the next cushion while we wait for the food.

"We're going to a family function this evening?" I finally ask, in a near-whisper.

Jackson looks at the ceiling and sighs. "Of sorts."

"What kind of function?" I draw out the words, not really wanting the answer I know is coming.

He grimaces and nods. "I'm so sorry. I completely forgot. Or maybe I just wanted to forget. I'm expected at my father's for dinner."

I stand. "Then I'll just go. You have dinner with your dad, and I'll head back home."

He stands and grabs my hand. "No. Please don't."

"Jackson, please don't take this the wrong way, but seeing as how we've just established ourselves as friends an hour ago, I don't think I'm ready for the whole 'meet the family' scene yet."

His face flushes pink, but I can't tell if it's out of embarrassment or anger. "It won't be like that." He lets go of my hand and holds his up. "I swear. I'll text him, let him know I'm going to miss dinner. I still need to go over after we eat, but it'll only take a few minutes. I just . . . it's like you needed your hug today. I need some support tonight, and I gave you that hug so now I figure you owe me. After that, we can go see Fiona. Her band is playing tonight."

"I don't know, Jackson."

He sighs. "Well, look, I can't make you go. But I've already ordered the takeout, so you might as well stay and eat."

I look up at him. There's a desperation in his expression, a fierce plea.

"Okay," I say. He sits back down, and I follow suit. "How did Dr. Booth know your father?"

He shrugs. "I'm not sure, but it's not surprising. Everyone seems to know my father."

I don't reply, hoping my silence will trigger some more information.

"I'm a little surprised he knew just from my name, though, especially since I keep my distance most of the time. I'm afraid I'm something of a disappointment to the Alderman."

I take a second to realize what he just told me. "Wait. Your father is an alderman? And how can he think you're a disappointment? You own your own business, you're supporting an entire Costa Rican family . . ."

"You're overestimating. I don't own the business. At least, not by myself. Jamie and my father are equal partners. Besides, I'm the son who couldn't follow in his great political footsteps. He might have dealt with my lack of political motivation if I'd stayed my course and completed my doctorate at Northwestern, but instead I dropped out to live in a Costa Rican hut for two years."

I smile at the last bit. "What made you do it? No offense, Jackson, but you don't really seem like a guy who does things on a whim."

"Not usually, no." He chuckles, dry as tinder. "Three years ago, things were going according to plan—a month away from my degree and already admitted to the graduate program, a fiancée, good friends. One month later, the fiancée went away with one of the good friends and my plan went a little topsy-turvy. I shut down.

"That's when Jamie staged an intervention and booked the Costa Rica trip. He said the change in scenery was necessary. To be honest, I didn't really have the willpower to fight him. I just . . . went along with it. Then we found the farm, and the rest is history."

"And you got your graduate degree in coffee instead?" The buzzer goes off, letting us know the food has arrived.

"Exactly how I prefer to think of it."

I'm beaming when he sets the Chinese food on his coffee table.

"Any issue with eating straight from the cartons?"

I shake my head and start unbagging the to-go containers. There are egg rolls, rice, kung pao beef, and Peking shrimp. I pick up an egg roll and take a bite, snapping into the crisp wrapper as steam billows out.

"Now that you've heard my sob story, you want to answer my questions? Tell me why you're at Hope House?" he asks.

It's all or nothing. Jackson just shared; fair is fair. I set my food down and pull up my shirt sleeve, revealing the three scars on my left forearm. They're ugly things, raised and bright pink. "Because I did this." I have to give it to him: he doesn't recoil, keeps a blank expression.

"Okay." He swallows and blinks. "Will you tell me why you did that?"

"I have depression. I've thought about doing this for as long as I can remember. This time I didn't talk myself out of it." A numbness washes over me. The scars seem like something that happened to me rather than something I did to myself.

"Why this time?"

I shrug. "Not sure. Had a bad day, drank too much, and there's a knife sitting on the counter next to the empty bottle of whiskey. There's nothing I can tell you that will put a positive spin on it. Or on me."

"How did you end up in the hospital?"

"Apparently I turned up my music too loud when I tried to kill myself, and my neighbor called the landlord on me. He found me after I didn't come to the door and he let himself in."

"How are you now? Better?"

"Yeah. I'm on meds when I wasn't before. When you're stable, the doctors say your illness is in remission, so I'm trying to think about it like I have cancer. There's no cure for it, and you can look and feel healthy, but there's always a chance it'll come back."

He swallows a bite before asking, "So, are you in remission?"

"The million dollar question. Not yet. I've only been on meds for a few weeks, and I'll need to be on them and stable for at least six months for remission."

"How long have you been at Hope House?"

"Not that long."

"How is it there?" he asks, taking another bite of his kung pao beef.

"Boring, really." I shrug. "I cook breakfast, lunch, and dinner. Have therapy twice a week. Now, I go to your shop. I spend most of my time sitting in my window looking outside, watching the people and traffic on Division."

He hops up and walks over to his windows. "Which window is yours?"

I walk over to him and point across the street. "That one there. What's the big deal where my window is?"

"I've seen you. I just didn't know it was you." He shakes his head. "It never even occurred to me it could be you. It was just a silhouette. I noticed you watching, though. Wondered what that girl was doing sitting there in the middle of the night." We don't say anything for a long few seconds. Eventually, Jackson breaks the quiet. "Come on. Let's finish our dinner."

We eat in silence. I'm wondering if my revelation was too much, if he's regretting his decision to keep me here. The willy-nilly hand holding.

*　*　*

As we get to his door to leave, he steps in front of me. "Kyle, thank you for telling me everything tonight, and for having dinner with me. It's been an unexpected pleasure."

I throw myself into his torso. This hug differs from the one on the sidewalk. This time he wraps his arms around, no hesitation, no holding of breath. "Thank you, Jackson, for being with me today. It's been my pleasure."

We stay like that, holding each other while I count. At forty-seven, he pulls away and opens the front door.

We take a cab to his father's and are silent on the way there, aside from Jackson giving the driver an address. I can't talk, my mouth suddenly dry, my tongue sticky from anxiety. I suspect Jackson's silence is from his own nervousness. His knee is bouncing against the door.

He's looking out the window, and there's distance between us I thought had evaporated with our time together today. He reminds me of the asshole Jackson I met on my first visit to the shop. Like that day, I don't want to look at his face. I couldn't take it.

As soon as the cab stops, Jackson turns to me and says, "Ready?" I shake my head.

He nods once. "It'll be fine."

I don't know if I believe him. But he pays the driver, gets out, then turns and holds out a hand for me. I take it. He squeezes once as he helps me out of the car, then lets go as we walk into the house.

His father's home is what I should have expected from the man I saw earlier this week: expensive. There's not one thing I can put my finger on, but every surface whispers money, and I'm immediately uncomfortable.

"Jackson," I say as I stop walking, my whisper echoing around the entryway.

He turns to face me, eyebrows raised in question.

I shake my head.

"Wait here?" He nods to an armchair at the foot of the stairs.

I nod.

"Okay. I'll be quick." He turns and walks into the next room before I can reply.

I sit in the proffered chair, not surprised that it's a little stiff and not quite comfortable. It's a metaphor for the room. Everything in the space is not quite something—the walls are not quite white, the lights are not quite bright enough, the artwork not quite beautiful, the smiles in the family pictures not quite genuine. It's like whoever decorated this space did it to keep visitors on edge. It's working.

I close my eyes. I need to stop psychoanalyzing the decor. Pictures of the day roll through my mind until I hear voices coming closer from the direction Jackson went earlier.

"I understand why you want me to, but I can't."

"You mean you *won't*, Jack. Don't think I don't understand the difference."

"You're right. I *won't*."

"You'll have to listen to reason eventually. It can't keep going like this. I won't allow it."

"Then I'll figure something else out, so it's not up to you."

His father barks out a harsh laugh. "Go ahead and try." His voice is mocking and mean.

There's silence for a moment. I wonder if there's anywhere I could hide in case they round the corner. I really don't want to meet his father.

"I need to leave. There are people waiting."

"Fine," his father snaps. "This isn't going to go away."

"I know," Jackson grumbles. "I'll talk to you tomorrow."

He comes into view, and, without realizing it, I've gotten up and am standing at the door. His face is flushed and angry, but his expression eases as soon as he sees me. It's not quite relief, but I can tell this place makes him tense, too. "Ready?"

I nod, open the door, and rush onto the sidewalk. At the street's edge, Jackson turns right and walks toward the corner.

"Where are we going?"

"Huh?" There's distraction in his voice, like he hadn't actually been going anywhere but *away*.

"Are we still going to see Fiona?"

He stops and turns to face me. "Do you want to?"

"Sure."

He nods and says, "Then let's go see Fiona."

CHAPTER ELEVEN

The blast of sound when Jackson opens the bar's door gives me pause. We make it only ten feet inside before Fiona runs over, her squeal audible over the opening band. She's decked out for the show in a red satin corset and black cigarette pants. She's so beautiful, I fidget at how inadequate I'm feeling in Jackson's sweater and my ratty jeans. I look at him for some reassurance and find him looking down at me. Just being here with him helps ease my outward anxiety, but my head is a mess of self-doubt.

"Oh, shit! Kyle, how did you get out?"

"Jackson called the doctor. He got me a free pass until midnight."

Fiona punches him in the shoulder. "Good job! You're all right, I don't care what they say."

"Thanks." He laughs. "How long until you go on? We have a schedule to keep."

"Thirty or so. These guys are using our drums and amps, so that'll save time on setup. I'm gonna let the band know I wanna hustle. We can plug and play as soon as they're done." She throws herself into me and gives the quickest of hugs, then runs down a hallway toward backstage and disappears.

"I knew Fiona would be excited to see you here. You want to grab a drink before she goes on?"

"That would be great," I say, smiling up at him.

We weave as a pair to the bar.

"What would you like? Have anything you want."

"Any old beer will do. I'm not picky." I shouldn't drink. My meds and alcohol don't mix well, but this is so nice—spending a night hanging out with friends, watching a band, and drinking a beer. It feels like normal. I feel like I'm normal for the first time in a long time.

While Jackson's getting drinks, I take my chance to look around. I've been here a hundred times, so it's not a new experience: tiny bar, tiny stage, people crammed in wall-to-wall. Some people are watching the band and bobbing their heads in time with the music. Others are trying to carry on conversations over the noise, practically yelling just to be heard a foot away. The bar smells like decades of sweat and booze.

Jackson comes back with two plastic cups of beer. He tips his chin. "Heads up. Here comes Jamie."

"Well, hello, Kyle," Jamie draws out in a singsong voice. "And hello, Jackson. What's up?"

"Hey, Jamie," I laugh.

Jackson leans in close to Jamie's ear and starts talking. I assume he's explaining how I ended up here with him, because Jamie nods twice, grins at me, and pats Jackson on the shoulder. "Well, see you tomorrow, Kyle," he says, walking away.

I stand on tiptoes to peer after him. "Where's he going? I expected some grief."

Jackson nods. "He's a good friend. I told him you were having a bad day, and I'd talk to him tomorrow."

"He could have stayed longer. I'm having a good day now."

"I didn't want to overwhelm you. Jamie can be a little overbearing."

"Oh, I know." You can't spend two seconds with Jamie without knowing.

We move to the front of the bar, just to the left of the stage. It's a great place to watch the show. Jackson positions himself behind me, a buffer against the cacophony.

The opening band wraps up, and though the bar is quieter now, I don't turn around to talk. So much has happened today, I'm grateful for the chance to be still for a few minutes. My brain is buzzing with the emotions swimming around: happiness, depression, gratitude, doubt. I don't dare break the silence.

Jackson doesn't say anything either, so he's probably dealing with his own emotions. Or maybe he's just content with the stillness, too.

Fiona comes onto the stage with a smile and a wave for me. Her band plays, and I'm pretty sure they're great, but I can't concentrate on anything but Jackson. Every now and then, his body brushes mine, this feathery touch against my back or arm. I wonder if he's a runner. Does he run to Humboldt Park to sit next to the lake? Or maybe he's a swimmer. All that lean solidity doesn't just happen without some kind of work. I let my mind wander, daydreaming about what he does when he's not being a coffee mad scientist.

Jackson leans down after a handful of songs and tells me, "Kyle, we need to go. You have to be back soon." It's little more than a murmur, even with the blare of the band fifteen feet from us. It's a caress of words, his breath kissing my ear.

The walk back to Hope House is slow. I think he feels the same as I do, not wanting this to end. Or maybe he's just keeping pace with me.

"Tell me about your mom. How much do you remember about her?" he asks.

"Bits and pieces. Honestly? Mostly the bad stuff. Maybe that's because there wasn't really anything good. Or maybe my kid brain is trying to protect me from the hurt of her leaving. I don't know."

"What kind of bad? I don't mean to pry."

"Well, she went through boyfriends almost as fast as she went through fifths of whiskey. Most of the time, she left me alone in our apartment, so I was relieved when I finally got to live with Grandma. Granted, Mom didn't tell me she was taking off, so I was alone in the apartment for four days before the landlord showed up with CPS." I chance a glance at him and am surprised by the impassivity of his expression. "What about your mom?"

"She died when I was two. I don't remember her."

I don't manage to remain impassive at his news and have to fight off tears. My chin quivers, and I bite the inside of my cheek.

"My dad left me alone most of the time, too. As soon as I was old enough, he sent me to boarding school. It sounds a lot like what happened to you, just with more money."

I smile up at him, my eyes glassy. "We're quite the pair, huh?"

"I think so."

* * *

He keeps his promise to Dr. Booth. We get back to Hope House, and he escorts me inside with thirteen minutes to spare. The security guard thanks him for taking care of me, then Nancy comes into the office.

"Kyle, so nice to have you back with us." She's looking at Jackson with scrutinizing eyes. "Dr. Booth was concerned today. He left explicit instructions regarding your return. I'm to escort you to your room immediately."

"Okay. Sure. Would it be alright if I say goodbye first?"

Nancy purses her lips. "I'm afraid not. You should get back to your prescribed schedule as quickly as possible. Let's not delay any longer, or I'll need to add it to my notes."

I don't like Jackson seeing this, me being handled like I need to be contained. It's humiliating. Nancy grips my elbow, pulling me from the room.

"Kyle, thank you for the unexpected end to my day," Jackson says from behind me. "I'll see you in the morning."

His words give me a thrill, but I can't give away how much I enjoyed my time with him. Booth is already going to pry, and I won't give him any ammunition. Nancy will tell him everything anyway.

I speed up, walking up the stairs with enough purpose that Nancy loosens her grip on my elbow.

"Dr. Booth would like a full check since you were away from the premises for so long. Take off your clothes."

"You're going to do a strip search?" I'm shaking now, scared about what's coming. "Dr. Booth made Jackson think me being gone was okay. Was it not?" I clench my jaw, grinding my teeth.

"He excused your excursion, but I was instructed to treat your return as a readmission," she answers, her voice colder than usual. "Miss Davies, I need to check for any evidence of self-harm or mutilation."

My eyes mist as I kick off my shoes. I'm crying silent tears by the time I'm naked, shivering from cold and fear. She looks me over, then runs her fingers over my skin, pausing at my scars. These minutes with Nancy's icy hands moving in slow motion on me are excruciating and mortifying. I close my eyes, breathe deep, and try to pretend I'm anywhere but here.

"You can put on your pajamas now. I will be in the hall. Let me know as soon as you're done."

When I do, Nancy reenters the bathroom. "Dr. Booth issued a mandatory order for all patients this evening. Because of the unfortunate incident this morning, everyone will take a sedative." She holds out the pill, and I take it.

"I . . . I had a drink tonight. A beer. Is this safe to take?"

Nancy nods. "It's mandatory, Miss Davies." She checks to make sure I swallow, then watches while I brush my teeth. She follows me to my bed.

When she walks away, I can hear her footsteps skip the stop at Joey's door. I hadn't thought about him for the past few hours, and a wave of guilt washes over me. I won't feel guilty over the time I spent with Jackson, though. Getting out of bed quietly, I go to my window and look over at his building. He's standing at his windows. I can't look long; Booth's pill is already kicking in, making me woozy and fuzzy around the edges.

I lie down and pass out before I can pull up my blanket.

* * *

The next morning, I wake up with a wicked case of cotton-mouth and a body that's not cooperating. The sun is bright through my eyelids, so I know I've slept much later than usual. I keep my eyes closed and lie still, hoping for consciousness to spread to my limbs. I normally refuse any medication to help me sleep, not liking the blank dreamlessness or the numb, weighted feeling the next day.

Nancy's explanation for the extra meds rang hollow, but I didn't doubt its veracity; I'm sure Booth sent orders to put the remaining residents down for the count after the shit show with Joey. And I'm sure my disappearing act didn't do us any favors. So I find myself at a loss again today, needing to make it up to Eddie and Mary and wishing Joey was here, too.

Lori's standing in the doorway when I open my eyes.

"Good morning, Kyle. Sleep well?"

I roll onto my side to look at her better. "Too well. What time is it?"

"Eleven. I was about to wake you up. No one came down for breakfast, but Eddie and Mary both got up about an hour ago. He'll want lunch and won't want to wait since you didn't cook yesterday. I calmed him down last night by getting some deep dish delivered."

"Good call. Thanks for handling that, Lori. I'm sorry that I disappeared yesterday. I wasn't intending to be gone so long. I just . . . lost track of time. I couldn't be here."

"I understand. Yesterday was tough, and you and Joey were close. I'm sure it was hard to see."

"Do you know anything you can tell me, Lori? Is he okay? Can I go see him?"

"He's not allowed any calls or visitors. I could try to get a letter to him if you like, but you should give it more time. You know I can't tell you what's going on, but I'll do my best."

I nod. "Is Mary okay? First the thing with the panic attack and then this. I feel bad for ditching her yesterday."

"Don't. You did what you needed to do for you, and Mary did the same. She wrote a letter to her sister and took a nap. I brought her a new book yesterday, and she read for a while in the evening. It worried her when you didn't come back on time, but she calmed down once she knew you were okay."

"That's good. I guess I should get up. Go make sandwiches." I stretch and yawn.

"Tell me or Bruce if you need anything."

"I will. Thanks again, Lori."

*   *   *

Eddie's standing outside the kitchen waiting when I get downstairs. He greets me with his usual "Hey, Special K!"

"Hey, Ed. Sorry about yesterday. I'll make it up to you, okay?"

He leans in, getting right in my face. "Whatever you say, princess. Just get me some goddamn food and don't fucking disappear again."

"There was food in the fridge. You could have made yourself something to eat, Eddie. What did you do before I got here?"

"Just the same as at home. I had some other bitch doing it for me."

I brush past him into the kitchen and pull out the makings of our sack lunches. I bang doors and slam things on the counters to cut off any more insults. He's trying to get a reaction, and my noisy display should be enough to make him think he succeeded in upsetting me. I make the lunches without looking up and assume he took the hint, because I don't hear another word.

After I make the lunches, I trudge back upstairs to take a shower, hoping to shock away my sedative-induced sluggishness with the cool water. It works enough to keep me moving, but not enough to get me out of my pajamas.

There's a stab in my gut when I realize I'm not going to make it across the street today. I'm just not up to it. I can't get dressed, can't walk across Division, can't make small talk with Jamie. I would like to see Jackson, but the lingering numbness of the sedative takes the edge off any desire. I peek at The Coffee Shop. It looks like business as usual. I head downstairs and make sweets for him, rather than sleep the entire day away.

I bake hazelnut macarons—easy enough—and package them while a casserole is in the oven. Lori leaves the cookies in Jackson's entryway for me. I repay the favor by sending her home with a dozen to share with her family.

After dinner, I go back to my room and sleep off the rest of the sedative. Jackson's at his window. He points and gestures, asking if I'm okay. I nod big enough for him to see from across the street, smiling at his sweet gesture and how much it reminds me of my conversations with Joey the past couple of weeks.

We exchange waves before I walk over and flick off my light, climb into bed, and pull up my blankets. I fall asleep with a goofy grin on my face, hopeful I'll see him in the morning.

CHAPTER TWELVE

I'm feeling more like my new old self—ready to get moving and ready to see Jackson, hoping to talk to him about the macarons Lori left last night. Nancy stops by the kitchen as I'm daydreaming. "Booth's asked that your appointment be pushed back. He'd like to see you at two, rather than ten."

"Okay, Nancy. Thanks for letting me know."

She doesn't respond, just turns and walks down the hallway. I hear her stop and talk to Mary about her now-rescheduled appointment with Booth, too.

Mary herself walks in shortly after. "Good morning, dear. It's good to see you finally. I was so worried about you when you didn't come back the other night. Are you okay?"

"I'm great, Mary. I mean, considering everything that's happened. I was worried about you, too. How are you handling it all? Have you heard anything about Joey? Lori told me yesterday I should give him time, and that's it." There's so much to talk about, between Eddie's and Joey's blowups. My brain's having trouble keeping up. Mary looks amused, and I realize I've pelted her with a ton of questions without taking a breath. "Sorry I'm rambling."

"Ramble away," she says with a chuckle. "And, no, I haven't heard anything."

"Are you sleeping okay? Your nightmares still bad?"

She nods. "I suspect they'll always be terrible. Sometimes they're more frequent is all."

Most days it doesn't make any sense why Mary is in here. She's the stereotypical grandmother—doting and kind—during the day. But then something will trigger her nightmares, and it all becomes clear. The screams woke me up on my second night here. A mugger stabbed her husband and he bled to death in Mary's arms right there on the sidewalk. They were married for something like a hundred years. Even though she ended up in here, I marvel at her strength.

"Let's get this meal over with," she says. "You must be anxious to go on your outing today, since I imagine you missed it yesterday. I couldn't even get out of bed with whatever they gave us."

"You're right. I managed to get up for a while, though. Eddie was pestering Lori about food, so I came down and made him lunch, then made some hazelnut macarons." I smile at her. "I saved some and hid them so he wouldn't get yours."

"You're so sweet to think of me. Maybe I'll take them back to my room, have a little snack before my appointment with the doctor. Now, let's go eat and get you out of here. You can go see whoever's got you all perked up these days." She nudges me in the ribs as she heads into the dining room.

* * *

While getting dressed, I worry about what's going on between Jackson and me, what to say about Jackson and me, what to say to Jackson, how to act around Jackson. It's been a long time since I've made a friend outside of Hope House.

The only thing about this that's simple is what to wear: I can't dress any differently since I have just four changes of clothes here. I still have his sweater, the only cold-weather garment in my current wardrobe. I could call Rebeca and ask her to bring more clothes, but I've chickened out on contacting her since Booth told her to fire me. I feel like that window has sort of closed.

Missing yesterday at The Coffee Shop has me at loose ends. Most of me thinks I should play it cool, not let on how much I've looked forward to seeing Jackson this morning, but a small part wants to throw myself at him and hug him until he forces me away. And the last, and not smallest part, wants to give in to my ballooning anxiety and stay here. But I don't want to fall into those old habits.

I've changed in the past few days, and I know our new friendship is part of the reason.

Having connections or putting expectations onto another person isn't something I've ever been able to do. I put them on my mom once, and look at how that worked out. The relationships with my grandmother and employers are the only steady things I've ever had, ever let myself have. I want to be able to put expectations on Jackson, though. He would be steady and supportive, steadfast and loyal. He's also unrealistically attractive, especially when he smiles. Daydreaming about his smile is becoming a preoccupation.

I sit down hard on my bed. I like him. I really fucking like him. And not just as a friend. Shit.

I squeeze the blankets in my fists as the panic washes over me. There couldn't be a worse time to feel like this, and Booth would definitely not approve. I mean, who dates a girl in a mental institution? My heart thuds. *Fuck.*

I'm pulling his sweater over my head as I walk out of Hope House, jaywalk, and push into the shop, heart in my throat. Jackson's not there, though. Jamie's alone, and he's distracted by a woman. She's leaning on the counter, and her breasts look like they're about to pop out of her sports bra. Her jacket is off, and she's pressing her arms in front of her, squeezing those breasts together and telling Jamie about a muscle she pulled in hot yoga this morning. I clear my throat over her shoulder to get his attention.

"Oh, hey, Kyle! How's my favorite girl?" He winks and shoots me a huge smile. His greeting is over the top; he must want my help getting rid of her, so I play along.

"Aw, I missed you, too. You know how upset I get when I can't see you every day." Batting my eyelashes a little, careful not to look at the woman. If she were Medusa, I'm positive I would turn to stone right now.

Jamie turns to her. "Yeah, well, I guess I'll see you around. Don't forget your coffee." He shifts toward me, shutting her out. She huffs and bumps my shoulder as she walks by but doesn't make too big a scene, since she'll probably be back in a day or two.

"What did I do to make me your favorite girl?" I ask him. "Maybe I should stay away more often."

"You got me out of that conversation, for starters. She's persistent. What are you having today? It's on me."

I order a flat white and Jamie starts making it. I'm stunned. I've never seen anyone but Jackson use the machines, not in the store or from my windowsill at Hope House. There's no sign of him. I stand at the counter fidgeting for a second, deciding if I should ask where he is, but retreat to my usual booth without a word.

"He's not here," Jamie says as he puts my drink on the table.

"What?"

"I know you're wondering where he is. He went home for a bit. His dad came by, and it put him in a foul mood, so I kicked him out. Told him to take a couple of hours. I can call him, though, let him know you showed. He'd want to know. He was worried yesterday."

"You don't need to call. I don't want to bother him."

"No bother," Jamie assures. "He'll want to know." He walks back up to the counter, leaving me with my drink. It's good. Better than any other, except Jackson's. A couple of minutes later, Jamie's back at my table. "He asked if you'd come up to his place. He wants to see you. You know where it is?"

"Yeah. I know where it is." I gulp down the rest of my drink and wipe my mouth with the back of my hand. "Thanks, Jamie. See you tomorrow?"

"I'll be here."

*   *   *

I walk up to Jackson's. He buzzes me into the building as soon as I hit the button, and he's standing in the doorway when I reach the top of the stairs.

I'm smiling, thrilled at the sight of him until I get a closer look. He's stone-faced, and nervousness punches me in the gut. Maybe liking him isn't the best idea. Maybe I misread our connection as something more than it is. But if so, then what was the thing with the window last night? Maybe our connection is just . . . an imagining of my depression? My anxiety is swirling, and it takes every shred of bravery I have not to turn around and run back to Hope House. I wrap my arms around myself when he moves aside to let me walk into the loft.

"Morning, Kyle. It's good to see you," he says to my back as soon as I'm inside.

I turn to face him. "Is it? You don't look happy."

"I had a difficult conversation with my father this morning."

"Oh." I don't know what else to say. I don't want to pry. I turn to look at Jackson, but he's looking past me into the kitchen.

"He brought those this morning." He nods in the direction of his gaze. "All filled out and everything. Just needs my signature. He even put stamps on the envelopes." Jackson's tone is biting, bitter. The kitchen counter is covered with colorful, glossy brochures. I walk over to get a closer look.

They're for law schools. Looks like every school in the country is represented, and beneath every shiny booklet is a filled-out application. Even if my brain weren't preoccupied with this morning's revelation, this would take some processing. I open and close my mouth to pose a question at least three times, but give up and look at Jackson instead.

His back is against the door, and he's watching me. His expression gives nothing away.

I raise my eyebrows, prompting.

"My father is trying to bend me to his will. He's stubborn, and I know he won't give up. This is the latest plan—get me back on the path of following in his political footsteps."

"But what about the shop? How can he expect you to walk away from that?" The volume of my voice rises with each word. By the end of the questions, I'm practically shouting.

Jackson looks at the floor. "The shop's losing money. Lots of it. And part of that money belongs to him. If I can't turn things around, I won't have any choice but to close. After that, I'm out of options. I do what he wants. And that's becoming the next Alderman Turner."

"But, Jackson, there have to be other options. Something other than making yourself miserable."

"Yeah, there are," he sighs. "But none that will make me less miserable than doing what he wants."

"There has to be something, Jackson. No offense, but you'd make a terrible politician."

He grins, a break in his desolate expression. "None taken. There's no way I can follow the plan. I'm much too disagreeable."

I shake my head. "You just aren't willing to fake it. It's one of your best traits."

He lets out a deep laugh, and I close the distance between us. He's smiling that full, knee-buckling smile now. His espresso eyes are all kinds of mischievous. "We talked about you, too."

"Me? Why in the world would you talk about me?"

"He wanted to know who was with me the other night."

"What did you tell him?" I swallow around the lump in my throat.

"That you're my friend." He looks at me for confirmation.

"Good. Yeah. Friends." I nod and look at the floor, trying to hide my disappointment.

"Do you want to know what else I told him?"

"What do you mean what else you told him?" I don't know if I want to hear what he has to say, but I'm desperate to hear it nonetheless.

Jackson puts a hand on my shoulder. The touch triggers me to raise my eyes to meet his. "I also told him you're smart, funny, beautiful, and have impeccable taste in beverages."

My brain is slow to catch up with his words. "Why did you tell him those things?" My voice is unsteady.

"Because they're true."

I study him for a moment, looking for truth or deception or anything in between. "Are they?" I finally ask.

He smiles and nods, then his expression turns somber. He sighs long and deep. "I'm sorry everything in my life is so uncertain right now. You need stability, and I can't give you any."

"Nah." I wave a dismissive hand. "You can lean on me." I'm nowhere near sure I can back up my promise. I shuffle my feet, then decide to put all my feelings out there, even if my timing is the shittiest of the shitty. "I really like you, Jackson."

"Um. Thanks." He lets the word fade off. "Are you sure? I mean, how can you be—"

I cut him off by throwing my arms around him and squeezing the bejesus out of him. "I just am," I say into his shoulder.

He squeezes back, a tentative tension in his arms. "I like you, too . . ." But it's definitely an ellipsis, not a period. He trails off like there was something else he was going to say.

"But?" I push.

"Nothing. But nothing." His arms tighten around me a little more.

"It's not nothing," I push. "What?"

He shoves away, out of my arms. "It's not a good time, right? You're not . . ."

"I'm not *what*?" I put my hands on my hips, an indignant pose if there ever was one.

His mouth opens and closes twice, but no sound comes out. He waves his hands in front of him, like he's trying to grab onto the right answer. "You're sick. That's what you said."

My righteousness evaporates. My arms fall to hang limp at my sides. "Yeah, I am," I say to my shoes.

"I just don't want to take advantage."

"Jackson, you didn't force me to come here. You didn't make me hug you. Yeah, I'm sick, but I'm not incapacitated. I can make decisions for myself."

"I know," he says too quickly and waves his hands again.

"Then what's the problem?"

"I'm just trying to do the right thing. For you. For me. I don't want to make things worse."

"Oh, that's really big of you."

He flinches, then hits a fist against his thigh. "I'm doing this wrong. You don't understand—"

"No," I interrupt, "I understand perfectly."

Jackson calls my name twice by the time I reach the door, but he doesn't chase me, and that tells me everything I need to know.

CHAPTER THIRTEEN

I run across the street and into the Hope House kitchen. I don't have long before my appointment with Booth, but I've got to get my shit together before going into his office. If he sees me like this, he'll skewer me alive, and I'm already in hot water after my late night out. In the forty-five minutes between Jackson's rejection and seeing Booth, I pace the five-step width of my room 364 times.

I'm not looking forward to my appointment with Booth. He's going to delve into my coping skills after the incidents with Eddie, Mary, and Joey. He'll want details about my disappearance with the son of an alderman. There's a hard, nervous knot in my belly. I have to put on a blank face in Booth's office this afternoon, and Jackson made that triply difficult. His friendship, at least for the couple of days I had it, was a soothing balm, his rejection a stinging slap.

Now, standing outside the doctor's office, I'm replaying the conversation in my mind.

Right on cue, the doctor calls me into his office.

"Good afternoon, Kyle. Please have a seat." He gestures to the chair opposite his desk. "It's been quite the week around here."

"Yes, it's certainly been . . . exciting. Good thing it's not like this all the time," I try to joke.

"Indeed. So, let's start with how you're coping with the incident in group therapy this week—Joey's outburst." He's diving right in today. It doesn't bode well.

"Okay, I guess. I was upset right after it happened, but I'm doing better now. I'm worried about Joey. He's a good friend."

"And the incident between Edward, Mary, and the security personnel? How are you doing with that?"

"Again, I'm okay. I was, well, I *am* worried about Mary. Her nightmares are back."

"That's not answering my question, Kyle. How are *you* handling the incidents?"

"I'm handling them fine."

He looks at me with raised eyebrows.

"Really. My anxiety's ramped up, of course. But other than that, I feel like I'm handling it pretty well."

"And what are you doing about your anxiety? Your chart indicates no other deviations from your regular medication schedule, other than the sedative I prescribed on Monday."

"I'm doing my deep breathing exercises, Dr. Booth. They're effective." I smile while passing on my bullshit compliment.

"Very good. I'm pleased to know you're taking advantage of the tools at your disposal." He moves into Caring Pose, and I brace myself. The more I see it, the more I fucking hate it. "Next, Miss Davies, I would like to discuss your absence on Monday."

Booth almost never uses our last names. He wants to be our "friend," which makes him more delusional than any of us. His use of my last name sends up all the red flags.

"Sure. What would you like to know, Dr. Booth?"

"Your friend—I'm assuming 'friend' is accurate—told me where you were on the phone, but I would like you to give me an accounting of your whereabouts yourself."

I play it dumb, like I didn't overhear Jackson's entire conversation with Booth. "I'm not sure what Jackson told you, but we went for a walk, had dinner, then attended a function before coming back here. I was upset about Joey and going for a walk on my own, but I bumped into Jackson on my way out."

I don't want Booth prying into my feelings for Jackson. They're too raw. I have enough self-doubt about what's going on and don't need Booth's two cents thrown into the mix.

"And this function you attended?"

I shrug. "A small gathering of Jackson's family and friends. I kept to myself." No lies there.

"I have to tell you, Miss Davies, I had great reservations about your being away from the facility for an extended period of time. My fears were somewhat allayed after I spoke with Mr. Turner, but I am given great pause by your seemingly rapid turnaround. Two weeks ago, you were unwilling to leave the premises, and now you're leaving every day, taking liberties with your privileges. I must be frank with you: although you've made tremendous progress, I urge you to reconsider the steps you are taking."

"And what steps would those be, Dr. Booth?" I wish he kept a clock in here so I could count the minutes until this is over.

"Entering into a relationship with Mr. Turner. I know you're not telling me everything, Miss Davies. You're omitting details about that evening because you and I both know your emotional recovery has not progressed enough for this."

"I'm not entering into any relationship with Mr. Turner," I snap, "other than friendship. I'm not leaving out any relevant details. I know I'm emotionally fragile, and I'm not going to do anything to cause any setbacks in my treatment." Even though I just did. "No one wants me to get out of this place more than me." I cross my arms, glare at him, and hope the anger hides my fear and sadness.

"I'm glad to hear you say that. You must be fully committed to my treatment plan if you are to reintegrate yourself into society successfully. It may not always be apparent to you, but I have your best interests at heart. Outside of this week's diversions, your charts say that you are making progress and are otherwise compliant. I hope that pattern will continue."

I relax. "Thank you. I am trying." Flattery will get me everywhere, and he loves nothing more than absolute compliance. Well, except himself.

"Good, Kyle. Good."

We're back to first names, so my compliment helped. He lays down his notebook and my file and closes them, then walks around to sit on my side of the desk so we're sitting face-to-face. He rests his elbows on his knees, steepling his fingers under his chin. I'm going to call this the "Aggressive Caring Pose." His face is inches from mine. This is the closest he's ever been to me. I panic but try to remain impassive on the outside.

"Wh-what's going on?" My stutter betrays me, opens the window to my anxiety. I make fists against my thighs and Booth turns my freak-out even higher when he takes both my hands in his.

I look down, not knowing what to make of the awkward alienness happening in my lap. Booth's hands are cold and slippery with lotion. He smells like Vaseline Intensive Care and too much cologne. "I have something to tell you, Kyle. I want to say something to you first, though. I want you to know I'm proud of you. You've made extraordinary progress in a short time."

"Okay . . . Thank you?"

"You're welcome," Booth replies. "Repeat after me, please: 'I have the potential to be exceptional.'"

"I have the potential to be exceptional?"

"Thank you, Kyle. Remember, though, it is a statement and not a fact in question."

He pauses, waiting for my response. I nod weakly. It's all I can manage. My brain is buzzing, trying to figure out what the fuck Booth is up to with this creepy hand-holding and affirmations shit. I need to get out of here.

"That's not all I need to tell you today. Something rather unfortunate happened this morning. I felt it was best for you to hear this from someone you know cares about you."

I think, *Are you sure you're the one who should tell me, then?* I nod at him and swallow.

"I spoke with Joey's mother this morning. There was an incident at the hospital."

I try to let go of his hands, but he is gripping mine too tightly. I lean away from him. "What kind of incident? Is he okay?"

"Kyle, Joey took his own life this morning."

I pry my hands away from his and hurl myself out of the chair. I'm sobbing. I hit the wall hard enough to dent the sheetrock. "Why didn't someone stop this?" I spin around and point at Booth. "Why didn't you stop this? You knew how fragile he was, and you kept pushing him and pushing him! This is your fault!"

"Now, calm down, Kyle. I understand you're upset. We're all upset. Joey was a very sick young man, and I know you need to blame someone."

I shake my head. I don't want to talk anymore, and I need to get the fuck away from Booth.

"Lori is waiting in your room with a sedative. You will take it to prevent a repeat of this week's events. You will take it at regular intervals until you are coping sufficiently. I'll look in on you tomorrow, but in the meantime, ask the nurses for anything you need."

I'm crying so hard, I can't hear half his drivel. I hiccup between sobs. "Can I go now?"

"You may. Please keep this to yourself for now. I'll inform Mary and Eddie later this afternoon. I should be the one to tell them."

I run to my room. Lori is there, waiting. She holds out her arms and lets me fall into her hug. "I'm so sorry, Kyle. He was such a sweet boy. We'll all miss him." She rubs a sweeping arc up and down my back. "You'll miss him the most of all of us, though." She lets me sloppy-cry against her for a while before saying, "I hate to do this, but I need to go to Mary's room. She's in with the doctor now."

I pull back, sniffling. "I got snot on your shirt," I say, pointing at her shoulder.

She snorts. "I'm a nurse. There's nothing you could get on me that would bother me. Oh, the stories I could tell . . ."

I give her a teary smile. "Can you tell me what happened? How he did it?"

She nods. "His mother gave me permission. But are you sure you want to know?"

I nod. "I've been worried for a while now. Worried about how he would ever get better. I think I need to hear."

"If that's what you want and you're sure you can handle it."

I nod.

"Joey had been in isolation since Monday, but last night, he calmed down completely and seemed okay. First thing this morning, they moved him into a regular room. His mom went to get breakfast."

I'm back to sobbing again but trying to keep quiet so she won't stop talking.

"The nurses said the bathroom light was on, so they assumed he was in there."

"He wasn't in the bathroom, was he?"

Lori shakes her head. "He hanged himself with one of the sheets. Tied it to the bed rail. His mom found him when she came back. The way he did it, Kyle, you can tell he thought it through. This wasn't a snap decision."

"That's the thing, though, Lori. We all think about it. *I* think about it. Mary thinks about it. I know Joey thought about it. I can't help but wonder, though, if Booth hadn't pushed him . . . If he hadn't ended up in the hospital again . . ."

"It's normal to think about the what-ifs. Take today to shut down and be sad. Tomorrow, get back up and keep going. You have to keep going. Remember that, okay?"

I grin at her through the tears. "Thanks. Where's that pill Booth left for me? I need to check out."

"This will make that happen," she says, putting a caplet in my hand.

*   *   *

We were hanging out in the kitchen, talking about cookies and laughing. Then he was gone. Poof. Vanished. I ran through the house yelling his name and couldn't find him. None of the doors would open except the one to his room, so I pushed inside, but it wasn't Joey's. It was the shitty cockroach-infested apartment my mom and I lived in when I was in the third grade.

Eight-year-old me was under a blanket behind the couch in the living room, hiding, because mom's new boyfriend was mad about something and throwing things. I heard him hit my mom and peeked around the couch to see if she was okay, but they were both gone. Poof. Again.

I was with my grandma. Poof. Then Rebeca. Poof. They vanished. I was standing in the middle of Division between Hope House and The Coffee Shop. Jackson was closing up for the day, locking the doors. I couldn't move, couldn't talk, couldn't yell. I watched, frozen, as he turned and walked westward, away from his home and me, and then vanished.

*   *   *

I bolt upright, drenched in sweat. I don't need a professional to tell me that my abandonment issues are rearing their ugly head. It's nearly dark outside. I go splash cold water on my face and shake off some of the dread exposed by my dream. Lori's in the hall when I come out of the bathroom.

"Hey, I wasn't expecting you to be awake. Are you okay?"

"I guess," I shrug. "Bad dreams."

"They must have been doozies to wake you up. Can I get you anything?"

"No, I'm okay. Just tired. Do I need to cook tonight?"

"Don't worry about it. Mary's in her room sleeping, too. Eddie, of course, wasn't upset. Bruce got him a burger and fries and he's happy as a clam. I'm leaving in a few minutes. I'll see you in the morning, okay?"

I nod and shuffle back into my room, going straight to my window and looking out. The traffic is dependably steady on Division. The lights are off in Jackson's loft. I climb back into bed, wondering what he's doing, and drift back to sleep.

*   *   *

The nightmares keep it up all night, popping me into consciousness twelve more times before I give up. It's early, but late enough that I missed Jackson's walk to the shop. I sit in the window until the sun is fully up. Nancy is pacing the hallway, making her checks. I don't look at her, though, assuming she'll say something if I need to make breakfast.

The Coffee Shop is busy this morning. There's a steady stream of customers, most of them regulars. Two faces I don't recognize go in and soon blow out the door, empty-handed and red-faced. I think of Jackson's iced coffee woman and smile, guessing he's the reason for their hastened departure.

I sigh, stand up, and stretch. Nancy walks by and says nothing, so I crawl back into bed, dragged down by the sedation.

I sleep into the day, wake up again, then sneak downstairs to make meals for everyone else. When Lori shows up I ask for more sedatives, and she gives them to me. Lori wakes me up again in the afternoon and tells me to get up and make dinner. It's hard, because of my fog, and I just put together grilled cheeses and canned tomato soup. I'm not hungry anyway. As soon as that's done, I get back in bed. None of the nurses bother me to do more than make meals or take pills. There's no sign of Mary. Later, I wake up enough to acknowledge Joey's weeping mother going down the hall as she retrieves his belongings. I want to get up, tell her how much I loved him, but I can't. It just hurts too much.

After two days of the same mindless haze, I realize that I know this tired. This is depression exhaustion, when nothing can override the need for escapist sleep. I've regressed, my illness slipped back. Slap some bandages on my left arm and it would feel like I'd time-traveled back to the hospital. The thoughts should worry me, but I honestly can't be bothered to care. That's one of the things about depression: you should care, but you just . . . don't.

On Saturday, I quit looking out the window. I'm not fit to be seen in this state, not suitable for public consumption. Booth said he would check on me, but either he didn't mean it or I slept through his visit. Mary finally comes by on Sunday. She sits on the side of my bed, rubbing circles on my back, while I feign sleep. She asks how I'm doing, and I don't answer. Eventually, she goes away.

On Monday, Lori comes into the kitchen while I'm making lunches and says someone came to see me, wanted to make sure I was okay.

"Who was it?"

"I don't know." She shrugs. "I didn't talk to her. She got mad when security wouldn't let her in."

"Oh, it was a woman." I'd hoped it was Jackson. Maybe he changed his mind.

"What was that?"

"Nothing. It was probably Fiona. You can let her in if she bothers to come back."

"Go by security and add her to your list. You'll have to do it, not me."

"It doesn't matter. I doubt there'll be anyone else for you to worry about." It's been nearly a week of no visits to the shop or seeing each other at our windows. Jackson would have come to the house by now if he cared. I swallow tears and go back to cooking.

"Kyle," Lori says to my back, "you can't keep this up. Remember how good you felt a few days ago. How happy it made you to go outside. Fight it, Kyle." She places a hand on my shoulder. "I can't make you, but you can make yourself. You don't want to end up back in the hospital. It sucks here, but it's so much worse there."

"I'll try tomorrow, okay?"

My brain has a definite fatalism, but that Fiona made it over here before Jackson tells me everything I need to know: he doesn't care about me. I finish dinner and head back upstairs. But on my way, I stop by the security office and add both of them to my visitors list, just in case. There's some part of my brain, deep in the back, that tells me believing in hope like that is still important.

Then I go back to sleep and dream about him walking away from me over and over again.

CHAPTER FOURTEEN

Mary starts coming in to give me daily updates. There's a new girl in the house named Phoebe; she moved into Joey's room and has anorexia, so she's thrilled the house chef isn't cooking much. Mary's taken over part of my task but says it's not the same. She's too scattered to plan meals for the whole week, so they end up eating sandwiches for days because she used all the other food. She begs me to come back, but I won't roll over, so she's forced to speak to the back of my head. I can't turn around. Can't make eye contact.

I lie here, looking at the wall, staring at the bumps and imperfections in the plaster, focusing on each defect for hours, and give the impression of sleep so everyone will leave me alone. My depression cycles through its favorite topics on shuffle: I'm alone forever, not good at anything, not worth anything, there's no point in keeping going, there's no point in anything.

* * *

I walked to the nearest bar, getting soaked by the storm in the process, took a seat on a barstool, ordered a double whiskey. And another. And another. I didn't let the bartender take my empties but lined them up on the weathered bar top instead. An acquaintance named Stewart took the stool next to me, chatting me up, getting more handsy with each successive drink. Dave the bartender called me a cab and made Stewart stay where he was when he tried to follow me. I went back to my shitty studio apartment and ate cold, four-day-old pizza standing at the counter next to the refrigerator and listened to old school country music on shuffle. I plopped on my bed, stared at the lights from the city that danced across my ceiling. The stress and exhaustion caught up with me. I cried and turned up the volume on Johnny Cash to drown it out.

I needed another drink and got a glass. Needed my butcher knife to stab apart the ice cubes in the freezer. On the fourth stab, I misjudged and nicked my left arm. The cut was a shallow slice, an inch above my wrist, and there was only a droplet of blood. I slid down onto the floor and made another tiny cut. There was more blood this time. The depressive thoughts were on shuffle like my music. I took a shuddery breath and made a deep, diagonal slice across my forearm. It didn't hurt, so I made another one, just for good measure. And another. I watched the blood pour out of the slits.

*   *   *

I wake up and reach for my forearm, feeling for the bandages, but the scars are all that are there. My personal pat-down stops when I realize there's someone in my room.

"I'm sorry, Kyle. This is all my fault."

It's Jackson. Fuck. I have no idea what to say to him. "No," I whisper and shake my head. My throat is sandpaper scratchy. Why is he here now? How many days has it been since I found out about Joey? I haven't kept up.

"Will you turn around and talk to me?"

I shake my head.

"It's been a week and a half since you came into the shop."

I pull my hands up, cover my face. "I was so tired, Jackson. Once I started, I just couldn't stop. This isn't your fault. It's mine." A tear runs down my cheek. I pull my knees up to my chest, trying to make myself as small as possible.

"It's okay."

"No, it's really not."

"Yes, it really is. You didn't do anything wrong. I did."

"I get it. You can go now." I snap and try to sound as mean as possible. Maybe he'll leave before the hurt gets even worse.

I don't realize he's come up right behind me until I feel his palm flatten on my back and he sits on the edge of the bed. He doesn't rub in circles like Mary but holds his hand still, anchoring me. "No, I can't. Not until you understand why." I don't say anything, so he keeps going. "I told you, everything is a mess. My life is a mess. Your life is a mess. Taking things further with us is a terrible idea. Maybe if you were better—"

"I didn't mean to do this," I interrupt, and take a deep breath so I can feel the increase in pressure from his touch. "Check out like this. You rejecting me. Then Joey dying. It was too much."

"What? Joey died?" The sympathy in his voice almost breaks me all over again. "When did that happen?"

"I had an appointment with Dr. Booth when I left your place that day. He told me then." I take another deep breath, Jackson's hand reliably strong between my shoulder blades. "I was so mad. So sad. I wanted to forget for a while."

"I'm so sorry, Kyle. I just assumed you were running from me."

The statement triggers me to roll over and face him, not caring anymore how shitty I look. I need to make eye contact so he can see the truth in what I'm saying to him. "No, I wasn't running from you. Well, not entirely, anyway. I assumed you didn't come here because *you'd* made up your mind about me."

"You're not wrong. That's what happened at first, yeah. After a couple of days, though, I realized how stupid it was, what I did."

"It was?"

He nods. "I hated myself for it."

I pull my eyebrows together.

"But Kyle, I need to be honest: I really don't know if I'm ready for what might happen if we take things any further. And I don't know if you are either. No offense, but we're both pretty screwed up right now." He gifts me with a smile and places his right hand on my cheek, wiping away a stray tear with his thumb.

I give a weak laugh. "We are, but what are we going to do about it?"

"I have a few ideas, but only one suggestion."

"What's that?"

"Could I lie down with you?"

"It would make me a lot happy if you would lie down with me. But only for a couple of minutes. The staff won't like it if they catch you." I scoot over to make room, then pick up his left arm, moving it under me, so I can position my head in the crook of his arm.

We're aligned, the length of my body pressed against his side. "You may not want me this close to you. I haven't showered in a while."

"You only tell me that after I'm already lying down?" he laughs. "Don't worry, I'm a gentleman. I won't say anything about how much you stink."

I poke him in the ribs. "You have no idea how humiliating this is for me."

"Don't be embarrassed. We all have our bad times. Some people are just better at hiding it than others. I've been hiding my bad times for years. Why do you think I'm an asshole to so many people?"

"I love that you're so honest. You're my hero for it."

"My being mean to people makes me a hero? I think you have that flipped."

"I don't think you're being mean, though. Just honest. They're not treating you or what you create with respect. They don't deserve any if they're not willing to give it."

He doesn't say anything, and I think I may have left him speechless. He takes a deep breath—his ribcage rises and his exhale brushes over the top of my head—pulls me closer and squeezes. I can feel him pouring his whole self into the embrace. I wrap my arms around him, hugging back with everything I can muster. I'm weak, the depression gnawing at my gut, but his embrace is restorative. I hear one of the nurses coming down the hall and climb over him, out of bed. He sits up, looking bewildered.

"Jackson, I told the doctor you were my friend. If they see me lying in bed with you, it'll create all kinds if complications. Booth made it clear he doesn't want me involved with anyone right now. He doesn't think I'm far enough in my recovery, and after my relapse this week, he'll be even more insistent."

Jackson stands and paces next to the bed. Lori gets to the window for her check, looks in, and moves on. "He's probably right."

I nod. He's looking at me, though, eyebrows raised, clearly expecting something more.

"Probably," I whisper, and wince at the bitterness in my voice.

His brows drop and pull together. "Can I ask you a question?"

"Of course. Anything."

"What's the one thing you've wanted more than anything while you've been locked in this place?"

I mirror him, creasing my own forehead. "What do you mean?"

He shoves his hands in his pockets. "There has to be one thing you've wished for. I mean, looking around, you don't have much with you. There has to be something you want, like . . . a book or music."

"There are lots of things."

"But what have you thought of every day, even when you were lying in bed?"

"Why?" I know I said he could ask me anything, but now that I understand his question, I don't want to answer.

His expression is almost pained, like he's embarrassed and frustrated at the same time. He looks at me, a plea. "Please tell me."

"I don't want to."

"Why?"

"It's ridiculous."

"I just . . ." He hesitates, like he's changed his mind about what he was about to say. "I just need to help. I need to take care of you."

"I can take care of myself," I snap. I want to pull the words back as soon as they're out.

"I know you can. I didn't mean it like that. *I* need it. It's been a miserable week wondering about you. I thought, maybe I could do something for you and it might be good for us both."

I sigh. It has been a horrible week, and spending time with him sounds like just about the best thing in the world right now. "What time is it?"

"About three. Why?"

"I can sign out for two hours. It's not too late yet. As long as I'm back in time for dinner. No more midnight extensions."

He smiles. "Well, let's go, then." He holds out a hand and starts pulling me toward the door.

"Wait." I pull my hand free. "I need to change. Give me two minutes."

I grab clothes, then run into the bathroom to change out of my pajamas and comb my hair. "Okay. Ready?"

He nods. I hold out my hand and pull him toward the door, feeling a glimmer of last week's energy stirring in me.

Out on the sidewalk, I ask, "Where are we going?"

He shrugs and smiles. "I don't know. You never answered my question."

My face heats. "Ugh. I really don't want to tell you."

"Come on. It can't be that bad." He puts a finger under my chin and lifts my face so I'm looking up at him. "It can't be any worse than what we've already told each other."

I sigh. "You're right, it's really not." I close my eyes, since I don't think I can look at him and tell him at the same time. "I want a really, *really* hot shower."

"That's it?"

I nod. "Yep. That's it."

"Why is that what you want more than anything?"

I huff and shake my head. "The water at the house doesn't go higher than lukewarm, because someone could scald and self-harm if it were too hot. So, every time I take a shower, I imagine it's hot and try to get out of there as soon as possible."

"What's the big deal? That's not humiliating. It's not like it's your fault."

I roll my eyes. "That's not the humiliating part."

He raises his eyebrows, prompting me to go on.

"I wanna shave my legs." I look at the ground.

He laughs.

"Don't laugh at me," I say in my best grumpy voice.

"Okay. Sorry. Look at me, okay?"

I meet his eyes but say nothing.

"Let's go to my place. You can shower and shave. You can use up all of my hot water if that's what you want. If it'll make you feel better."

I smile. "I'm gonna use up all your hot water." I grab his hand and pull him down the sidewalk.

CHAPTER FIFTEEN

As soon as we're in the apartment, the excitement hits and I start rambling. "I want to wash my hair with real shampoo and shave my legs. I want to feel normal again for a minute. Can I borrow your razor and soap and shampoo? I'm not allowed to keep any of those in the house."

"Kyle, anything I own, you can have it. Anything you need."

I throw my arms around his neck, jumping up so my feet don't touch the ground. Luckily, he catches me. "Thank you. I've really, really missed hot water." I drop to the ground and walk toward his bathroom.

I'm glad I hadn't seen myself in the mirror yet, because as soon as I do, all of my bravery evaporates. I've got the world's worst case of bedhead, and circles under my eyes. I take a deep breath and turn on the shower. Steam billows into the bathroom as I undress, then step under the spray. I turn, tilt my head back, and let the water run through my hair and down my back. There's a perverse rush of desire as I wash with Jackson's shampoo. It will be nice to have his smell on my skin. Until my next shower at Hope House, that is. I smile at the stupid thought of lying in bed tonight and sniffing my arms.

I realize there's no razor in the shower, so I call out, "Jackson?"

"Yeah?" he answers through the door.

"Where's your razor?"

"Oh, sorry. Top drawer."

I grab my towel and wrap it around me to keep from dripping all over his floor. A smile breaks through when I pull open the drawer, possibly the most organized in the history of drawers. Its contents are lined up parallel to one another, evenly spaced. What I don't see, though, is a razor.

"I don't see it."

"It's on the right. Beside the toothpaste."

Of course he can tell me its exact position.

I look again and find it, only it's not what I was looking for. I'd assumed it would be a plastic drugstore razor, not a legit old school one. Silly me. The thing is essentially a switchblade, and as soon as I flip it open, panic punches me in the chest.

I've used knives at Hope House, so I'm not sure why this particular blade swoops me right back to that night on my kitchen floor, but it does. I drop the razor and stumble back away from its clatter until my back hits the bathroom door.

"Is everything okay in there?" Jackson asks, with a gentle tap on the door.

I jump away from the vibration. I can't breathe, so I can't answer, just drop to the ground and scoot back against the wall.

My fingers scrabble for something to grab onto, needing more than my fist-making for comfort.

"Kyle?" Jackson asks again, his voice a little panicked.

I still can't answer. I'm shivering, teeth chattering, from the panic attack. I hug the towel tighter and pull my knees to my chest.

"I'm coming in, okay?" The door opens and Jackson sweeps the room with his gaze. When he spots me, curled on the floor, he hurries in and crouches in front of me. "What's wrong?"

I rock and squeeze the towel, then look up at him. I bet I look like some demented Blythe doll, eyes huge with fear. I shake my head. "P-panic attack," I wheeze.

Jackson, bless him, sits beside me, pulls me next to him, and wraps an arm around my shoulder. I burrow my head into his bicep. He rubs circles on my back.

Slowly, the panic recedes, and my breathing begins to even out. I ease my death grip on his sleeve and smooth the fabric. "Sorry," I'm finally able to choke out.

I don't know how long we've been here, but the room is filled with steam from the shower. Jackson's face is dewy with humidity. "For what?"

"Freaking out."

"You don't need to apologize. What happened?"

I nod my head at the razor on the floor across the room. "The blade . . . I don't know why."

"Shit, Kyle, if you'd said something . . . I didn't realize."

"I didn't either." I shudder. "I use knives every day . . . I don't know why this one . . . why it made me freak out." I laugh nervously. "Maybe shaving my legs wasn't such a good idea."

Jackson walks over and turns off the shower, then picks up the razor. "I could do it."

"Do what?"

"Shave your legs. I could do it for you."

I pull the towel tighter around me. "No way. I'm like half-yeti at this point. I'd be too embarrassed."

"You should see my legs. They're gruesome." I laugh, and he taps the toilet lid. "Sit here." Looking at me, he adds, "Please."

I hesitate for another couple of seconds before complying, still unsure.

His gaze is steady on my face. He goes down onto one knee with the other in front of him, like he's proposing, and says, "Now, give me a leg."

"Huh?" I can't decide if this is demented or the sweetest gesture ever.

"A leg," he repeats. "Let me take care of you. Rest your foot on my knee," he says, tension in his voice. I stick out my right leg, placing my foot on his thigh. "Be still. Be very, very still."

He sits the razor down beside his foot and produces a tube of shave gel. He squirts some into his palm and smooths it from my lower thigh to my ankle. Then he picks up to razor and places it on my ankle, letting it rest there. "Ready?"

I nod, but he isn't looking at my face anymore, just studying the foot on his knee. "I'm ready."

Slow and steady, he pulls the razor in a straight line up to my knee and rinses it under the faucet. Then, just as slowly, a second line. And another. He grips the back of my leg, just above the knee. He squeezes a little every now and again, pulls and tugs to position me how he needs to complete the task.

I close my eyes—his hand on my thigh, the slide of the razor. It's overwhelming. I work to steady my breathing and clutch the towel tighter to my chest.

"Kyle, please be still."

He works, and I can tell, even without looking, that he's applying all of his care and concentration to the task. He finishes my right leg and skims both hands from mid-thigh down to my ankle even more slowly than he moved the razor.

I start my anti-anxiety deep breathing to steady myself, to keep from trembling.

"Left leg, please."

He repeats the process with the same meticulousness. He moves at the same speed, but I'm becoming more unsteady with every swipe, every squeeze of his fingers behind my knee. My left leg takes eons. He completes the final swipe on the inside of my thigh and places the razor on the bathroom floor. He drifts his hands from thigh to ankle, same as he did on the right, then surprises me by running his thumbnail down the arch of my foot, applying enough pressure that my ticklish instinct is overridden by the sensuousness surrounding me like shower steam.

"Jackson," I whisper. I can't figure out what he's doing, what this means.

The sound of my voice wakes up some part of him, and he pulls his hands from my leg. "It's not long until you need to head back. Go ahead and finish up. I'll be waiting for you out there." He hikes a thumb over his shoulder, pointing at the other room.

Needing a minute to recover, I bury my face in my hands. When I think I've regained some semblance of composure, I dry off. I can't leave the bathroom until I'm fully clothed, unsure what just happened here. I know that it was absolutely the sexiest thing that has ever happened to me and, at the same time, the most confounding. I clench and unclench my fists and pull on my jeans. He was right when he said we don't have much time.

When I open the bathroom door, Jackson is sitting on the couch. He switched out his wet clothes for chinos and a T-shirt and looks completely unaffected, typing something out on his laptop.

"Hey," I croak. I don't know what to do with my hands, so I sort of flap them around for a second before finally shoving them in my pockets. I'm standing there pigeon-toed, my mind a blank buzz.

"Sorry. I got an email from Costa Rica and needed to respond right away."

"Is everything okay?"

"Nothing that can't be dealt with. Just a customs issue. I need to go to the office here. He needs to go to the office in Porto Caldera. We'll get it taken care of."

"Oh. Well. That's good."

"Come sit by me?" He sets the laptop on the coffee table and pats the couch cushion next to him.

I don't say anything, not trusting my voice or my instincts. My brain can't keep up with the boomeranging events of this afternoon. Two and half hours ago, I was practically catatonic. Now, I'm confused and more than a little bit aroused. I sit on the opposite end of the couch, putting as much distance between us as I can without seeming standoffish while I try to settle myself.

"Feel better?"

"Yes. Thank you for the shower." My face heats.

"My pleasure."

I knot my fingers together, close my eyes, take a breath. "Thank you for bringing me here." I frown. "I don't like having you at the house. I never know what will get back to Booth. Plus, I don't want Eddie seeing you in my room and giving me more shit." Jackson frowns but says nothing, so I keep going. "I want to talk to you about last week."

"Okay."

"You said you liked me. Did you mean it, or did you just say it because I did?"

"Kyle, if you haven't figured this out, I don't say anything I don't mean."

"Right. But. Could you say it again, please?"

"Yes, Kyle," he says patiently. "I like you."

"Okay." I exhale. "Can I ask you one more thing? Will you kiss me?" If he rejects me again, then I'll just go back to Hope House and be catatonic for a few more weeks. No biggie.

He sits motionless for few seconds before standing. At first, he's moving away from me, but then he takes the step and a half over to me and extends his right hand. I take it, and he pulls me up and against him. "You said it yourself. It's a bad idea."

"I know. But will you do it anyway?"

He takes another half step forward. "Kissing you has been my sole preoccupation for a while now."

Jackson puts his hands on my hips and backs me into the wall. Then, yes, he kisses me.

I know I asked for it, but I'm still a little surprised when it happens. One of his hands stays on my hip but the other moves to the nape of my neck and tugs at my hair, pulling my head back to where he wants it. He presses me harder into the wall, and it feels like he's kissing me with his entire body. He starts with this lingering, closed-mouth kiss. It's the perfect first kiss for a man who uses the word "willy-nilly": it's a little chaste, and leaves me a lot wanting.

Then there's another one, more lingering, more open and hungry. I think he's done, pulling away, when he nips my lower lip. I gasp in surprise, and the next kiss moves another step away from chaste. His hand slides from my hip, under my shirt, and comes to rest against my lower back. He moves his lips from my mouth, skimming my cheek and then my jaw with just his breath before biting playfully at my neck. I yelp, and the noise must shock him; he pulls back, moving both of his hands to my shoulders.

He's blushing. "Sorry. I got a little carried away."

"No need to apologize. You just surprised me. Feel free to do that anytime the need arises, Jackson."

"I'm not sure I'd ever stop."

As soon as I'm on my own feet, he lets go, pacing away. He puts his hands to his face and rubs. He took all my wits with him, so all I can do is stand there, my mouth hanging open.

He's the first one to speak, keeping his back to me. "Well, now I've got even more to be preoccupied with." His ribcage heaves.

"Yeah, there's no way that's a bad idea."

I shuffle my feet. My time is nearly up, and I don't want to go because more of those kisses has just been pushed to the very top of my hierarchy of needs. No more food, only Jackson. But what if I end up with no more Jackson and I'm left starving? I swallow the thought.

"Hey, you remember the first day I came into the shop, right? The day you yelled at me for standing with the door open?" I ask.

He pulls his bottom lip into his teeth like he's making himself stay silent. He looks like he wants to argue, but after a couple of seconds, he nods again.

"I have to tell you, that was the first time I had left Hope House since my admission. I had been watching the shop from my windowsill every morning. I was so intrigued by the two of you; Jamie was always smiling, and you always . . . not."

He huffs a single laugh.

"I thought about you all the time and why you never smiled, because even with my depression kicking the crap out of me, I still smiled sometimes. I also thought about what it would be like to see you smile. I wondered how it would change your face if I could ever manage it. And then I did manage it, and your smile, Jackson . . . man, it's everything."

The corner of his mouth tugs up. "You know what's everything about you?"

"What?"

"Those cookies." He smirks. "I almost made myself sick on them."

I had completely forgotten about those. "Did you get the others?"

His brows draw together. "What others?"

"The chocolate cakes and the macarons?"

"Those were you?"

I nod. "I forgot to tell you."

"Kyle, what do you do for a living?"

My face heats, even though I don't know why I'm embarrassed by the answer. "I'm a pastry chef."

"Really?" He paces farther away, into the kitchen. "I don't know why I'm surprised. I shouldn't be, but I am. You know Jamie's been bugging me about putting food in the shop." It's a statement, not a question. Maybe he heard us talking on that first day in the shop.

"Uh-huh. He told me."

"Oh," he says, the tone unclear. He doesn't sound shocked or angry. I can't tell what he is. He paces away another step, to the far wall of the kitchen. "We need to go. Your time is up." His voice is even more of a mystery to me now, weirdly flat and emotionless. He walks over and tugs my hand, pulling me closer.

"How many minutes?"

"Four."

"Then we'll need to make this quick." I smile, put a hand behind his head, and pull him to me. I kiss the hell out of him, needing to know that he's okay. That we're okay. When we pull apart, I desperately want time to collect myself before going back, but I don't have the luxury. "Stay here. I'll see you tomorrow."

He nods and swallows hard as I close the door.

I run back to Hope House. Even without a watch, I know I'm late. Maybe Booth will forgive a couple of minutes. I must look like I just ran a marathon, flushed and out of breath. Hopefully, who-ever's on duty in the security office will be busy with something else and not notice my tardiness.

Luck must be on my side: the sign-in log is out on the desk and there's no guard. I scribble my name and keep running up to my room, fingers crossed that my four extra minutes went unnoticed.

CHAPTER SIXTEEN

Dinner is slapdash, since I didn't have time to cook anything substantial: grilled ham and cheese with potato chips and pears. It's going to draw ire from Eddie, but it's the same meal my grandma served on my first night in her custody. It's a sense-memory-hug on a plate. I'm edgy.

The two hours in Jackson's loft were overwhelming. I hate to think Booth is right and I'm not ready for what's happening, but my brain is having trouble keeping up. I want to run back across the street and smother myself with all things Jackson. It's a foreign feeling; attaching myself to another person isn't something I've even considered before. Maybe it's growing up the way I did, maybe it's the depression, but giving someone else any part of me always seemed horrifying, like a waste of time and energy.

At the same time, I'm worried about his reaction to me being a pastry chef. I was afraid he'd be angry because I'd kind of lied by omission, and he wasn't that. He *was* upset, though. It's the why and how that are gnawing at my brain all afternoon.

While I'm cooking dinner, I resolve to keep myself together, focus, do everything Booth says, and get out of here.

"Hi, Mary."

"Hello, dear. How are you? I've missed you."

"I know, and I'm sorry. The Joey thing combined with . . ." I pause when I realize I haven't told her about Jackson. "Well, other stuff. It was just too much. I'll try to do better. At least what I'm supposed to do every day. How are you? I'm so sorry you had to deal with Eddie on your own all this time."

"I've been better and I've been worse. I can deal with Eddie. He doesn't give me nearly as hard a time as he does you and Joey." She notices her slip and reaches in her pocket for a tissue. "*Gave* Joey." She sniffs. "Now I'm sorry. I keep forgetting he's not here."

I give her a big hug, patting her shoulder. It's interesting, hugging Mary after Jackson, comparing the two—how she's softer than him, more fragile. How I don't *fit* into her the way I fit into him. "It's okay. If I hadn't spent a week in bed thinking about it, I'd be doing the same thing. Let's eat some dinner and get things back to normal around here, okay?"

"Sounds good."

Mary doesn't set a glass of milk next to the fourth plate.

"I thought there was a new girl? Should I not have made anything for her?"

"Phoebe will be down for dinner because she has to be. And yes, you needed to make a plate for her. But don't be offended if she doesn't eat. She's sweet. I think you'll like her."

Right on cue, Phoebe walks into the room and stares at me as she sits.

"Hey. It's Phoebe, right? It's nice to meet you. I'm Kyle."

"Hi," she whispers, and adds a little wave. She jerks her hand back, pulling it into her sleeve, as Eddie and Nancy walk in together.

"Good evening, Kyle. How nice of you to join us," Nancy says.

I ignore her snarky tone. "Hey."

"What's up, Special K? It's about fuckin' time you got your ass out of bed. The food's been shit this week."

"Maybe I can make it up to you a little. The making it up to you isn't going to start now, though. Just sandwiches tonight, but it'll get better tomorrow."

"Well, thank fuck for that." He turns to Phoebe. "Hey, Feebs, whatcha gonna do once Special K over here puts chocolate cake and muffins and shit in front of you? You gonna do your bird act or try the old binge-and-purge?"

"That's enough, Eddie." Nancy shoots him a look, then her eyes move to Phoebe. "I will need you to take at least ten full bites of food this evening. After that, you may be excused."

Phoebe looks at me, embarrassed, from under her curtain of waist-length brown hair. I grin, letting her know I'm not going to bother her about what's happening. She reaches out and picks at the crust of her sandwich.

The rest of us eat. Mary and I stay quiet while Eddie regales us with a recap of the Rambo marathon that was on TV last night. His explosion sounds send crumbs flying out of his mouth, and I shield my plate the best I can. I'm sure to "ooh" and "ahh" in all the right places so that Eddie will know I'm listening. I couldn't care less about what he's saying, but I have to admit that his wild gesticulating, crumb-spraying recap is the most entertaining movie review I've ever seen.

"Then there's this huge fucking helicopter with all these guns and missiles, and it flies over the ridge, and there's just Rambo. Alls he's got is a fucking bow and arrow, but the arrow has an explosive tip. He shoots the fuckin' arrow and BOOM!" Eddie's arms fly out. "The fucking helicopter explodes and blows up those commie motherfuckers. It's epic, man. So fuckin' epic! Hey, Mary, next time it's on, I'll come and get you. Maybe watching John Rambo fuck up a whole bunch of dudes will help you get over this PTSD bullshit you've got going on. See a bunch of other dudes die and maybe seeing your old man die won't seem so bad. What would the doctor call it, Nance? You know when you see so much of something it doesn't fuck with you anymore?"

Mary's got her tissue out of her pocket again, making confetti.

"Eddie," Nancy warns.

"I'm trying to help, Nance. Just putting' in my two cents." He shrugs as he shoves the last quarter of sandwich into his mouth. "See ya." He pushes back from the table, his chair hitting the wall behind him, and walks out of the room.

"Well, wasn't Edward in fine form this evening? I think I'm going to retire to my room for the night," Mary says. She suddenly looks so, so tired. "Thank you for dinner, Kyle. It's wonderful to have you back with us again. Goodnight, Phoebe. You let me know if you need anything."

I finish my last few bites of food and leave Phoebe alone at the table, still picking apart her sandwich with Nancy whispering over her shoulder.

* * *

My old sleep pattern is back since there was no sedative alteration yesterday. I wake up at five and lie there for an hour, fighting the urge to sit on the windowsill. Once I can't stand it anymore, I get out of bed and get dressed. The Coffee Shop is already open for the day. I don't dawdle but head downstairs to start breakfast. It's pancakes this morning. They take more time than muffins, so they'll keep me occupied. I barrel through the morning, picking tasks that take time, keeping my brain distracted. I'm trying to wait until mid-afternoon to check out. I'm not as concerned about going to the shop today as I am with hanging out with Jackson, and that may not happen until the shop closes. Tomorrow I have an appointment with Booth that will take up a whole chunk of my morning.

At two thirty, I'm in the security office, practically running in place with pent-up energy.

"Hey, Kyle. What's up?" Bruce asks.

"Just gonna check out for a while. Maybe grab a cup of coffee."

"Aw, man. Didn't the doctor talk to you this morning?"

"Uh, no. About what?" Shit. This is not good. The other times Booth talked to me outside of our regular appointments, he told me I wasn't meeting expectations. And then he told me that Joey was dead.

"Your off-site privileges. He revoked 'em yesterday." Bruce isn't ruffled at all by this conversation. He's probably told a hundred patients the same thing.

I, however, am very fucking ruffled. I clench my fists to stop myself from picking up the clipboard on the desk. I want to throw it at his head. Maybe take it to Booth's office and hit him in the face with it a couple of times. "Why? Is it because I slept so much this week? I'm better now. I promise." Why am I pleading my case here? Booth is the only one who can do anything to change it.

CHAPTER SEVENTEEN

I'm standing outside Booth's office for my appointment five minutes early. I couldn't sleep last night, tossing and turning thinking about how to handle the doctor and Jackson.

Eventually, reason prevailed, and I picked a course of action for the doctor that didn't involve violence: do whatever the fuck he tells me to. It seems easy enough, but surely the good doctor will throw some wrench into my plan. He never makes things too easy.

"Miss Davies, you may come in," Booth calls.

I take my seat. "Good morning, Dr. Booth." My smile is weak, but at least I put in the effort.

"Good morning." His voice is terse. He's leaned forward, forearms on his desk, studying me.

I scratch at the spot of green icing color on my jeans so I don't have to take part in a staring contest.

"It's been another exciting week, hasn't it?"

"Yes, sir." Keep the answers brief.

"How do you feel you've dealt with it? The nurses' notes this week are not positive."

"Not well. I didn't use my coping skills." Use keywords, so he'll know I've been paying attention.

"At least you are aware of that mistake. They also informed me that you exceeded your two-hour time limit for off-site yesterday."

"Yes." I bite my tongue so I don't add that it was only a couple of minutes.

"You know how I feel about punctuality. This is your second offense, and the reason I suspended your privilege."

"For how long?" Don't argue with him.

"That all depends."

"On what?" Fucker.

"Last week, you were insistent that you were not in a relationship with Mr. Turner. Then, this week, he was added to your visitors list, signed into the facility, and you left with him. Holding hands," he says, ignoring my question.

Shit, shit, shit! I didn't even think about that. I was so happy Jackson showed up and we were leaving; I lost my head for a minute. I can't think of anything to say to Booth to fix it.

"Then, you were tardy for the second time."

"I'm sorry, Dr. Booth." It's lame, but the only thing that seems appropriate.

He ignores my apology. "I have several topics to address with you this morning, so we will not linger on the subject. I have made my feelings about your readiness for any sort of romantic entanglements clear. I cannot force you to obey, even if you should."

My head drops. There's a threat behind those words. I was so apathetic in the hospital; I signed over my right to make medical decisions to the doctor. There didn't seem to be any harm in doing it. I've realized my mistake, though. Booth can keep me here as long as he wants. Until he deems me competent. Until I'm compliant.

"Although I cannot entirely ignore your setback and the rule-breaking of last week, I would like to tell you how pleased I am with your general progress since admission. For the most part, you have been committed to my programs and schedules. It is unfortunate that your reaction to Joey's death was so extreme, but I am confident that future counseling will help you develop more effective coping mechanisms. That being said, I believe you are ready for the next step in your treatment plan."

I jerk my head up to look at him. "What's that?"

He moves into Caring Pose. "Transition. Preparing for your release."

I light up like a Christmas tree. Color me surprised. Of all the things I thought he could have said, that wouldn't have been on the list. "I'm ready, Dr. Booth. I want be back in the world. I want to live my life again."

"I know you do, Kyle. The first step will be finding you gainful employment."

"Okay. I can make some calls—"

He holds up a hand. "We have an agency that will take care of finding a position. One you will want to keep after your discharge."

"Is there paperwork I need to fill out?" I fidget, excited about the prospect of getting out of here for more than two hours at a time.

"Not now, no. There's nothing for you to worry about. I have spoken with them and provided any relevant information regarding your interests and availability. They should get back to me later this week, and I will notify you once a plan is in place."

"Oh," I say, not entirely comfortable with how this is progressing. I want to pick my own job. But I wanted a chance at a fresh start more, and that's what this is, so . . . I take a deep breath and accept the doctor's plans. "When will I start?"

"As soon as the agency gets back with an acceptable position. Until you receive the employment placement, though, I require *absolute* compliance. Your off-site privileges will remain suspended until that time. Any deviation and I will reverse the course of your treatment."

"Okay." I'm not thrilled with that stipulation, but I can deal for a few days if it means getting out for good.

"And, Kyle? Once you begin working I still expect you to keep up with your assigned tasks in the house, so you will need to plan accordingly."

"I can do that." Another deep breath.

"I know you can. You can go now. Take the appropriate steps, and you'll be discharged in no time."

He gives me a huge, creepy smile, and I get out of there as quick as I can.

* * *

The 117 minutes from my last visit to Jackson's apartment play in my head like a film reel running fast, then slow. Chunks fly by in a quadruple-speed blur. Other bits move in frame-by-frame and let me see every happiness and hurt in fragments of suspended time. Our kiss is super-slow, lasting what feels like an hour in my replay. The initial press of his lips is eight minutes, the brush of his thumb under my breast is four. The flicker of our matinee keeps my mental projector busy. I can even feel the flap, flap, flap of the film running out at the end.

Jackson came by the day after my appointment with Booth. Turned out, Booth suspended my visitor privileges, too. The man knows how to drive home a point, I'll give him that. So, for nearly a week, I haven't seen Jackson. I can't bring myself to sit in the window.

On the sixth day, Lori comes into the kitchen while I'm kneading bread dough and funneling all my frustrations into it. I've worked the dough so hard it's turned into a gluten brick.

"Kyle, the doctor wanted me to tell you that we should get the information about your job today. You should plan on starting tomorrow, so your off-site privileges have been reinstated. You can go out today if you need anything to prepare."

"Thanks. I think I'll do that." I throw the dough in the trash and head upstairs to get dressed.

* * *

It's freezing out, and I still don't have any cold weather clothes other than Jackson's sweater. The wind bites through the single layers on my legs and lower arms as soon as I hit the street, but the sting is invigorating instead of painful since I haven't been out in a week. The Coffee Shop is closed, so I put my head down and walk to the Division East Bridge instead. Once there, I turn and face downtown, sliding my arms through the same beams as that day with Jackson. I stand there until my forearms are numb with cold, thinking about him and what tomorrow might hold. This outing is supposed to be for job prep, but how can I get ready with no idea where I'm going?

I walk back toward Hope House with no more insight or pre-paredness than before I left. Hopefully, the job Booth finds will be a good one. My options are limited; even if the job sucks, I can't walk into coffee shops around the city and tell them, "Right now I'm in a mental institution, but next month, I'd like to bake cookies for you!"

I scroll through my mental contacts as I walk, going through the list of reputable bakeries, ones with creative pastry cases that could give me some artistic license. I'm list-making, not watching the sidewalk in front of me, and run into someone. I mumble an apology and walk around them. A man's hand grabs the arm of my T-shirt with force. I shove hard enough that he releases his grip, then realize it's Jackson.

"Jackson? What are you—? Oh, my gosh, I am so sorry! I didn't know it was you."

Seeing him for the first time in nearly a week is overwhelming.

"It's okay. You were distracted. What are you thinking about?"

"A lot." I sigh and change the subject, not wanting to use our little bit of time talking about my job prospects. "What are you doing?"

"Looking for you. I saw you leave Hope House earlier, but I had to finish closing the shop, so I couldn't get away immediately."

"Why?"

"I wanted to see you. I've missed you." He grabs my hand. As soon as he feels how cold it is, he takes the other and cups them between his own, then brings them to his mouth, blows warm air into them, and rubs.

"Oh." I look down. I was sure he'd be mad about my recurring vanishing act. Why wouldn't he be? And I just shoved him. I'm too agitated to raise my head.

"Kyle, will you look at me?"

I shake my head in refusal. My hair falls into my eyes. I need a haircut.

"Why not?" There's a trace of hurt in his voice.

"I don't know what I'll see when I look at your face." I start to tear up but try to hold myself together. I shiver.

He must pull up to his full height, because now he's blocking the wind that's gusting down the street. He puts our gathered hands under my chin, pushing up, but I pull back enough that he can't force my face upward.

"Please don't make me, Jackson." I shake my head again.

He pulls our hands back toward him and doesn't let go. He's not saying anything. I start silent counting to keep my anxiety at bay: twenty-seven, twenty-eight, twenty-nine . . .

"I won't make you, even if I want you to more than anything."

A tear slips out and runs down my cheek. Shit. I'm not even sure why I'm crying—maybe because I know I shouldn't be here with him. Booth would kill me if he knew. He might put the brakes on my transition.

"Please don't cry." Jackson takes one hand away from our bundle and wipes the moisture from my cheek with his thumb. "I've been doing a lot of thinking this week. I've made some decisions and would like your opinion."

"I don't have much time. I've got to be back in a few minutes and can't be late. Booth told me he's willing to start my transition, you know, to release me, and there can't be any rule-breaking."

"So you can leave again, right?"

I nod.

"Okay. You can give me your opinion tomorrow. Will that be okay? Will you come see me tomorrow at the shop? Jamie can cover for me."

"I don't know. I'm supposed to start my new job tomorrow."

"Oh," he says, disappointed. "But that's great news."

"Yeah. It is. I'll try to come by, but I can't promise anything."

"I guess I'll just have to take it. It can wait a little while."

I pull my hands away and shove them into my pockets. "I gotta go." I start walking the last two blocks.

"Kyle, wait." Jackson's right behind me, but doesn't try to spin me around to face him. "Can I tell you one more thing before you go? I'll tell you while we walk, okay?"

I nod, and he pulls up beside me.

"I'm not quite sure how to say this. I've been thinking about it for days, what I was going to say once I had you in front of me again, but nothing was right. Now, I'm finding myself at a loss for words."

I smirk at his rambling but keep walking. The need for punctuality is the only thing greater than my desire to hear what he has to say. "One block to go. You're on the clock." I didn't mean for that to come out so snippy.

"I've missed you. That's all it comes down to. I've missed you in the shop. I've missed you on your windowsill in the morning. I can't put it more plainly than that."

I look at him for the first time since right after I ran into him. Those brown eyes are twinkling like crazy, probably with nerves. I reach out and smooth my index finger over the creases between his brows. His expression relaxes. I grab his left hand and entwine my fingers. "Me, too. I'll come by. Not tomorrow, but the day after. Okay? I'll have to figure out a way so Booth won't find out."

I pull away from him and step into Hope House's entryway. The door is nearly closed when it pulls open behind me. I turn around and start to ask him what he's doing, but before I can get a word out, Jackson backs me into the wall. Quicker than a hiccup, he pulls me into a hug, my hands holding tight to fistfuls of his shirt.

"I'll see you soon." He pulls away and opens the door, letting in a whoosh of arctic cold, and leaves the alcove without looking back.

I use all of my fifty-three remaining seconds of freedom to collect myself before I walk back into captivity. This isn't the first time it's felt like I'm trapped here. But it is the first time I've felt this measure of desperation for freedom.

CHAPTER EIGHTEEN

It hits me halfway up the stairs to my room: Jackson just hugged me. In the Hope House entryway. On camera. "Shit! Shit! Shit!" I mutter to myself. Booth will find out. I just know it. This could put the brakes on me getting out of here. I clench my fists hard enough to break the skin on my palms, when the painful sting makes me stop and take the prescribed calming breaths. I have to keep it together for a few more hours. Then I'll have some freedom.

Just last week, I promised no rule-breaking, do whatever it takes to get me out of here. Booth said it: no more Jackson Turner. Why do I keep thinking I can put one over on him? Booth has the power. I know it, he knows it, and he's done everything he can to remind me of it since I got here. Once the release papers are in my hands and Dr. Booth can no longer decide about me or my life, Jackson and I can see each other again. But until then, keeping my distance will be the best thing for both of us. I don't want to stay away, but I have to. If Booth finds out, I have no doubt he'll revoke my privileges again, send me ten steps back. I'll tell Jackson everything the next time I see him. Man, this sucks.

I walk into the bathroom to wash the blood off my palms.

*   *   *

I spend the evening baking muffins for the rest of the week's breakfasts, then make a grocery list to cover the next two weeks, hoping that'll give me enough time to adjust to my new schedule before I have to do these tasks again. The possibility of getting out of here has to be my focus, present happiness be damned.

When dinnertime rolls around, it hits me—I really don't care what ends up on the table. Mary's my friend, so I'd rather keep her happy, but Phoebe's still a mystery, and since she's anorexic I assume she doesn't much care what's on her plate. And Eddie . . . well, at this point, he can just fuck off. I make an extra pile of sandwiches, pour some chips in a big bowl, and leave it all on the dining room table before going back to my room.

When I reach the top of the stairs, Lori's walking down the hall with an envelope. "Here's the information you need for tomorrow morning. He said if you have questions, that Nancy can help you once she gets here."

"Okay. This is great. Thanks. Did he tell you anything? Did he get me something good?"

"He said he found something suited to you, so I would assume you're going to a bakery, but that's just a guess." She shrugs, then places a hand on my shoulder. "I just want you to know how proud I am of you. It's been tough around here the past few weeks, and you've handled it well. You'll handle your job, too. I'm rooting for you."

Tears well up in my eyes. "Thanks. I'm ready to get the hell out of here."

"You do whatever needs doing. You don't need to be here anymore. I know that and you know that. You just have to prove it to Dr. Booth."

I nod. "I'm going to get my stuff ready for tomorrow. Dinner's already on the table downstairs."

"Okay. Maybe I'll see you tomorrow? Depending on your new schedule."

I rip into the envelope and am immediately disappointed. The piece of paper inside doesn't tell me much. Booth gave me an address and a map showing an intersection in Little Italy. There's just a note telling me to be there by eight in the morning and a transit card to pay for the train. I drop onto the bed, sagging with disappointment. Why is this lack of information such a surprise? This is so typical of Booth. Of course he's reminding me he's the one in control, even as I earn my freedom. That fucker.

As much as I've lamented my wardrobe choices in the past few weeks, now it comes in handy. Do I want to wear the red shirt or the blue one? The jeans with the spot of red food dye on the right thigh or the ones with the frayed hem? With the clothes folded in my chair and ready for the morning, I take off Jackson's sweater, fold it, and lay it on top. Since he gave it to me, I've worn it every day except laundry day. I'm sure it doesn't smell like him anymore, but now and then, I swear a whiff of espresso is still there. It's probably my imagination playing tricks on me, but I don't mind.

It takes a long time to fall asleep because my brain won't be quiet. I should probably give Jackson's sweater back if we can't see each other anymore. I dread telling him. He said he'd wait, but how unreasonable would it be of me to expect it? We hardly know each other. Will I even have the guts to tell him? Maybe I should just chicken out and hide myself away until Booth releases me. But how long will that be? With Booth, who knows? He could be expecting a week, or a month, or a year. There's one certainty: he won't tell me.

The swirling thoughts are so different from what's usually going on in my brain. I enjoy the insomnia a little, even if it's going to bite me in the ass tomorrow morning. My brain is usually just a dull hum of activity. This is the biggest change since I met Jackson, the *feeling* everything. For years, I've been flat and numb. I thought I'd just been wired that way, but apparently it was actually depression.

Honestly? It's nice to feel something for once. Even if it's not all good.

*   *   *

Nancy gives my shoulder a not-so-gentle shove to wake me up.

"Time to get up so you won't be late," she says. She has enough confidence in her authority to walk right back out of the room. She knows I'll get up.

I shuffle across the hall to the bathroom and splash my face with cold tap water, trying to shake off the tired. Getting ready takes only a few minutes, way less time than Nancy gave me. It's thirty more before I need to head to the L station down the street. Peeking out the window, I see The Coffee Shop is already open. Two booths have customers, reading the paper and drinking Jackson's magical brew. I'm jealous. The 7-Eleven coffee I'll have to get instead will pale in comparison. Maybe this job will have decent coffee for the employees? I can only hope.

"You know where you're going, right?" Nancy's questions snaps my attention away from the view across the street.

"Yeah. I can get there."

"Go, then. You do not want to be late on your first day. Dr. Booth would not be pleased."

And so, not bothering to respond, I leave for work.

* * *

It's a good thing I left early. I've been standing on the sidewalk outside of Frank's Pizza for five minutes wondering what the fuck Booth was thinking. Maybe he wasn't. Or maybe this is just one more of his mind-fucks. This isn't a place for me to reestablish my career. Maybe it's not meant to be. I'm pretty sure Booth is the only one who has any of the answers.

At eight, I walk through the door. It looks like every other old-school pizza place in Chicago. Maybe in the world. Red-check-print vinyl covers tables that have folded cardboard under at least one leg to keep them from wobbling. Walls covered with prints from *The Godfather* and pictures of a guy who I assume must be Frank, with every local politician and semi-celebrity who's ever been in here. One thing I do know about this place, if it holds true to my experiences? It'll have incredible pizza.

"Hello?" I call out.

A guy bursts through the swinging door at the back of the room, and I stumble back in shock, from both the force of his entry and the sight of him. "You the newbie?" he asks in a voice that's pure grit.

I just stare at him, unable to answer. He has to be at least six and a half feet tall and is dressed like a skinhead—huge black steel-toed boots, tight jeans with suspenders, and a white T-shirt. His head isn't shaved, though. He's got what would be a mohawk if he put enough styling product in it. And it's neon pink.

"Yo!" he yells, waving a huge hand in front of my face. "You okay, lady?"

"Yeah," I squeak.

"Well, you can talk, so that's one thing outta the way. What do you want in here? We don't open 'til eleven."

I hold up a finger, then shake my head. "Sorry. I'm here to work. I'm the new girl, Kyle."

"Kyle, huh? Good thing he told me it was a new girl and not just your name or I woulda assumed you were a guy." He scratches the shaved side of his head and furrows his brow like he's confused by it all.

"I get that a lot." I'm making fists in the sleeves of Jackson's sweater, but they're not doing as much for my anxiety since I cut my fingernails off last night—the edge of pain takes the edge off the jitters. Super-short nails are a requirement of working with dough, and I assumed Booth would put me in a bakery. "My mom had a screwed up sense of humor, apparently."

He booms out a laugh way bigger than I was expecting. Everything about this guy is big. "Well, come on. Time's wasting. We got a ton of shit to do before lunch." He puts a ball cap on and walks toward the doors he just came through.

"Um, I don't wanna sound dumb, but what exactly am I doing here?"

"Frankie didn't tell you?"

"No. I haven't met Frankie. He may have told the, um, guy who got me the job, but it didn't make it back to me."

We walk into the kitchen. It looks pretty standard. Prep stations for salad, pizza ovens, and a couple of burners for pasta.

"Frankie told me you were gonna handle the dough for me. Said you're some kind of whiz kid."

I pinch the bridge of my nose, trying to stave off the headache that's sure to come.

"Maybe with desserts, but definitely not with pizza dough. I haven't made pizza dough since my first year of culinary school. I'm trained as a pastry chef."

"Fuck! I knew Frankie was gonna pull this shit. Him and his favors." He paces, kind of. The kitchen isn't huge, and his legs are so long there's only room to take two steps back and forth.

"Look, I may not know shit about pizza, but I do know how to work. If you show me what to do, I can keep up. I'm a quick learner, and I need this job. I won't let you down . . . uh, you didn't tell me your name yet."

He stops pacing, turns, and studies me. After five seconds, he thrusts one of his huge hands toward me. "I'm Trace."

"Nice to meet you, Trace," I say, shaking his hand and mentally shaking my head. With a name like Trace, where does he get off making fun of my name? "Where should I start?"

"You ever work a sheeter?"

"Uh-uh." I shake my head. "I've only ever done desserts and a little bit of bread dough in a pinch." I see him make a face that's just short of an eye roll and add, "I swear, I really am a fast learner. Show me what to do, and it'll get done."

He walks into a storeroom off the main kitchen filled with lid-ded plastic trash cans. Well, shit. I hope this huge guy isn't some kind of serial killer about to shove my dismembered body into one of these things. "This is gonna be your spot." He gestures to the room.

"My spot?"

"This is the dough room. There's your mixer." He points to an ancient Hobart commercial mixer in the corner. I know what that is. Then he nods at the trash cans. "We keep the dough in these to rise overnight."

"But, they're trash cans," I say, wondering what the health inspector would say if they saw this.

"Yeah, but we don't use 'em for trash," he says, like I'm slow. "They're the only thing big enough to hold as much dough as we need in a day."

I want to argue, ask about health codes, but bite my tongue when I remember that this job is my ticket out of Hope House. "What do I need to do first?"

He pops the lid off one of the cans, and the smell of yeasty goodness fills the room. "You wanna get some flour outta that bin over there and spread some over the counter for me?"

"Sure." I know how to do this without further instruction.

As soon as the counter is flour-dusted, he picks up the trash can and flips it over above the counter; the dough slides out in a glutenous blob.

"You're gonna punch this down, then section it into 250-gram balls. There's a scraper and a scale on the shelf. You need me to show you how to do that?"

"No, I know how to do that part."

"Good. I gotta keep working on prep for the line. You get going on that. Let me know when you've got the first can done, and I'll show you what to do next. You're gonna need this, too." He hands me a red bandanna and circles a finger at my face. "You know, for your hair."

I don't know how to deal with his thoughtful gesture. "Thanks. I didn't think about that this morning." Actually, I *did* think about it. But I don't have a hat at the house, and we're not allowed bandannas or scarves.

"Shout if you need anything," he says.

We head to our separate workstations and make pizza.

An hour later, after making and weighing what feels like a thousand balls of dough, my shoulders and back are screaming from the onslaught of the day's labor. And it's only nine. Trace comes in and shows me how to work the sheeter, a machine that turns those balls of dough into pizza crusts, and how to prep the pans with a dusting of cornmeal and the flattened dough. The assembly line isn't exciting. It's mindless and boring. On the one hand, I'm pissed at Booth for sticking me with this shitty job that surely pays minimum wage, but, on the other, it gets me out of the house every day and will eventually get me out for good.

At ten, the restaurant fills with staff: another cook, a dishwasher, a busboy, and a number of waitresses. I can hear the kitchen's busy din, but my little room is calm and separated from the chaos. I work my way through most of the bins by the end of the rush.

"Good job today," Trace says from behind me. "You weren't kidding when you said you'd keep up. Get outta here. I'll clean up for you. The night guy'll use the rest of this and make tomorrow's batch." He gestures at the trash cans of dough.

I'm disappointed that I won't be making anything from scratch but try to school my expression so Trace can't see it. "Okay, thanks. Same time tomorrow?"

"Yep." He walks back into the kitchen and starts wiping down his station.

I grab my bag and walk to the train station.

CHAPTER NINETEEN

"Hey. Good first day?" Bruce asks before I've even made it through the door of the security office.

"Yep." Even though the job is boring, now that I've been back in the world all day, I'm filled with a restless energy, a need to create. The Coffee Shop was still open, and I was tempted to stop, but I didn't. Booth might know when I get off work, and I don't want to be in trouble with him on my first day out.

"Hello?" Bruce is waving a hand in front of me.

"Sorry, Bruce. I spaced."

"Did you hear what I said?"

I shake my head. "Sorry."

"Quit apologizing. You with me now?"

I nod and feel my cheeks heat.

"I was saying, Doc wanted to go ahead and see you as soon as you got back. Head on down." He tilts his head toward Booth's office. "He's waiting for you."

"Sure. Thanks." I hand Bruce my bag so he can lock it up and head for Booth's office.

Before my knuckles hit the door to knock, he says, "Come in, Kyle."

I look at the floor all the way to my usual chair. Unsure about why Booth wanted me here and restless isn't a good combination. I need a minute in my own head to work back to a place where I can deal with the doctor.

"How are you?"

"Fine," I say to my knees. The denim is pale with flour dust.

"And how was your first day of work?"

"Fine." Just an hour ago, I would have been tempted to tell him how much the job sucks and how angry I am about being shoved in a room by myself all day and doesn't he know how overqualified I am and there's no way I'm keeping that job for long once he lets me go. But now, I'm not. He doesn't care about any of that. Compliance is my key to freedom.

My restlessness doesn't have anything to do with Booth, but the job at Frank's does have me itching to create something of my own that doesn't involve flattened disks of dough. Well, unless that dough was pie crust. And I could fill it with something like an almond cream or bittersweet chocolate pastry cream. I should do both of those things. Maybe tonight, after dinner . . .

"Frank's is one of the best Italian restaurants in the city. You could do much worse." He must sense my hesitation.

I look up at him. "Frank's is great. The guy who runs the kitchen seems nice." Those two things are both true enough. It's not Frank's that's the problem, it's what I do for Frank's.

He nods. "Good." He opens my file and leans forward, elbows on the desk. "And how are you?"

"Fine."

"You seem . . ." He hesitates. "Preoccupied."

"Sorry, Dr. Booth. I guess I am."

"What's on your mind?"

"Baking stuff," I hedge. No need to give him more than needed.

"Ah. Still thinking about your job, then."

It's a statement instead of a question, which surprises me a little since he's not prying further. I leave him with the assumption and nod.

"Good. That's good news." He shifts in his seat, like he's trying to get closer, but I have the feeling if he scoots any more forward, he'll fall out of his chair.

I wipe my hands together and they rub together as if fine grit sandpaper covers my palms. I cringe.

"What? You're making faces, Kyle."

"Oh, sorry. I just . . ." I hold up my hands. "There's flour all over me. I need to take a shower."

"Well, that can wait. It's been nearly a week since we've seen one another." He smiles. "At least it's been an uneventful week."

I tip up one side of my mouth, too, and nod.

"Well, maybe not so dull for you, though." He wipes his face of expression and looks at me over the top of his glasses.

I stare back at him and try to parse my week for what was exciting enough to have him nearly glaring at me. At least, anything that he'd know about.

Jackson.

It hits me, and I struggle to pull in my next breath through the stab of anxious pain. Booth knows I saw him, might have seen me with him. Shit. Work was distracting enough to make me forget to worry.

I don't say anything to Booth but am guilty enough to look away and down. Today, I'm wearing the jeans with the frayed hem. I wish this chair didn't have arms, or were wider, so I could sit cross-legged. That way I could reach the threads, give my fingers something to do. As it is, I'm looking down like the universe's answers are around my ankles.

Booth clears his throat and says, "Who have you loved?"

The question is so far out of left field, and so unlike our typical discussions, my head snaps totally up. Well, at least he distracted me from the anxiety. "Huh?"

"It's a perfectly simple question. Who. Have. You. Loved?"

"What? Like, ever?"

He nods. "Yes, Kyle. Like, ever." His answer drips sarcasm.

His snark shoves me off balance. He's not taken this tone with me before. I shrug. Maybe for most people the answer would be simple—mom, dad, grandparents, their first boyfriend—but it's not so clear-cut for me. "Uh. My grandma."

"Who else?"

"I probably loved my mom at some point, but I don't really remember it." I scrunch up my face at the thought of her. Booth and I talked about her in the hospital, so he knows the story.

"Anyone else?"

I shrug again. "I don't know."

"No grandfather? Boyfriends?"

I shake my head.

"So, no relationships with men?"

"Not unless you count my bartender," I joke.

He looks over the top of his glasses again. "This is serious, Miss Davies."

I wipe my nervous smile. "I know. Sorry. Just trying to lighten the mood."

"No, you're diverting."

I look at the diploma over his shoulder. Vanderbilt. I always pegged Booth as an Ivy Leaguer, but he's putting on as much of an act for me as I am for him, I figure. I don't say anything, because he's right.

He leans forward again, drawing my eyes back in his direction. "There's a point to this."

I swallow.

"So, no men?"

I shake my head. "I guess not."

He takes Aggressive Caring Pose. "I suspected as much." He squints, like he's trying to see me more clearly. Maybe my outside has started to match my inside and gotten a little blurry around the edges.

I shift in my seat and move my eyes back to the wall above his shoulder. This concentrated studying is uncomfortable.

"I've been thinking a lot about this relationship of yours with Mr. Turner."

I open my mouth to protest, but he holds a finger up to stop me. I slam my mouth shut.

"I'm trying to understand why you're so determined to defy me. I've made my position clear?"

It takes me a second to realize that was a question, so there's an awkward pause before I answer, "Yes. You have."

"There's a bit of a rebellious streak in you. Perhaps a bit of delayed adolescence." He arches an eyebrow. "We could go with the tried and true interpretation of your actions, say you're looking for a father figure." He smiles.

I squirm in my seat. He's smiled more today than usual. It's creepy. I want him to go back to smug, pretentious Booth, not this guy who's trying to be my "pal."

"That's not it, though." His smile fades. "You actually like him. Maybe even care for him."

I bite my lower lip and nod. "I think so."

"That's far more troublesome. At least from my perspective."

"Why? Isn't it good to know that I *can* care for someone? I wasn't entirely sure I could. It's a bit of a relief."

"You make an excellent point. It is beneficial for you to know that." He picks up his fountain pen and scribbles a note in my file. I imagine it reads, *Patient confirmed to have a heart.* Booth continues. "I want you to think about the timing of this revelation of yours, though."

"Okay?"

"The past few months have been traumatic. Both your grandmother, the one person you've loved, passing away and your suicide attempt happened within a short span. Correct?"

I nod and run my fingers over the scars on my forearm. They've faded in the past couple of weeks, now just pale pink, raised lines.

"The most traumatic since the abandonment of your mother?"

I nod. His phrasing irks me, though; it makes it sound like I left her and not the other way around.

"What if, and not to think the worst of him, but what if Mr. Turner abandons you?"

I open my mouth to respond, but Booth holds up his hand like a crossing guard. "Hell is paved with good intentions. I'm sure he has no ulterior motive." He smiles again and the sarcasm is back, although subtler this time. "There's no devious plan to hurt you, but it happens. It happens every day."

I sigh. "I know."

"And your long history of untreated depression makes this kind of emotional risk especially dangerous for you."

I close my eyes and sigh again, weighing his words. After a minute, I say, "Are you saying I should never be in a relationship? That I'm too damaged now?"

He barks a laugh, and I throw my best glare at him. "No," he says, shaking his head. "Anything but. I think a supportive partner is the penultimate goal for everyone, especially those with an illness like yours."

"Oh."

"At the same time, though, consider your reaction now: that you're too damaged. That's exactly the self-perception you need to correct before proceeding. It's trite, but you have to love yourself before you can love someone else, Kyle." He grins weakly, the pity evident behind his expression.

I look at his diploma again and blink away tears.

"This is painful, but it's important. Maybe the most important thing you need to learn before your release." He closes my file and leans back. "You may go. Have a good evening."

I nod and drag myself into the hallway.

All of the energy I had when I walked into his office has vanished. Now, I just want to take a shower and go to bed. Mary can figure out dinner. I prepped enough sandwiches to survive the zombie apocalypse. They won't go hungry without me.

* * *

I can't sleep. I lie in bed replaying Booth's words in my head. "You have to love yourself before you can love someone else." It is trite, but fuck if it's not true. I don't love Jackson but think maybe I could eventually. I'm not crazy enough to think I'm in love with him. I'm not. I like him. A lot. A lot a lot.

The longer I lie in bed watching the headlights outside sweep across my ceiling, though, the more I think Booth might be right. That I always assumed my messed-upness was the fault of my shitty childhood and not an inherent flaw in myself is the biggest problem, that I placed the blame solidly on my mom's shoulders instead of accepting any for myself. How much of me ending up here is on . . . well, me?

Every recipe has a ratio, a balance of wet to dry, sweet to salt, pastry to filling. I need to figure it out on my own. I mentally parse the metaphor. The flour is me—the foundation. The milk is my childhood—a building block. My depression is the sugar— too much and my mental cake sinks in the middle. My job is the baking powder—lifting me up in spite of all the sugar. The only thing missing is the eggs—the emulsifier. They bring the mixture together. Is Jackson the eggs? I don't know.

I shake my head and close my eyes. This is ridiculous. The metaphor is dumb. I begin to drift off way after the rest of the house has gone quiet other than the occasional squeak of Nancy's shoes on the linoleum. The last thing that goes through my head before I finally fall asleep is, "I need eggs."

*   *   *

I wake up groggy and tired from not enough sleep. I shuffle to the bathroom with my toiletry bag and shower, hopeful the cool water will wake me up. After, I sit on the windowsill for a minute while I rub my hair with the towel and watch The Coffee Shop. I want to see Jackson, but, at the same time, I don't.

Putting off the discussion isn't helping; I need to tell him I can't see him. Not until I'm out of Hope House. Not until I figure out if he's eggs.

I shake my head. Of course the stupid analogy's stuck in my head now. Fuck. I get up and finish getting ready for work.

Outside, I can see Jackson behind The Coffee Shop's counter. He's scowling at a man in a business suit at the front of the line while Jamie's grinning madly. I smile and walk to the train station.

I'll do it this afternoon. I'll tell him I can't see him anymore.

CHAPTER TWENTY

I run a hand over my hair a block away from Hope House, smoothing it down the best I can, and breathe deeply. My clothes are smudged and streaked with flour and dough, but there's nothing to be done about it. Going into the house and changing isn't an option. Once inside, I won't be allowed to leave again until tomorrow, and I have to get this over with.

When I get to the door, The Coffee Shop is closed. Jackson is sitting just inside, but he's not alone. His father is standing at the door and opens it as soon as he sees me. I have no idea how he knows what I look like. Maybe he saw me at his house, but I'm not sure how. He definitely knows, though. I can see it on his face.

Going in is my only option, but I wish more than anything it weren't. I don't want to be in a room with this cold, domineering man. And I want to tell Jackson that I can't see him in front of his father even less. I just want to get it over with and leave.

Mr. Turner stares at me, expression blank. He looks long enough that it feels like one of those staring contests from elementary school, but I know I'm going to lose this one. I don't have enough of a competitive streak to take him on. I want to end it, so I blink first, then look down at my shoes.

"Miss Davies, I presume." He doesn't hold out his hand to shake.

I think that was a line from a movie—James Bond or Indiana Jones. I rack my brain. Or maybe it was a book. Or maybe I'm crazy and grasping at straws to avoid the situation standing in front of me. He huffs, and the noise draws me out of my reverie.

I don't want to irritate him. So instead of trying to comb through my mental file of books and movies, I force myself to look up. Our eyes meet for a heartbeat, and I nod. It's hardly a twitch of my chin, but with the way he's studying me, I know he sees it. His eyes are glacial. They're close in color to Jackson's, but where I'd always thought of Jackson's as something warm, his father's . . . well, they're cold. What's brown and cold? Iced coffee? My mind blanks. I've got nothing. I shiver and look at Jackson. He's staring at the tabletop, unblinking. I wish he'd turn my way.

"Are you cold?" Mr. Turner asks. The question itself is solicitous, but the tone matches the chill in his eyes.

"No." I choke on the word and have to clear my throat.

"Would you like something to drink?"

Jackson doesn't move.

I shake my head. "I'm fine." I'm anything but fine. My insides are riotous. I grab the strap of my messenger bag and squeeze tight. "Thank you."

"Good. Shall we sit?" He moves to the booth where Jackson sits, closest to the door and farthest from where I usually sit, and gestures for me to go ahead with a sweep of his hand. I move with deliberateness, thinking about every muscle as I slide into the seat next to Jackson, as close as I can get without giving away my need to touch him. Our thighs brush.

"It's a pleasure to officially meet you, Kyle. May I call you Kyle?" I nod.

"I've heard *all* about you." He says it like he knows everything.

I suspect that accentuation is his first move in the game we're about to play. I don't kid myself either. Just from the little bit Jackson's told me, I know this man. At least, I know his type. Mom dated guys like this. They didn't have money, but they played with control. Usually their control involved fists instead of words, but it's really all the same if you put enough force behind the sentence or the punch.

"All good, I hope," I say with a stupid giggle. I can do my Booth routine with this guy, or at least some version of it. At least, I could if my heart and brain would stop racing. *Calm down*, I think, and dig my fingers into the sides of my thighs. At the movement, Jackson grabs my hand, twining our fingers, and flexes. I sigh in relief.

Mr. Turner doesn't respond for a second, like what I said or did was unexpected. "Oh, of course." He smiles weakly. "Of course." The repetition is forceful, assured. He moves his hand over his sleeve, smoothing a nonexistent wrinkle, and says, "Jack speaks highly of you."

"Who? Oh, Jackson. Yes. I speak highly of him, too." Damn, that was awkward. And dumb. *Be cool.* "He's been very kind." I look at him and smile. He's looking out the window. If not for the fact he's holding my hand with some serious force under the table, I'd think he was ignoring me.

"I'm sure he has," Mr. Turner nearly snarls. He stares at me again. The long, unblinking looks creep me out.

I look outside. The cars on the street aren't moving. The school two blocks down lets out about now; the kids and carpools jam up traffic in the afternoon. I need to get back home. "I'm not sure what's going on, why you're here, but I need to go home and get cleaned up." I keep my eye on the Honda Civic in front of the store. It's got a silly paint job. Homemade and multicolored. The paint is clumpy in spots.

"Then I'll get to the point." He claps his hands together. It's too loud in the empty space. It startles me as it echoes around, and pulls Jackson into the conversation; his head jerks up and he glares at his father.

I nod for Mr. Turner to continue. I don't entirely trust my voice. Half of what I've said since walking in here is awkwardness exemplified.

"Jack tells me you're a baker."

I nod again.

"An unemployed baker."

I shake my head. "No. Not unemployed." I open my mouth to add more, but slam it shut. It's none of his business.

"If you're working, that would certainly explain," he says, and flicks a finger at me, "the mess."

"I just got off work," I say slowly. "That's why I need to go home. To clean up."

"Yes. Kyle, I have a business proposition for you. Well, *we* have a proposition for you."

Jackson tries to pull his hand free, but this time I'm the one holding tight. I don't want to let him go yet.

"What kind of proposition?" I shiver again.

He nods. "You want to ask her, Jack? It was your idea, after all."

Jackson looks at me for the first time. His eyes aren't warm now but filled with trepidation, and maybe shame. "I want you to bake for me. Well, we want you to bake for us." He winces and nods in his father's direction.

The world stops. There might as well be nothing other than this booth in the universe. All I can recognize is my racing heart and the whoosh of blood in my ears. Jackson raises his eyebrows and looks at me with hope. He looks at me like I'll save him from the machinations of his father, but I'm not his savior. I can't be.

I yank my hand from his, even with him holding tighter as I pull, and cross my arms. I flick my eyes back and forth between the men and fight the urge to curl into a ball, give in to the panic attack that's blurring the edges of my vision. I shake my head.

Jackson frowns, then dons the impassive mask he wears for customers. "Oh."

Mr. Turner smiles a Cheshire cat grin.

I shake my head harder, hoping to impart the message that there's more to the gesture than the word "no," but I need a minute to compose myself. Bile rises to my throat, stinging. The bathroom is less than five seconds away. I run and barely make it before the remnants of my breakfast come up. I lay my arm over the toilet seat, resting my forehead on top.

"Are you okay?" Mr. Turner asks from behind. He sounds freaked out and unsure.

"Just . . ." I swallow. "Give me a minute."

"Take all the time you need." I hear him walk away from the open door. "I told you it wouldn't work," he says to Jackson, the surety back in his voice.

His words trigger me into action. I don't have much time, only a few minutes before I need to be back at Hope House. I jump up, flush, and pull a handful of paper towels from the wall dispenser. I wipe my face and blow my nose, trying to put myself right enough to finish the conversation. Apparently, I just threw up my panic attack. The need for fight or flight has fled. I breathe deep and walk back into the shop, still scared shitless over what I came to tell Jackson, but now resolute.

Jackson's back to staring at the table. His father's fiddling with his phone.

"Sorry. I don't know where that came from," I tell them and wince. My throat burns.

Mr. Turner tucks his phone away. "Absolutely fine. Do you need anything?"

I shake my head. "Look—"

"Look—" he says at the same time. "Go ahead."

"I don't have much time. I need to get back."

"I assume, from your reaction, you will be declining Jack's offer."

I shrug. "I don't think I *can* accept." I look at Jackson. I can be straightforward with him, but not with his father. Mr. Turner makes me waver.

He turns my way and mouths the word "please." He looks desperate, like he's drowning.

My heart stutters, and I have to press my fingers against my chest at the pinch. "Why . . . How . . . Do you know . . ." I don't finish any of the questions, unsure how to put what I'm feeling into words. I don't want to tell him no. Telling people no is difficult for me in the best of circumstances; I don't want to be anyone's source of disappointment, but declining his offer is painful on a whole other level. I'll let Jackson down and reject my own wishes at the same time. This offer is exactly what I want and can't have. Why did he have to ask me now? Why couldn't this have happened after Booth lets me go?

I close my eyes and sigh. I can't say yes. I can't be Jackson's savior.

"Do I know what?" Jackson asks, pulling me from my thoughts.

"I can't do it," I blurt. My voice is a little too forceful, too mean. There's spite there, directed not at Jackson but at Booth. There's no way for Jackson to know that, though, and, when I look up, it's all over his face.

"Oh," he says, his voice as blunt and spiteful as mine just was. Only, I suspect, his ire is intentional.

I fight the urge to run, but Jackson and the door are the same direction. I could run to him or right past him, out the door and back to Hope House. I don't know which one I want, which one I need. So I stand still and keep my head down. "Sorry. That didn't come out right."

"Oh?" Mr. Turner asks.

I had forgotten he was here, standing right next to me.

I look at him, blinking.

He looks surprised.

"But, I really can't do it." I turn back to Jackson.

"I see," he says, voice blank.

"But you don't. You can't see." Tears pool and threaten to spill over. I should have known I'd turn into a blubbery mess, and I don't want to cry in front of Mr. Turner. I don't want him to see more of my weakness. "I want to. It's exactly what I'd like to do. I've thought about how great it could be."

"Then do it," Jackson pleads. "It *will* be great. For both of us."

I shake my head again, pull in as much air as I can, and hold it. "How would I do it, Jackson? I'm a patient in a mental institution, not just your neighbor." I see Mr. Turner out of the corner of my eye, and that gloating grin is back. Jackson hadn't told him that part. "Did you forget about that?"

"No," Jackson snaps. "I did not forget. But I thought—"

"You thought what? That I could make you cookies while I'm cooking dinner for the crazy people? Or were you planning on talking the doctor into letting me come work for you? 'Cause let me tell you, that's not gonna fly." My throat's on fire, I'm so angry. My entire life is a string of bad luck and worse timing. Jackson could have been my first real chance at happiness. Instead, I'm forced to end it all, and in front of his father. That's the cherry on top of the fucking sundae.

"We could figure it out. My father—" He stands and looks at his dad.

I nod my head in his direction. "You think he's going to go to bat for me?" I bark a sarcastic laugh.

"If you'd just take a chance. Show him how extraordinary you are. He'd listen."

I stare at Jackson. "You told me yourself, you've spent your entire life trying to get him to listen to you. Why would he change now?"

Mr. Turner is stunned. Hell, I'm stunned; I can't believe I just said that in front of him. I can't be Jackson's savior for the shop, but maybe I can do something for him.

Jackson's head drops, and he sighs. "I can't believe you're doing this to me," he whispers.

"I like you so much, Jackson, and if this were six months from now, maybe I could give you a different answer. But today, right now, I can't. I'm sorry. I *have* to do this." I walk to him and reach for his hand. It's hanging limp against his thigh. I squeeze, but he doesn't react, and doesn't squeeze back. "I am genuinely so, so sorry." I turn to Mr. Turner. "Thank you for the offer."

I push through the door and run across the street, hoping to make it to my room before the tears really get going. The security office is empty. I'm relieved I don't have to explain why I'm upset. I get upstairs without any staff sightings, close the door behind me, and sit next to my bag of clothes.

I cry with my back to the door until the streetlights turn on and illuminate my room in orange.

CHAPTER TWENTY-ONE

It's been two weeks since I let Jackson down and threw him away, tossed him at his father's plans. I wish I could say I've spent those two weeks forgetting him, washing my hands of the whole ordeal. Instead those fourteen days have been spent wallowing in the memory of his pleas and anger and disappointment.

The only thing I've managed to do in those days is go to work. All my time has been in the dough room. It's just me, the mixer, the sheeter, and approximately ten million tons of pizza dough. Trace is there every day. Music blasts from his cheap radio over the prep station. Sometimes he sings along, and I pretend he's talking to me. Other than a greeting in the morning, yelling for more crusts, or noticing it's quitting time, those sung lyrics are the only words spoken to me all day. But, then, there's not a ton of opportunity.

Frank's is busy. The lunch rush is frantic, but ever since I got the hang of things, I've been able to hold up my end of the bargain. The job sucks. It's mindless. My brain doesn't help with that. Most of the time it's just . . . blank. Every now and then my mind will drift to Jackson. Focusing on him doesn't do shit for me, though, except make me more depressed than I already am. I shut down the thoughts as soon as they show and settle for the numb buzz that's always been my brain's depressive default. The monotony of working the dough into crust is an effective time killer, so I knead and pass the time.

I don't have the energy to protest, anyway. But then again, what would I fight against? I turned away the only thing in my life worth fighting *for*.

The Coffee Shop is still open when I walk by this afternoon. Jackson is cleaning the windows, and I stop and stare. I miss him. He sees me, then turns and walks away, the window cleaner running in rivulets down the glass.

When I get to Hope House, I sigh and go inside, staring at my shoes and fighting back tears. In my room, I lie down and turn to the wall. This is where all my late afternoons are spent these days.

"Kyle?" Mary says from the doorway.

"Yeah?" I say. I don't turn to face her.

"I'm leaving."

I roll over and sit up. "What?"

There's a suitcase on the floor next to her. "I told you earlier this week. Remember? I'm going to live with my sister. It'll be good for both of us."

I shake my head. "I didn't remember." She came into the room a couple of days ago and talked to my back, same as after Joey died. I didn't hear a word.

She takes two steps into the room and holds out both arms. "Come here, sweet girl."

I get up from the bed, and she closes the distance, throws her arms around me, and squeezes tight. I start to sob. I don't know if I can make it through this without her.

"It'll be okay. You don't need me," she says, like she heard my thoughts.

"Yes, I do. I'm so sorry, Mary."

"Don't apologize." She pulls back and takes me by the shoulders. "You're tough, Kyle. Tougher than I'll ever be."

I shake my head. "No, I'm not."

"Yes." She nods. "You are. And one of these days, you'll figure it out for yourself."

I look at the floor, and she squeezes my shoulders.

"Who's gonna come in and talk to me when I'm sad now? Eddie?" I joke.

She smiles. "You'll be fine." She turns, and walks away.

I sniffle, wipe my cheeks with the back of my hands, and fight the urge to chase her down the sidewalk. I go back to my position on the bed and lie there until I fall asleep.

*   *   *

I have an appointment with Booth this afternoon and no idea what he'll say; I haven't heard from him since the day I started work. It's not uncommon to not see him, though. If he leaves his office other than to moderate our group sessions, I don't know about it, and since he keeps his office door closed all the time, who knows how much he's even here. The disconnect between his absences and his over-the-top attentiveness when I do see him messes with my head.

An hour into my shift at Frank's, the first can of dough is worked out, and I leave my little room.

"Hey, Trace?" I call out over "London Calling."

"'Sup?" he asks, reaching up and turning down the music.

"I have to cut out a few minutes early today. I promise I'll get everything done in there, though." I throw a thumb over my shoulder, toward the dough room.

"You clear it with Frankie?"

I shuffle my feet. "Uh, kind of? I left a note on his desk. I haven't seen him this week. So, if he didn't come and tell me no, then I can count that as a yes, right?"

Trace laughs. "Why not? If you get all your shit done, I don't care when you leave."

"Cool. Thanks. My doc's a bitch about being on time. I can't mess stuff up with him."

He goes back to chopping bell peppers; I take that as my cue and head back to work.

I manage to get out an hour before I usually do, although to be honest, I didn't really need to leave early. Booth set my appointment so I could walk straight into his office from work, but I'd rather have a few minutes to take a shower and wash off the flour. Every day it covers me like a second skin. All of me and my clothes wind up a shade lighter from the even dusting of white.

Because I'm back early, The Coffee Shop is still open. I stop and watch the windows, both hoping to see Jackson and not. But he's not there today—at least, not where I can see him—and the wave of disappointment and relief I feel reminds me of, well, the disappointment and relief when he is. Jamie's behind the counter looking at his phone. I speed walk the rest of the way to Hope House's door, then run up to my room.

There's no sign of Lori in the hallway. I need to let her know I'm back before getting into the shower, so I head downstairs to find her. The house is quiet. No one has moved into Mary's room yet, and Eddie has some part-time job during the day. Phoebe's probably in her room. She stays there most of the time, same as everyone else. Well, everyone but Eddie.

Bruce is in the security office playing on his phone. There's not much for him to do right now.

I go back to my room, assuming Lori will show up in the next few minutes. I sit on the windowsill and watch the traffic. I wish there were some way to undo what I've done to Jackson. I've sunk so far down in the past two weeks; my depression is at least as bad as it was before the hospital. I can only hope that getting up and going to Frank's every day will at least give me the appearance of functionality. I sigh. I just want to go home. I don't know how much longer I can live across the street from The Coffee Shop. It hurts too much, this constant reminder of him.

"Hey," Lori says from the doorway, making me jump. "Sorry to startle you. I didn't know you'd made it back already." She smiles like she's happy to see me. "You ready for your appointment? It's in five minutes."

"Yeah. I didn't realize it was that soon. I'll head down in a minute. I just need to change out of my work clothes first."

While changing, I try to pull myself together enough to put on my happy and healthy act for Booth. By the time I walk into his office, I've managed to smile.

"Well, well, Kyle. What's got you so happy today?" he asks, slipping off his glasses to chew on the right arm.

"Nothing, doc. Just smiling." I shrug. I've got this suck-up act down pat. If I can keep it up now, maybe I can get out of here.

He puts his glasses back on, pulls my file off his desk, and opens it across his lap. "I trust your employment is still satisfactory?" He doesn't wait for an answer. "I must admit, it thrilled me when the opportunity came up. I can only imagine how rare positions like these are. Especially ones so well suited to a baker of your caliber."

I literally bite my tongue to keep from laughing at him and nod. Nearly anyone who came off the street could do my job at Frank's with a day or two of training. The dough room's a glorified assembly line. And, really, not at all glorified if I'm being honest.

"I assume you're eager for today's appointment."

There's no point in telling him otherwise, so I sit still and quiet.

"Maybe hoping for some progress on your discharge?"

If I knew that's what we're talking about, I would have been more eager. "A little," I fib, while fiddling with a loose thread on my T-shirt's hem. "Will there be any progress? I've been doing great at Frank's. I mean, at least that's what Trace says. I've been on time every day and finishing all my work and cooking here and I haven't used any of my off-site other than to go to work. And I'm rambling now, so maybe I'm a little more antsy than I thought. Sorry." I've got the loose thread wrapped around my fingertip three times, pulling out stitches on the hem and cutting off the blood flow in my finger. "Oh, and I quit seeing Jackson Turner, just as you asked," I tack onto the end of my chatter. Saying his name makes my heart stutter and stab.

"That is all excellent news. My reports on your progress from the nurses here have noted an increase in your sleep, and, although it's disappointing, I don't think it's unexpected. Going back to work full time after an extended break would make anyone tired."

I can't believe he's attributing all the time I'm spending in bed to going back to work, rather than my depression, but there's no way I'm going to be the one to correct him.

"Your reports from your supervisors have been excellent. I am also pleased to hear you have reassessed pursuing a relationship with Mr. Turner."

I nod, not knowing how to respond. The whole situation with Jackson is still so raw and painful, I don't want the hurt to show. He closes my folder, places it back on his desk, then hands me a sealed manila envelope.

"What's this?" I ask, taking it from him.

"Your next step." I don't know what that means. I slide a finger under the flap to open the package, but Booth stops me just as the paper tears. "Wait. I would prefer that you not open that here. It can wait until after our session."

I lay the envelope in the chair next to me and rewind the loose thread around my finger.

"Oh, don't be disappointed."

I must have frowned without realizing. I carefully straighten my face to a neutral expression.

"What's in the envelope is just details. I would prefer to give you the news myself."

"Okay?" It seems like I never get to say that word to him without my doubts drawing it out to about three syllables.

"I see no need for any unnecessary suspense, so I'll cut to the chase." Again, I almost laugh. No need for unnecessary suspense? What does he think he's been doing the past few minutes? "I've already begun processing your discharge from Hope House and expect to finalize things by the end of the week."

I wasn't expecting this. Especially with the huge backward slide my depression has taken since the confrontation with Jackson two weeks ago. I've been practically nonfunctional outside of Frank's for fourteen days. How did none of the nurses notice? Or did they just not tell Booth? If that's the case, I should make them cookies. Or a twelve-tier cake. I hoped for this, of course, but Booth has managed to blindside me with unexpected news yet again.

I inhale the deepest breath I can, then release it in a burst. My heart is pounding. "That's awesome. When—"

He holds a finger up. "Please hold any questions. I believe the contents of the envelope will answer most of them," he says, pointing to the chair next to me. "I will be out of the office on Friday and, therefore, unable to see you off. Now is the time for me to tell you what a phenomenal young woman you are, Miss Davies."

The switch to using my last name, usually an indicator of trouble, makes me want to frown and worry about what he's going to say next, but I'm so elated, I can't. I smile hugely.

"Remember, I rarely issue such grandiose compliments to the patients in my care, but I believe you are deserving. You have limitless potential. I beg you not to squander your gifts."

"Thanks?" I say, not sure what to do with that. It feels uncomfortably like the speech he gave me after Joey died, so I'm halfway waiting for the other shoe to drop.

"You are welcome," he replies, both smiling and ignoring the question behind my statement. "It has been a distinct pleasure. But I'm getting ahead of myself. This will not be the last we see of one another. After your discharge, I will expect you to keep appointments with me twice monthly to review your progress. Any regression will necessitate readmission. Are you amenable to this?"

Why is he asking? I don't have a choice. And if regression means readmission, then why am I being discharged after a pretty huge decline? I nod. "For how long?" I ask, figuring it's the safer route.

"There's no way to know. When I am satisfied that your illness is fully in remission, I will consider signing the paperwork to reinstate your authority over any health care decisions. At that point, you will be free to do as you please."

"I'll do whatever you say, Doctor." My complete acquiescence should be enough to get me out of his office.

He beams at me. "Then we are quite done. I'm sure you are anxious to get to your room and pack."

"Absolutely," I agree. First, though, I want to get into that envelope.

"Address any issues you may have with Lori. She has access to the pertinent information." He waves a hand, dismissing me. His attention is already back down on his desk.

"I will. Thanks."

I grab the envelope, run up to my room, and rip it open. I cough out a bitter laugh at the "information" inside: an appointment card for two weeks from today. Typical. Of course Booth won't give me more than he absolutely has to. Why did I expect anything else from that man? I sit on the windowsill, smiling.

The Coffee Shop is dark now. They closed while I was at my appointment. I wish I could tell Jackson, but I can't.

And, anyway, would he even want to know? He doesn't care what happens to me now.

CHAPTER TWENTY-TWO

The casserole I scrape together for dinner is disgusting: a mixture of canned vegetables, cream of something soup, and ground beef. Eddie's plate is quickly emptied, though, and he's scraping it clean while I'm still pushing the mush around on my plate. My head is stuck on Jackson, wishing and thinking of a way to fix things before I'm gone. For some reason, it feels like once I'm not across the street from him, the possibility of an "us" will cease to exist. Poof. Gone. Like it never existed.

Phoebe never came down, and Nancy hasn't checked in like she has every other night, so I assume they're together. Eddie's unusually quiet. It's not like him to not fill the silent spaces with chatter about some inane nonsense.

He throws his fork onto the plate with a clatter that jars me out of my thoughts. "What's up, K? You ain't talking for some reason. You ain't even looked up from whatever this shit is you made for dinner. Something happen?"

"Yeah, Ed." I sigh. "A lot of somethings happened."

"You wanna talk about it?" He leans back in the chair and puts his hands behind his head.

"What, you wanna be friends now?" I snap. I didn't mean to sound so sharp, but I also don't want to deal with his games tonight. I'm in knots with wanting to fix things with Jackson before the end of the week, at least ease my own guilt a little. "I don't think I can handle you fucking with me today. I've met my quota this year."

"I'm not trying to fuck with you. I'm not all bad, you know."

"Oh yeah? Could've fooled me."

He smiles and nods. "Yeah. I like fucking with people. It's fun. I may not be able to feel shit, but I can listen. I've seen a lot in my life. I might even be able to help you."

"Since when do you help people?"

"Well, I don't have to." He sounds hurt, but I know he's not, since Eddie's got no feelings. "I was just offering because it seems like you're all fucked up over something. Who else are you gonna talk to? Phoebe will squeak and hide under her hair if you even look her way. Doc's put the kibosh on the fella across the street. That pretty much leaves me, right?"

That was the most surprising string of sentences Eddie's ever spoken, at least to me. "Wait. What? How do you know the doc put the kibosh on Jackson?"

"I know all kinds of shit, K." He shrugs. "You'd be amazed what you hear in this place if you weren't holed up in that shitty room all the time."

"Like what?" Engaging him probably isn't a good idea, but he's piqued my interest. Maybe there's some other motive to Booth's quashing my relationship with Jackson. Maybe it's not just because of me.

"Like I said, all sorts of shit. Pick a person, and I'll tell you something you don't know."

"Okay. Tell me something I don't know about you."

He leans farther back in the chair and laughs. I have to sit on my hands to keep from reaching out, afraid he'll tip all the way back. He's playing nice right now, but experience tells me to tread lightly. "That's a fucking cop-out. I ain't gonna prove shit telling you about me."

"I know." I smile. "Just call me curious."

"Sure, sure," he says with wariness, looking at me sideways. "I'll play your game for a minute. You better not be trying to fuck with me."

I hold my hands up in mock surrender. "Not fucking with you, I swear. I don't feel right asking about anyone else. It's none of my business."

"I call bullshit. That's part of being in this place. No secrets. You're not allowed."

I laugh—he's so, so wrong, but he's also cut right to the heart of something.

"What do you want to know? I got no secrets."

I shake my head. "I don't believe that for a second."

He shoots me a wicked grin, leans forward, stares at me for a few seconds, and says, "I've been living here for two years."

"Wh—" I can't finish that thought. Eddie's good at shocking people, and that tidbit was a classic example.

His grin turns into a smug smile, and he leans back in his chair again, tipping so far that the back hits the wall. "Didn't know that, did ya?"

I watch him for a second, trying to determine if he's telling the truth. It's pointless. "Hell no. Why in the world would you live here for two years?"

"Because I want to."

"But . . . *why would you want to*?" It's unfathomable; I've been trying to get out since the second I got thrown in.

"Why wouldn't I? I got a roof over my head, cable TV, a full belly, and a clean bed to sleep in. This joint's better than what's waiting for me out there." He throws a thumb over his shoulder.

"What? Your old lady doesn't have all that luxury ready and waiting for you?"

"She ain't got shit waiting on me. I got the run of this place and get to fuck with all you nut jobs. Why would I give that up?"

"But isn't the whole point of this place to get out of here?"

"Yeah. I just gotta have a temper tantrum once in a while, then the doc has to keep me. I'm a danger to myself and others, see?" He winks.

I huff a laugh and shake my head. Eddie's manipulations weren't a secret, but having him spell it all out is a mind-fuck. "Shit."

He cackles. "You gonna tell me what's got you all twisted up now?"

I hesitate. I don't relish the idea of spilling my guts to Eddie, but he's right. No one takes him seriously. I presume everything he does and says to be part of a game only he's playing. "You promise you won't tell?"

"Why the fuck would I do that?" he snaps. It's a glimpse of his volatility. I want to keep that part of him under wraps.

"Tell me about what you've heard. Like, how do you know about Jackson?"

"Sure, sure." He tips his chair back to level and leans toward me. "Doc got a bee in his bonnet after you vanished a few weeks ago. Had Nancy and Lori and Bruce in his office and was asking them questions about where you might have gone, who you might have been with."

"What did they say?"

"Nothin'. They didn't know shit about where you were. He shoulda asked me. I saw you and that fella over at the fancy coffee place when I was coming back from work."

I laugh.

"They were all in a tizzy about it. Ol' Mary musta torn up a case of them tissues that night between you and Joe."

Oh, God. Mary said she was worried about me, but that was it. I had no idea how much stress that night had put on her, especially since it did the opposite for me, easing my stress over Joey. I clutch at my chest. It's hard to breathe.

"Now, don't get all worked up. I ain't gonna tell you shit if you start cryin'."

I close my eyes and shake my head. "I'm not gonna cry," I wheeze. "I just didn't think . . ." I don't need to finish the sentence. The urge to push away from the table and go back to my room is strong. "You didn't answer me, though. Why'd Booth put the kibosh on Jackson?"

He grins and shrugs. "Does it to all of us." Eddie straightens in the chair and moves into an uncanny impression of Caring Pose. Then, in a dead replica of Booth's voice, he says, "Your emotional recovery has not progressed enough, Miss Davies."

I stare at him, open-mouthed.

"Right?" He lifts an eyebrow, grins, and leans back in the chair again.

"How—how did you know he said that exact thing to me?"

He crosses his arms. "'Cuz he says the same fucking thing to everybody. You know how many times he's said that to me in the last two years? How many times he's tried to get me to ditch Carla?"

"Who's Carla?"

He knits his brows and looks at me like I've lost it. Maybe I have. "My old lady. Ain't you been listenin'?"

"Oh. I didn't know that was her name."

"Doc's been trying to break us up since the first time he met me. Using that bullshit about my emotional stability."

There's nothing to say. Over my time here, I'd never equated Eddie's psychopathy and drug use to my depression, thinking it was kind of like comparing a Pomeranian with a Great Dane—they're both dogs, but not much in common besides that. Apparently, to Booth, there's more overlap than that.

"You know what I told him?" He raises both eyebrows.

I look at him, eyes wide with wonder. "What?"

"I told him to go fuck himself."

I smile, imagining Booth's reaction. "And?"

"And nothing. Nothing else to say. She's my lady and ain't no doctor gonna change that, and if I ever move outta here, she'll be waiting 'cuz I'm her man." He slams a hand on the table, jarring me out of the stupor I'd fallen into since his Booth impersonation. "Well, K, nice talk. I'm gonna go watch TV."

He picks up his plate and carries it into the kitchen.

I don't move, even as I hear the television turn on down the hall. I sit still, replaying the conversation in my head, surprised and confused by the turns it had taken. I'd never tell Booth to fuck off, at least not to his face. For the first time, I envy Eddie's bizarro relationship and am jealous of his particular brand of unstable stability. He has someone to love who loves him back, and I hate him a little bit for it.

Nancy walks into the dining room. She's been gone for a long time. "How was your dinner? Is everything okay?"

"Sure," I say with a nod. "Everything is fine. Could you get the soap for me? I need to get the dishes done so I can go to bed."

She doesn't say anything, just pulls out her keys, unlocks the cabinet, takes out the bottle, and squirts some soap into the sink. She stays quiet as she puts the soap back in the locked cabinet and leaves the room.

I get ready for bed and am under the covers before she makes another appearance. I turn my back to the window and stare at the drywall until I drift off.

* * *

Waking up early for so many years has its benefits. I prepped the breakfasts for the week, so I'm out the front door in less than thirty minutes and crossing the street. The Coffee Shop is unchanged, and my nerves are reminiscent of the way I felt on that first visit.

Lying in bed last night, I realized I can't leave Hope House without seeing Jackson again and at least attempting to explain why I said no—why I had to say no. Why I can't be with him. Booth was right; I'm not ready.

I close my eyes and take a deep breath before pushing through the door.

Jackson looks up from his espresso maker when I walk in and frowns, but quickly flattens his mouth. He looks sad and tired, same as me. I step into the line and wait my turn behind the two customers already there. Jamie's smile doesn't waver.

"Hey, Kyle. Long time, no see. What can I get you?"

"Yeah. It's been a while." I look down at my semi-reflection in the steel counter, then take a deep breath. "*Café chorreado*, double strength."

"Ooh, the hard stuff. You drinking it here or are you headed to work?"

Well, Jackson told him that much about our last conversations. I look back up. "Both. I should have time to drink it here before work, though." I hand him a ten and wave off the change before heading to my seat.

The shop is busy. I haven't been here this early in the morning before. Watching it in the window isn't the same as seeing the rush in person, though. I was going to talk to Jackson, but I may not get the opportunity. Not unless the line lets up for a while.

"Here you go," Jamie says and places my order on the table.

"Thanks," I say to his back. He's already halfway back to his post at the register before I get the word out.

Weeks ago, Jamie told me the double pour-through wasn't for the faint of heart. He wasn't kidding. My heart beats stronger and faster after a couple of sips. I'm pretty sure I can feel my blood pressure increase. If nothing else, I should really be able to crank out the pizza crusts today. At least until the caffeine peters out.

My cup is empty and there haven't been any gaps in the line long enough for me to pull Jackson away to talk. This is probably a conversation best left private, but I need to have it and don't want to have to wait because I'll lose my nerve. I walk to his end of the counter. "Hey," I say, loud enough to be heard over the steamer.

"Hello." He doesn't look away from the drink he's working on.

"So, um, how are you?"

"Fine. You?" His words are clipped and terse.

"Okay, I guess." Maybe this isn't such a good idea. I didn't think he was angry, but hurt. Maybe I was wrong. "I wanted to talk to you for a second."

"What about?" He hasn't looked at me since I walked over.

"About us."

"There is no 'us.'" He makes air quotes as he says it. "So there's nothing to talk about."

I wince. He is pissed. I can't blame him. "Look, Jackson . . ."

He jerks down the lever on the espresso machine. I know it takes some force, but not that much. Fuck. I ball my hands into fists and squeeze. "Hey, I know you're pissed and have every right to be, but I came to try and explain. I need to explain. Tell you how sorry I am."

He looks down at the counter, the resignation clear in the sag of his shoulders. "Are you?"

"Of course," I answer too loudly. In my peripheral vision, every head in the place turns toward me. I continue, just above a whisper, "Booth really wants me to stay away from you, and for a long time I didn't get it. But now I do."

"Then go. Stay away."

I look at my shoes, sure my resignation looks a lot like his from a moment ago. "I just . . . Just want to try to explain."

"What's to explain? I asked for your help, you said no. That's the end of it."

"But that's not all." I throw my hands up in exasperation. "I *couldn't* say yes. Not if I want to get out of Hope House. Not if I want to get better."

"So, I'm making you worse."

"No. Kind of." I drop my hands and stomp my foot. "This is coming out wrong. It's not your fault, but hurting you—that *fear* of hurting you, or of being hurt—made me worse."

He sighs and turns to grind espresso for the next customer. The noise gives me a second to mentally compose myself. I'm screwing this up.

As soon as the grinder is quiet, I say, "Jackson, it's not you. I can't have anyone or anything else in my life. I don't deserve it." I hang my head to hide my shame.

"You could have had me." He says it so bluntly, so resolute. But it's so quiet I almost don't hear him.

The pang in my chest at the declaration threatens to double me over. I rub my sternum and wince. "But could I? Really?"

"Yes!" he yells, a little too loudly. Everyone looks at us again, and he looks at me. The anger, or maybe it's frustration, rolls off him in waves, knocking me backward.

I didn't really mean for him to answer my questions; they were mostly rhetorical. Or maybe they were for me. I don't know. Standing in front of him makes the need to stay away from him both easier and more difficult. That desire to run to him and the need to run away are tearing me in half.

I shake my head. "No. I couldn't. I'm the problem here, Jackson. Booth keeps telling me, and I hate him because he's right. I'm not ready for a relationship. I need to get better, need to deserve you first, and I can't begin to deserve someone like you. Not yet."

I pull my hands into the sleeves of Jackson's sweater, making my fists.

He slides the to-go cup toward the customer and wipes his hands on his apron. "Jamie, can you take over for a second?"

"Um, yeah. Sure." There's a grumble from the people in line.

"You don't have to stop. I don't want to make your customers mad. Maybe I can come back . . ." I know I won't. I'm moving tomorrow. There won't be time.

He puts a hand on my lower back and steers me into the back room. "They can wait. I can't talk about this in front of everyone." He's so close I can smell his soap and breathe deep to take in as much as I can.

In the café behind us, there's a loud clatter, followed by Jamie cursing under his breath. "Do you need to see—"

"He'll be fine." Jackson cuts me off.

Now that we're sort of alone, I want to tell him how nice it is to see him, how much I've missed him, but can't. Really, now that we're alone, I'm tempted to give in to my want and hug the holy hell out of him. That desire presses in on all sides, so I cut it off before I can't ignore it anymore. "I need to get to work. Don't wanna be late."

"Wait," he says, even though I haven't moved yet.

"I can't be late. I'm being released, and I can't screw it up now."

"You're getting out?" he asks. And that's it. That's what I hate to crush: his hope.

I nod. "Tomorrow, I think."

He frowns. "So soon?"

"Is it soon? It feels like it's been forever."

He shuffles his feet and bites his lower lip.

"I need to go. I'm sorry, Jackson." I turn to leave. I need to get to the street before the tears start—I can cry on the train—but he grabs my arm and stops me.

"I just . . . I just wanted to . . ."

I turn and look up at him. There's so much sadness in his expression, and I can't deal with it.

"You can do it. I have faith in you." His voice is so earnest on top of the woe.

"How do you still have faith in me?" I ask. "After everything I've done?"

"I don't know," he says, and brushes past me into the main shop without a glance.

I cry until I get to Frank's.

CHAPTER TWENTY-THREE

It's my last dinner here, and I'm exhausted. I've been cooking since my shift at Frank's ended, prepping food for the next couple of weeks in an attempt to stave off my worries.

Starting tomorrow, it's just Eddie and Phoebe here, and neither of them are candidates to fill the position of cook. I chuckle darkly, though perhaps I shouldn't, at the thought of anorexic Phoebe putting plates of celery and carrots on the table. Eddie already gives her shit for not eating; she would hide in her room at every mealtime just like Joey. I can't imagine dinners will be much of an event around here until Booth fills the two empty rooms.

I stop by the living room before heading upstairs. The rat-a-tat of machine guns tells me Eddie is exactly where I thought he'd be. "Hey, Ed," I say, peeking around the corner at him sprawled on the couch.

"Sup, K?" He doesn't look away from the TV.

"I guess I wanted to say goodbye."

"Aw, K. I didn't know you cared."

"To be honest, I'm not sure I do. But I know I'm not going to forget you anytime soon."

"Don't go gettin' sentimental on me now." He's still watching the action movie as he speaks. "The best fucking thing you can do once Doc signs those walking papers is get as far the fuck away as you fucking can from this fucking place and don't let 'em fuck with you ever again."

I laugh. "You just used 'fuck' as a verb and an adjective. Nice."

"You just proved my point. Some smart bitch like you don't need to be in this shithole. You're too good for it. So walk out that goddamn door tomorrow and don't fucking come back. Don't fuck it up and don't let the door hit you in the ass on the way out."

He never looks away from the TV screen, but the faraway focus of his eyes tells me I'm dismissed. I head back to my room and get ready for bed.

I'm more than a little nostalgic now that moving day has come. I should say goodbye to Phoebe, too, but I don't. I can't go into her room. Haven't since she got here. It was Joey's room, and it would hurt too much to go in and have him . . . not be there.

I take my seat on the windowsill and look over at The Coffee Shop. It's dark inside, but every now and again a car's headlights will glint off one of the steel surfaces and the inside of the store twinkles. I've never noticed it before. Maybe it's just my mind playing tricks on me, wanting my memories of this place to be beautiful.

Out of the corner of my eye, I catch movement in Jackson's loft. He walks past his windows. My heart twinges. He walks toward the kitchen, then back again. He stops and looks my way, almost as if he saw movement like I did. I know that's not it, though, because I've been still as a statue since I spotted him.

He stares for a long moment, looks at the floor, turns, and walks away from the windows. I bite my lip, staving off tears. Jackson turning away from me is exactly what I deserve. I stay in the window long after his loft goes dark.

* * *

Sleep isn't happening tonight. I spend hours awake, alternately staring at the drywall and crying. For weeks, one goal has remained: get out of Hope House. Now that it's happening, though, I don't know if I want to go. That goals list I made for Booth bounces in the corners of my mind. I've managed only one item—getting a new job—and Booth did that for me. In a few hours, I'll be back in my old apartment, alone.

After hours of wallowing and staring at the beige wall, I give up and go to my morning post on the windowsill. I can't imagine Nancy will process my discharge at 5:00 AM, so there's no reason this morning shouldn't look like most of the others. After I spend a few minutes staring at the street, unblinking until the lights blur and streak, Jackson walks out his front door. My lids flutter until my focus returns, and I watch him move toward The Coffee Shop, unsmiling. A wave of guilt punches me in the gut, same as every other time I've seen him since I turned him down. A tear trickles down my cheek. I pull my knees tighter to my chest and dig my fingernails into my upper arms.

I've really made a mess of my so-called recovery. Not only am I still a disaster of emotional wreckage, but now there's a trail of victims in my wake. I have to do what's right when I leave this place: leave and don't look back. Don't cause more harm to myself or anyone else.

The Coffee Shop's lights turn on, and I watch with both pain and detachment. I stare until the shop's lights and steel surfaces blur and my eyes scratch and throb. I can't bear to see but can't bring myself to look away.

"Good morning," Nancy says from the door. "Dr. Booth processed your discharge yesterday before he left. You may leave when you're ready."

I wipe the tears away with my sleeve. My cheeks are raw from crying and doing this same thing all night long. "Really? That's it? I can just . . . leave?"

"No," she answers, as if my questions are the stupidest thing she's ever heard. "Bruce has papers for you to sign and the rest of your belongings. You'll have to wait until he's available."

I scramble out of my seat. "Is he available now? I'm ready."

"I'm afraid he's not. You may want to reassess your readiness as well." She points a finger at me and sweeps it up and down.

I'm still in my pajamas. Oops. My face heats with embarrassment. "Um, yeah, so I guess I'll get dressed first and wait until Bruce is ready, then."

She nods, turns, and walks away without a word.

"Fuck you, you fuckin' has-been!" Eddie's yell echoes down the hall. *That* explains why Bruce isn't available.

I smile and wonder if his blowup is real or fake. The past couple of days with Eddie have given me an entirely new perspective on his behavior. I shake my head and walk across the hall to the bathroom to brush my teeth.

An hour later, I've been sitting in the security office waiting for Bruce for forty-five minutes, my never-unpacked bag in my lap. I'm squeezing it like a kid with her favorite stuffed animal—taking comfort and hoping none of the grown-ups take it from me. Surely there's no going back at this point, but Booth has earned no trust from me. He could still pull some shit.

"Morning, Kyle. You been waitin' long?" Bruce walks around, sits at the desk, and smiles at me.

"No. Not too long."

"You're flying the coop, huh?"

"I hope so." I grin at him.

"No worries, now. You just gotta sign a couple of things and you're good to go." He shuffles through a stack of papers and pulls out two. He lays one of them facing me on the desk. "This one's your discharge. Booth's already signed it." He points at the bottom of the page. "You just need to sign right underneath that." He hands me a pen.

I take my time with the signature; it needs to be perfect, with no doubt it's my name.

As soon as I lift the pen, Bruce picks up the paper and puts it on top of his stack, then turns and unlocks the cabinet where my messenger bag and phone are kept. He places them on the desk in front of me. "You need to check these. Be sure everything's there. The phone's probably dead, but we can plug it in if you want to be sure it's okay."

"I'm sure it's fine. I trust you."

"That's nice, but I'm not the only one in here, you know. Check 'em for me, will you?"

I open my messenger bag and look inside: two pens, a tube of lip balm, keys, and my wallet. "It's all here."

"You wanna plug in your phone and check it?"

I shake my head. "I'll do it when I get home." I hit the power button and nothing happens, but that's to be expected when it's been sitting in a drawer for weeks. I drop it into my bag.

Bruce slides the second piece of paper across the desk. "This one just says you have all your stuff and nothing's missing. Sign there, at the bottom."

I scribble this signature, not caring if it's as perfect as the last.

"That's it. You're free, Miss Kyle." He stands up and holds out a hand.

I juggle my army bag when I start to stand but catch it at the last minute, then shake Bruce's hand. "Thanks, Bruce. See you in a couple of weeks."

I turn, jog down the steps, and push out onto the sidewalk a semi-free woman. Across the street, Jackson is at the espresso machine and Jamie is at the register, tending to a line of customers.

Just leave, Kyle. It's for the best. I pull the sleeves of Jackson's sweater over my hands, then walk to the corner to catch the bus home.

CHAPTER TWENTY-FOUR

Leaving Hope House was easy. Walking away from The Coffee Shop and Jackson wasn't, but I know my decision was the right one. The bus ride back to my neighborhood was uneventful. Walking into my building and up to my door was no problem. But now that I'm here, I can't open the door. I'm not sure how long I've been standing here with my apartment unlocked, just . . . unable to turn the knob. My heart's racing, and I can't catch my breath. I drop my bag, rest my forehead on the jamb, and close my eyes. Breathe in slowly. Exhale. Three. Four. Five.

After the ninth breath, I bite the bullet and open my door. I throw myself inside before my panic can take over and slam it behind me. Everything's the same as I left it. I halfway expected it to look different, like some imaginary crazy fairy would have visited in my absence and made all my thrift store furniture and milk crates shiny and new. Nope, it's still crappy and old. I glance at the kitchen. I half expected a smudgy pool of dried blood, but the floor is its normal grimy gray. Maybe there was some sort of suicide cleanup fairy.

The refrigerator is empty. I don't need to look in the freezer. It was empty except for ice the night I left.

Like a fist to the chest, it hits me: I have to get rid of the knife. I pull open the second drawer and it's not there. It's not in the top drawer either. There's standard silverware, measuring cups, a rolling pin, my offset spatula . . . but nary a sharp-edged tool.

"Fucking Booth!" I yell. He has to be the one responsible. It's one more reminder of how abnormal I am, how unhealthy. Booth still doesn't realize that I don't need him to tell me; I tell myself every day.

I slide onto the floor, the same spot as that night, pull my knees to my chest, and cry. I haven't cried like this, these body-wracking sobs that leave me breathless and sore, since Joey died, not even over Jackson. These tears are the same kind, though—I'm mourning. But this time, the person who's dead is me.

How did I not realize it before now? I'm not the same girl as the one the paramedics carried out. It's like those three slices with my butcher knife sloughed off all the thick skin and calluses I'd developed over the years. Now I'm all shiny, pink, and raw. The wrongs hurt more acutely, and the rights are more ecstatic. That horrible night made me feel.

I'm feeling it all now—the rights and wrongs of the past few weeks. My throat tightens; it's hard to breathe. I pull my kitchen towel off the oven door and push it to my face, sobbing until it's drenched with snot and tears.

Even after those stop, I don't get up. I need a plan if I'm going to make it. If I don't want to end up where I was three months ago.

After hours on the floor, I grab my bag and jog out to the street, then practically speed walk to the store. I fill my cart with condiments, yogurt, a toothbrush, and the largest knife they carry, throwing in the makings of a salad at the last minute. Three blocks from home, I detour and buy a new blanket for my bed.

Back home, after juggling too many bags to carry comfortably, I throw it all down on the floor and get to work. I open my windows wide, then carry my new blanket and my clothes from Hope House down to the laundry room, adding Jackson's sweater to the basket last. And then, I clean. No surface is untouched by my rag, mop, and brush. The kitchen floor is last. A new toothbrush and an almost-full container of cleaner scour and strip the tile. I scrub the blood-stained grout lines until any evidence of that night has disappeared—until my kitchen floor is as shiny and new as me.

After salad for dinner, I take a shower. I've been delaying it, saving the best part of my day for last. I strip naked in the living room just because I can, walk into the bathroom, turn the hot water knob until it's full-blast and the cold tap a fraction of an inch, then step under the spray. It feels spectacular. Once clean, I put my hands flat on the tile under the showerhead, lean forward, and let the spray run over my shoulders until the water turns cold. I'm overheated in the best way, so put on only a T-shirt and wrap myself in my new dark green blanket, cocooning in the warmth.

At seven thirty, it starts snowing and I fall asleep.

The next morning, my trip into work takes an extra thirty minutes because of ice on the El tracks. I'm losing my shit because I hate being late and don't want to fuck up my freedom on the first morning. When I speed walk into the kitchen at Frank's, Trace gives me a look but doesn't say anything.

"Sorry, Trace. I moved yesterday and didn't know it would take almost an hour to get here."

"No biggie. I know you'll catch up. Where'd you move to?"

"Ravenswood."

"Why'd you move all the way up there? Cheap rent?"

"It's a long story." I don't want to get into everything about Hope House with Trace. He might know already, since Booth got me the job here, but I'd rather not be the one to broach the subject. "It's a nice enough place, just a long way from here. I'm gonna get to work."

"Sure," he says, returning his focus to the prep table.

* * *

At the end of our shift, Trace walks to the doorway of the dough room and leans on the frame. "You wanna grab a drink?" he asks.

"Maybe some other time. I'm beat." I'm wiping down my table at the end of the shift.

"You sure? Happy hour next door started ten minutes ago."

"Yeah. Drinking's not really my thing these days."

"Hey, to each his own. You know where to find me if you change your mind."

"Sure thing. Thanks."

I turn around to smile at him, but he's already gone; all that's left of him is the shadow of the swinging door he just pushed through. I walk to my locker, tossing the kitchen towel in the laundry on my way, and grab my bag. Digging out my lip balm, I pause. What's the harm in having a drink? Surely I'm allowed to have some kind of life now. And what am I going to do except go home and fall asleep on my couch again? I throw my bag over my shoulder and scurry to catch up with Trace.

He's already at the far end of the bar, sitting and chatting up the bartender like it's his second home. Hell, maybe it is. I hop onto the stool next to him. "Hey."

"I thought you said drinking wasn't your thing," he says, grinning.

"It's not. Well, not anymore. But I figure a couple of beers can't hurt."

"You could stand to relax some. That's why I asked you."

"What do you mean?"

"Dude, you are too fucking tense. I mean, don't get me wrong, you're doing awesome, but I don't think I've ever seen anybody so uptight."

An image of Dr. Booth pops into my head. "I'm not that bad."

"Yeah, you are. But you'll chill eventually."

"Maybe." I sigh and look at the bar top, scratching at a bubble in the lacquer. "Look, maybe this wasn't a good idea. I should probably head home."

He grabs my arm when I start to scoot off the seat. "Shit, man, I didn't mean to offend. I was trying to help. You know, make friendly and shit. Don't leave."

For someone as intimidatingly large as he is, Trace sure has an effective sad face: he looks like I just kicked his puppy. I settle back onto the stool. "Okay, but you have to be nice."

"I promise. I have a terrible case of foot-in-mouth disease." He smiles.

He's got a gap between his two front teeth that make his smile just a little goofy and a whole lot adorable. "It's cool. I'm just in a kind of weird place right now. It's stressing me out."

Trace gets the bartender's attention and holds up two fingers. I look around while she gets our beers. It's a typical old neighborhood bar—too dark to see the years of grime, slightly lopsided pool table on the other side of the room, a neon Old Style sign hanging above the bar. I figure that's what we're getting and am disappointed when the bartender puts a different bottle in front of me. In the name of relaxing, though, I pick up the beer and take a huge gulp.

"I've been meaning to ask you. What kind of name is Trace?"

He frowns at me. "Nothing special. Just a name."

"Not with that face, it's not." I wag a finger at him. "Come on! You got to make fun of my name from the get-go."

He swallows his mouthful of beer. "I didn't make fun of you. I just thought you were a guy."

"Close enough." I take another sip, pacing myself.

Trace is not pacing himself, although his tolerance is definitely a lot higher than mine; he drains his bottle and holds up a finger for another. "So, how's the job treating you so far?"

"Wow, that was a super-shitty subject change."

"Nice, huh?" He grins at me. "Really. Whaddaya think?"

"It's okay. Not really my thing, but it should pay the bills. At least, I assume it's paying the bills." I rub my hands over my face. I hadn't thought about the logistics of rent, utilities, and everything since I left Hope House. Booth was paying the bills while I was in there. Hopefully, Frank's pays me enough to cover rent.

"What do you mean, you assume it's paying the bills? You don't know?"

"You caught that, huh?" I groan and rub a hand over my eyes. "It's a long story."

"I've got time."

"I know, but I don't really want to tell it." I peek over at him. "Sorry."

He studies me for a second, like maybe if he looks at me long enough he'll be able to see what I don't want to share. "No biggie. So long as it's not gonna fuck up your work."

"It shouldn't."

Trace's next beer showed up while I was hiding behind my hands; he drinks half of it in one go. "Speaking of work, you're a pastry chef, right?"

"Yeah."

"Then why are you working in my dough room?"

"Part of the same long story. "

"And you don't wanna tell it."

"Nope," I say with a pop.

We sit in silence, drinking our beers. Trace orders another round as soon as my bottle's empty. "You said no more than two, right?"

"Yeah." The silence is getting awkward. "So what do you do when you're not at Frank's?"

"I've got a second job at a bar over on Western. I work the door four nights a week."

"Makes sense. I think you'd be a pretty good deterrent for anybody up to no good."

He laughs. "That's exactly what they said when they hired me. You'd be surprised by what people will try, though."

"What's the craziest thing you've seen?"

He regales me with tales of drunken shenanigans until my second beer is gone and he's gone through three more. I reach for my bag and pull out my wallet.

"This is my treat." Trace pulls out his wallet and slaps two twenties on the bar.

"But—"

"You can pay next time."

"I don't know if I can afford to cover your tab." I elbow him in the ribs.

He nudges me back. "I wouldn't expect you to. Why do you think I work two jobs?"

I laugh and hop down from the stool, weaving a little as we walk toward the door. "Sorry. Two's my limit for a reason."

Trace puts a hand on my elbow to steady me. "No problem, lightweight."

It's dark out when we exit the bar, and I take a second to get my bearings. At least the snow has stopped, though. Now there's just a pile of grimy sludge at the curb. "I'm that way," I tell him, tipping my head toward the train station.

"Cool. I'll walk you."

"Don't go out of your way. I'm fine. I promise."

"It's no problem." We walk, and I'm still a little dizzy but I hope not enough that it shows.

"Thanks for coming out with me. Maybe we can do it again."

"Yeah, maybe." I look up at him. He's so tall, my neck twinges at the angle.

"Maybe tomorrow?" His eyebrows lift hopefully.

Shit, he's hitting on me. My mind is scrambling for an excuse to get out of this. I'm grasping at straws. My life outside of Frank's is pretty empty right now. "Um, I think I might have something to do tomorrow. I'm not sure. Let me check."

"Oh. Um, okay." His voice drops with disappointment.

"Sorry. I suck at this." I stop walking. It takes him a second to notice, so he makes it another two steps before he stops and turns around.

"What's that?"

"Huh?" I don't understand the question.

"What do you suck at?"

"Letting people down. I hate it."

He closes the distance between us and puts a finger under my chin, lifting my face to look at him. "Hey," he says, grinning. "No worries. I just figured it was worth a shot."

"Thanks." My face heats. "It's not gonna be weird now, is it?"

"What? Work? Nah." He waves a huge hand at me. "We'll pretend it never happened. Friends?"

I smile at him and nod. "Friends."

We start walking again.

"Hey, Trace? If things were different, I'd probably have said yes."

"If what was different?"

"The long story. I'm a lot messed up."

"Aren't we all?" He sighs.

"Yeah. I guess so. I'm in the middle of a bunch of stuff right now and trying to get my shit back together. I'll start rambling about it if I let myself. Shit, I really suck at this."

"Nah, you don't suck. You're overwhelmed."

He's right. That's exactly what I am.

"If you ever feel like telling that long story, though, I'm all ears."

"Thanks." We reach the station. I'm pretty sure Trace doesn't usually walk this direction, so we need to go our separate ways. "This is my stop. See you tomorrow?"

"Yeah. Tomorrow."

He leans down. I turn my head to ask what he's doing and end up pressing my lips to his. We both freeze. His lips are soft and warm, and my immediate reaction is not to pull back but to sink into the comfort. So I reach up and grab his bicep to keep him in place. My hand on him is all the encouragement he needs. He sweeps his lips back and forth across mine—once, twice, three times, four times before I come back to my senses and jerk back.

"I can't . . . can't . . ." Unsure what it is I can't do other than kiss Trace, I turn and run into the train station, leaving him standing and staring at me on the sidewalk outside.

CHAPTER TWENTY-FIVE

"Pepita!" Rebeca squeals, running out from behind the counter.

I wrinkle my nose at the nickname, but she ignores me, trots over, and wraps me into a hug. "Are you ever going to quit calling me that?" I ask, trying to pull back, but she just squeezes tighter.

"No. Besides, you secretly love it."

"Oh, yeah, it's great being reminded of that time I made myself sick on pumpkin seeds and puked in the middle of State Street."

She finally relinquishes her hold and takes a step back. "You look good. How are you? Are you okay? When did you get out?"

And there it is. That awful look, the mix of condescension and pity. It took less than a minute. I know she doesn't mean anything by it. It's the default expression for everyone who knows about what I did. The nurses in the psych ward all wore it like a mask; Fiona had it for a split second when she saw the scars that first time. Now Rebeca has it, too. The brain must be hard-wired for it. That look is the entire reason I couldn't come back here after leaving Hope House. As much as I hated Booth for making the decision for me, right now, with Rebeca looking at me with those sad eyes, I'm grateful. I have to fight the urge to turn around and run away.

"I'm fine. I got out a couple of weeks ago." I shove my hands into my pockets so I don't fidget.

She lets out a breath. "Good. I wanted to come see you, but the doctor—"

I hold up a hand. "I know. He told me. I'm glad you didn't."

We stand there long enough that the silence feels suffocating. The bakery is closing in a couple of minutes, so there are no customers or background noise to temper our awkwardness. Finally, Rebecca breaks the standoff. "Come on. Let's go in the office. Sit down and talk. You can tell me what you're doing these days." She walks to the front door and flicks the lock and turns the sign to "Closed."

The office looks the same as it did months ago: orders tacked ten-deep to the cork board on the wall, piles of invoices stacked on the desk in a system only Rebeca understands. There's comfort in the consistency. Then Rebeca sweeps the invoices into a single pile, and I have to fight to keep from taking it from her and organizing; I know she'll put them all back into the same stacks after I'm gone.

She sits in the squeaky rolling chair and pulls a bottle of tequila and a shot glass out of the desk drawer.

I lift an eyebrow at her as I sit in the metal folding chair on the other side of the desk.

"Don't make faces at me. I figure we could both use this."

"Why would you think I need that?"

"No offense, Pepita, but I lied before. You don't look so good. You're so pale. Didn't they ever let you out of that place?" She pours a shot and downs it, the glass hitting the desktop with a thunk, then slides the bottle and glass a few inches closer to me.

I put a hand to my cheek, as if I can feel the lack of color there. "They let me out sometimes."

"Well, you need to get out more. Walk in the sun."

"I did a little today. I was off." I was going stir-crazy in my apartment after the disaster with Trace last night. I went to the lakefront and ran for miles, even though it hurt like a son of a bitch and I probably won't be able to move when I do have to go back to work. I fucked up big time last night just because his comfort felt good. I used him, and it wasn't nice, and explaining it is gonna suck.

"Where are you working now?"

"This pizza place called Frank's," I say while pouring myself a drink. "The doctor got me the job."

"I'm glad you've got something decent. We miss you here, though. I hated replacing you."

That's my cue to throw back my own shot. With a mouthful of alcohol, I don't have to tell her the new gig's not so great. "I know. I miss you, too." I study the wooden desktop's decades of wear so I don't have to look at her.

"You know I get it, right?"

"Get what?"

"Why you don't want to come back."

I lift my eyes. "Yeah?"

"Yeah. But you should know something."

"What's that?" I go back to studying the scratches on the desk, looking for patterns.

"I'm the only one who knows, you know, about . . . um, what you did."

"Well, that's good, I guess." I scratch at a groove in the wood with the tip of my index finger, the callus there catching on the edge.

Rebeca pours and drinks another shot. "Okay," she says, her voice louder and more forceful. "No more of this sad talk. Tell me what you're doing besides working at this pizza place."

"Nothing."

"There's something. You're blushing. You can't lie to me, lady."

"I'm not blushing, it's the tequila. I haven't had more than a couple of beers in months, and I haven't eaten today." I leave off the part about how the tequila mixed with my meds is gonna knock me on my ass.

She pulls a sleeve of saltines out of her desk and throws it at me. "Here. Have a cracker and spill."

I smile, tear open the wrapper, and shove a saltine in my mouth. "Fanks," I tell her through the mouthful, intentionally spraying her desk with crumbs.

"Gross. I didn't think that through. I should have known you'd one-up me. That's what I get for trying to be a smartass with you."

"It is. Bow down to the queen." I do my best sitting-down curtsy.

"Sure thing, Your Majesty." She flips me off.

I laugh so hard I snort, and then laugh even harder. We're both howling, doubled over; it's amazing.

Wiping a tear from her eye, she says, "Quit changing the subject. What's the blush about?"

I shrug. "Nothing, really. I've just made a mess of things with a couple of guys."

She leans back in her chair and puts her hands behind her head, reminding me of Eddie at Hope House's dining table. "A couple of guys, huh? Things were busy at the institution." She laughs.

"Oh, fuck you," I say with a smile. I haven't smiled this much in as long as I can remember. My cheeks hurt. "One was stupid. I'll fix it and it'll be awkward for a while, but it'll be fine. The other guy's not so simple." I rub my hands over my face.

"Tell me," she says bluntly. "You've never gotten this worked up over a guy, so it's gotta be good. I'm thinking he's probably not just some guy."

"Ugh." I groan into my hands. "No. But he has to be."

"Why?"

"Well, first off, do you really start a relationship with someone when you're locked in the crazy house? That's gotta be a mistake."

"Maybe. Maybe not." She shrugs. "Besides, that place wasn't exactly a 'crazy house.' It was classier than that."

"Was it? Four nutso people not allowed to have shoelaces or sharp objects and surrounded 24/7 by nurses and security guards. I'm pretty sure it fits the bill."

"Well, when you put it that way . . ."

"See? You already agree and I haven't even gotten to the second point yet."

"Okay. What's the second point, then?"

"I'm about a million kinds of fucked up. The doctor says I shouldn't even try dating until I'm fixed."

"What does that mean?"

I shrug. "I have no idea. I mean, I kind of do, but not really." I don't want to go into the specifics with her. "I don't even know why I'm still thinking about this guy. I shouldn't be."

"I bet I do."

"Yeah? Why?"

"I'm just making a stab in the dark here, but I figure he's probably better than the usual pickings at the bar down the street." She tips her head to the right.

"That doesn't take a genius. Anybody's better than them."

"True, but how many of those losers have you gone home with over the years?"

"No comment."

"And how many of them have you come into my office and talked about the next day? Or even thought about again?"

"Zero."

"So why are you thinking about this one?"

I sigh. She's not going to stop until I give her something. "Because he's not just some lame drunk. He's . . . I don't know, just *different*. And it sucks."

"Oh, man. You've got it bad."

"No, I don't. Well, I could, but I can't."

"You mean you won't."

I tip my head at her. "What do you mean I won't?"

"You won't let yourself be happy."

"What are you talking about? I am happy. Well, at least I was before I did this," I say, pointing at my forearm.

"Really?"

"Yes, really. I loved this job and you. I had a roof over my head. It was good."

"Yeah, but you weren't *happy*. And the way I figure it, you're still not."

I frown at her, at a loss for words.

"Look, I get it—why you didn't come back here after that." She points at my arm. "Because your life sucked."

"Hey! It didn't su—"

"Yes. It did. Well, not me and the bakery, of course. We're fucking awesome. The rest of it, though . . ." She doesn't need to add the rest of the sentence.

I put my elbows on the edge of the desk and rest my face in my hands. At least the shot has taken the edge off my anxiety enough I don't need to make fists, but I do begin silently counting.

At twenty-two, Rebeca speaks again. "There's no way you're not lonely, Kyle. You work alone, you live alone. I assume those things haven't changed."

I shake my head.

"Then do something about it." She does another shot and slams the glass on the desk.

I peek at her through my fingers. "Like what?"

"Don't be dense." She rolls her eyes at me.

I yell into my hands. "Why does this feel like some sort of drunken therapy session?"

"Because it is. Consider this your intervention. That uppity doctor may not tell you this, but I will: you gotta put yourself out there. Take a chance on not being alone."

A tear rolls down my cheek. "It's too scary," I sniffle, "and the doctor says I'm not supposed to because I'm not ready up here." I tap my temple. "He's probably right."

She stands, walks around the desk, and puts a hand on my shoulder. "Sorry, Pepita. I didn't mean to make you cry." She rubs circles between my shoulder blades.

"I know. I just . . . I just don't think I can do it."

"Do what?"

"Be with him."

"Of course you can. People aren't made to be alone."

"But *him*, specifically. I don't deserve him. Besides, I hurt him. He doesn't want me, anyway."

"I find that hard to believe. Does he know how awesome you are?"

"Maybe."

"You don't even know." She shakes her head. "I'm gonna guarantee he sees exactly how fucking spectacular you are. And even if you hurt him, he'll get over it if there's a chance of getting all up in that." She waves a hand in my direction.

I laugh through the tears.

"If you like this guy and he likes you, then fuck all the other stuff and just be together."

"You make it sound so easy."

"It is."

I shake my head. "Maybe for you."

"Nah." She shakes her head back at me. "The only easy part is deciding to do the thing that makes you happy. The rest of it's really fucking difficult."

Her phone buzzes on the desktop. She picks it up and reads the incoming message. "Speaking of the rest of it. The kids are losing their shit wanting dinner, and my idiot husband still hasn't learned how to turn on a stove."

"Thanks, Rebeca." I give her a watery grin. "It was good to see you. Sorry about everything."

"Don't apologize. Just make yourself happy. And don't be a stranger, okay?"

"Okay."

I turn and walk out of the bakery. It's dusk. I need to buy something to eat before going home. At the grocery store, I get a cart and push through the aisles, grabbing anything that sounds good—salami, a slab of overpriced French Gruyère, capers, cornichons, artisanal mustard, rosemary crackers. This will blow through most of my paycheck, but it's not like I have anything else to spend it on.

At the end of the spree, I have twenty dollars left and use it to buy a bottle of decent wine and a corkscrew to go with my gourmet picnic. The tequila got me buzzed; might as well finish the job and have drunk snacks. They're way better than tipsy snacks.

I spread out my bounty on a tray, turn on the television, and open the wine, not bothering with a glass. The last five minutes of *Sixteen Candles* is on. Samantha's about to walk out of the church and spot Jake Ryan leaning on that bright red car. I love this part. As a kid, I imagined Jake Ryan showing up to rescue me. Jackson kind of reminds me of Jake—the dark hair and eyes, basically the same clothes.

I fall asleep on the couch again and dream of argyle sweaters.

CHAPTER TWENTY-SIX

*Grandma and I were in the kitchen making dinner—roast chicken—
and she was letting me chop the carrots and onions for the big pan.
Sunday dinner was our one big meal of the week. We'd be eating
chicken salad sandwiches for the rest of the week. She was letting me use
her knife. It was the biggest one in the drawer, and the wooden handle
was worn down and shiny from use. I was telling Grandma about the
big Home Ec assignment due on Tuesday and how stressed out I was
about making pie crust in front of Mrs. Donovan. "When I'm nervous,
I always tear it," I told her.*

*The knife blade slipped and sliced deep into my thumb. The blood
came fast, ruining the vegetables before I got the white flour-sack towel
wrapped around it. "Uh, Grandma. I messed up."*

* * *

I wake up confused; I fell asleep less than an hour ago.

Omitting my injury, this is one of my favorite dreams. I smile at the memory of my first pie. Mrs. Donovan never would have guessed what she was starting with that assignment.

I've started running. Every morning, when I would have gotten up to go to the bakery, I get dressed and run. I go until I get a stitch in my side and breathing hurts. I close the distance between Jackson and me, jogging past The Coffee Shop and Hope House and hoping for a sign, something to tell me I'm deserving, I'm worth a chance. Every morning so far, I've come up empty and make the return trip to my apartment as fast as I can.

This morning, though, The Coffee Shop isn't open, and there's a "For Lease" sign on the door. I stop, hands on my hips, and heave for a breath that won't come. The windows of his apartment are dark. I run down the sidewalk to his building's entrance. His last name is missing from the mailboxes. All that's left is a tacky rectangle. I press my index finger into the stickiness.

He's gone.

I struggle to pull in breath, even more than I was already from running. My fingers tingle, and I try to shake off the anxiety. The numbness of the impending panic attack ignores my effort, though, and creeps farther up my arm. I jerk on the locked entry door, hoping it'll magically open, with no luck. If I'm going to break down, I could go across the street to Hope House. Bruce would let me in.

That thought allows some reasonableness to break through my alarm. I can't go to Hope House in the middle of a panic attack. How quickly would Booth lock me back up if that happened? He might not let me leave again. The last thing I want is to be trapped after working so hard to get my freedom back.

I stand in Jackson's entryway for a long time, long enough for the sunrise to start coloring the sky in pinks and purples, and breathe. In through the nose, out through the mouth, until my heart's not pounding against my ribs. I clench and unclench my fists until the pricks of pain recede from my fingers.

"You can do this, Kyle." Mary said it. "You're stronger than you think. Be strong. Be strong." I chant into the empty space, letting the words bounce and echo around me.

Turning left out of the building so I don't have to see the sign in the window again, I run home. It takes twice as long to get back to my building as it did to get to Jackson's, my muscles wobbly and weak from the panic attack, but I get there. In my apartment, I strip and collapse in the empty bathtub, then turn on the shower. The spray rains over me. I curl into a ball and let it cover me like a blanket while I cry into the air pocket between my thighs and chest.

Why did I tell him no? Surely there's a way I could have said yes. Jackson would have had a plan. But now I've completely fucked it up, and he's gone, and The Coffee Shop's gone, and Jamie's gone, and Fiona. Shit.

I finally turn off the shower and get dressed for work, then spend the bus ride searching for Jackson Turner on my phone. There are what feels like a million results, but nothing recent. It's a common name, after all. There's nothing about him without his father, other than an article in *The Reader* about The Coffee Shop. I feel stupid now that I never got his phone number, but what would I have done with it in Hope House? It's not like I would have called him with Eddie listening in.

When I walk into Frank's, I nod at Trace but don't look to see if he caught it. My mind is so wrapped up in the morning's events that I don't really care. Things have been super weird and awkward since that sort of accidental kiss. He's not really talking to me unless he has to, so not saying hello will fit right into the pattern.

I head into my room. Once the red bandanna is tied over my hair, I get to work. This may be one of the most boring jobs in the history of boring jobs, but at least it's an effective tool for taking out my frustrations. After an hour of pounding, kneading, and rolling crusts, my shoulders are burning. I need to slow down if I'm going to make it through my shift. I slam my fists on the metal tabletop, then put my hands on the edge, hang my head, and sigh. Fuck.

I've got to figure this out. Got to get my shit together.

I've been kneading for about an hour, my mind turning things over as much as my hands are turning over dough, before it hits me: Booth's list. I need to finish it. As fucked up as the Hope House program often felt, he turned out to be right more often than not. I still hate his smug ass, though.

Four things. That's all. It should be simple enough. Finding a new apartment should be first, and probably the easiest. I can barely even walk into my own kitchen without thinking of the incident. I'm going to take my time with it, though. Find a place that makes me happy. And if it has a nice place to work on baking ideas nearby, all the better.

I can do this. I can do this without Booth or Mary or Joey or Jackson. I know it.

"You okay in here?" Trace asks from the doorway.

I startle at his voice, not expecting him to come in here, let alone talk to me unless it's to yell because I'm behind. I turn to face him. His eyebrows are pulled together in concern. I nod and huff. "I'm fine. Just frustrated."

He nods once, and I can hear a million unsaid words behind the movement. He's frustrated, too, and it's mostly with me.

He stands away from the jamb, and before he can walk away, I say, "Hey, Trace."

"Yeah?"

"I'm sorry about the other night."

"S'okay." He drawls the two words into one.

"No." I shake my head. "It's not. It was really shitty of me. I wish I could take it back."

He winces.

"Not like that. I just, I . . ." I trail off, unsure how to put my feelings into words. "I wasn't kidding when I said I'm all kinds of fucked up."

The corner of his mouth tips up.

"Or when I said I suck at this."

He smiles. "You really do."

"I just—"

He cuts me off. "Stop. Thanks for the apology. I think I suck at this, too." He gestures between the two of us, and I'm not entirely sure what part of this he thinks he sucks at but understand the gist of it.

"Can we start over?"

"Friends?" He tilts his head.

I smile back at him and nod. "I'd like that."

"Happy hour after work?" He nods in the direction of the bar.

"Sure, but you're not paying my tab this time. And I can walk myself to the train."

He blushes, and his smile fades a little, but he says, "Okay," then turns and walks back into his space.

I think, as he's walking, that I see his shoulders shudder with laughter. Trace and I could be great friends. And I just inadvertently accomplished one of the items on Booth's list. I go back to work and smile until my cheeks hurt.

* * *

Apartment hunting sucks. I was *very* wrong about this being the easiest item on the list. I've been looking at anything and everything in my price range for weeks. I shudder thinking of the place I went through right before this one, where there was rat shit in the refrigerator. How in the hell did a rat even get into the refrigerator? And the droppings might not have even been the worst part. No, that distinction might have to go to the toilet in the bedroom. Not a separate room or a wall dividing the space. The toilet was right next to the bed, like that was a perfectly normal thing. They say "Don't shit where you eat," but not doing it where you sleep is probably a good idea, too.

And so I've decided that if the new apartment thing might have to wait, I can at least make my old apartment feel new. I'm totally taking advantage of my new friend Trace and making him help me move in a new bed I found at a thrift store on Monday. It's a huge four-poster that reminded me of Jackson's. I was fretting at happy hour about how to get it home, and Trace just volunteered his truck. I don't think he was offering himself, but he's stuck with me now.

The pickup is mostly rust and sounds like it's wheezing its last breath every time he hits the gas, shuddering and jumping. But we made the trip.

My new bed weighs about ten million pounds, and by the time we get the whole thing upstairs, we're both sweating and out of breath. Since it needs to be assembled, the whole floor is empty, so Trace lies flat on the hardwood, arms and legs extended like a snow angel.

"You want a beer?"

"Is it cold?" he asks without moving from the pink carpet.

"It better be." I carry two beers over and sit cross-legged on the floor next to him. His shirt has ridden up and there's a swath of stomach exposed, so I touch the cold bottle to it, making him jump.

"Shit!" he yells and scrambles away from me.

I laugh. "Sorry, but I had to do it. You left me no choice."

"Yeah, yeah, yeah," he grumbles, his cheeks blushing pink.

I pass him a beer, and he twists the top off, then takes a long drink. I forgot how fast he drinks. "I've only got a six-pack, so pace yourself."

"Oh, I've got the two-beer limit this time. I gotta drive home."

"So, um," I mumble. "Thanks for your help."

"What are friends for, right?" He smiles brightly, genuinely.

"Right." I smile back and throw back my own swallow of beer.

"You need help putting it together?" He looks at the bed frame stacked against the wall, then back at me.

I shake my head. "Nah. I should be able to get it."

He hops up, drains the beer bottle, and sets it on the kitchen counter. "I better get going. Gotta work tonight." He pulls at his sweaty T-shirt. "And I need to take a shower."

I start to get up, but he holds up a hand, stopping me.

"Stay there," he says, and I settle back down. "You've got my number, right?"

"Yeah."

"Call if you need anything else."

"Sure," I say, even though I know I won't.

He walks to the door and turns just before it closes behind him. "See you on Monday."

And then he's gone and I'm alone. I close my eyes and absorb the silence. A wave of loneliness washes over me, but I shake it off the best I can. Today the bed. Tomorrow I'm going to put new tile in the kitchen. The hardware store had some that just sticks on top of the existing floor. It's not permanent, so the landlord can take it out if he hates it, and I don't have to look at the grimy gray tile anymore. Don't have to imagine the blood stains on the grout.

Out of sight, out of mind. At least, I hope so.

CHAPTER TWENTY-SEVEN

I'm going out tonight with Trace; there's some rockabilly band he wants to see. He asked and I hedged, not wanting him to think it was a date. Then I remembered I promised to take him out in exchange for his help with the bed, so I agreed while being very transparent that I was clearing my debt.

In Hope House, I grumbled about my clothing selection, but I gotta say, having my entire wardrobe isn't much better: the choices still suck. I end up in a pair of jeans-turned-shorts and a black tank top. I'm showing way more skin than usual, but it's the only thing I tried on that wasn't smothering in the early summer heat. Hopefully, all the skin won't give Trace the wrong idea.

I'm early, and the bar is relatively quiet. The place just opened last week and still smells like fresh paint. It makes me anxious; I'm more comfortable in grimier joints. There's only a handful of people milling around, mostly band members from the look of their pompadours. I grab a seat in the back corner and send a text to Trace letting him know I'm here.

I scroll through the employment listings on my phone while I wait. Pastry chef openings are rarer than rare, so even though the job at Frank's is good enough for now, I'm looking. Trace will be pissed when I find something else, but he'll understand. Eventually.

Trace throws himself onto the seat across from me, smiling his gap-toothed smile. "Hey! Sorry I'm late."

"Nah, I'm early." I smile back, then pull my debit card out of my back pocket. "Tonight's my treat, but go easy on me. What are we starting with? Beer?"

"Yep."

I walk to the bar, its new surface shiny even under the dim lights. I step into a narrow space open at the end closest to me and lean forward on my elbows. It's jammed with people lining up for the bartender to get their night started; the bar's gotten a lot more crowded since I first walked in.

The bartender is working at the other end of the bar with his back to me, gesturing with one hand as he slides a drink across the bar with the other. There are about ten other people gesturing and waving in the distance between us, so I pull out my phone and keep scrolling through the classifieds while I wait for him to work back my way.

I'm absorbed in my job search, trying different keywords, looking for anything that might fit, when he comes to the man next to me and says, "What can I get you?"

It's Jamie. I watch while he makes the guy's whiskey soda, trying to figure out what to say. I'm not prepared for this. As much as I want to avoid him, though, I'm desperate to talk to him. I want to blurt out all the questions: Where is Jackson? What's he doing? Is he okay? Does he talk about me?

"What can I get—" Jamie cuts off when his eyes lift to meet mine. "Kyle?"

I can't read his expression. It's not happy or sad or mad or glad, so I hold up a hand in greeting. "Hey."

He clears his throat and blinks slowly. "What can I get you?"

I didn't realize my hand was still up in my lame-ass wave, so I try to play it off by using it to hold up two fingers. "Two Old Styles."

He grabs two plastic cups and steps over to the tap. "You here with somebody?" he asks while the beer pours.

"Yeah." I nod, then shake my head when I realize he's probably asking if I'm on a date. "Just a friend. From work."

"Oh. What've you been up to?" I can tell he's striving for casual, but there's a tension in his posture, a stiffness in his spine.

"Not much. What about you?" I try for casual, too, and I'm pretty sure I fail miserably. My voice is too tight. My hands are balled in fists between us. I know all of this, and yet it's so hard to un-tense.

He sets the cups of beer in front of me and points a finger at the new guy, who's taken a place at the bar next to me and is wordlessly asking his order. "You know the shop closed?"

"I saw. What happened?"

He stops the tap and levels a hard gaze at me. "I think you know."

My face heats with embarrassment. *Shit.* I look at the bar top and scratch at an invisible spot. I open my mouth to explain everything to Jamie, everything that I said to Jackson on that day: that I couldn't, *why* I couldn't. But instead I just say, "Yeah. I think I do."

While he works with his back to me, I take the opportunity to escape the mortification and hurry back to the table. Trace smiles when I sit back down, then gulps down half the beer. "Thanks." He wipes the back of his hand across his mouth. "If it's gonna take that long, you might need to get me two at a time."

I shake my head and take a drink, swallowing past the nausea creeping up my gut.

"You okay? You look like you're gonna be sick."

I gulp and blink fast a few times. "I might be."

"What happened?"

"You know that long story I didn't want to tell?"

"Yeah."

"The bartender's part of the story." I take a long drink, emptying my cup. "Maybe we both need two at a time tonight. I don't wanna go back up there, though."

And even as I'm swallowing the gulp of beer, I know what I'm doing is beyond stupid. I can't drink more than a beer or two with the anxiety meds. I'm as likely to end up passed out as anything else. Right now, though, I don't care; I just want to ease the ache in my chest.

"You start a tab?"

My debit card is still in my back pocket, and I'm even more embarrassed. On top of everything else, I'm a thief. *Shit.* I shake my head. "I just wanted to get away. I forgot."

Trace holds out his hand and wiggles his fingers at me. "Gimme. I'll take care of it."

I give him my card, and he pushes out of the booth. While he stands at the bar waiting for Jamie's attention, I close my eyes and breathe, trying to calm down. With everything between Jackson and me, I only had the occasional fleeting thought about Jamie. I've never seen him anything but smiling and jovial, or at least putting up that facade. I want—no, need—to ask him about Jackson. It may be my only chance. And the one certain thing about the whole fucked-up situation of the past few months is that I need to see Jackson again.

I put my arms on the table and rest my head on them, blocking out the light and some of the sound. I stay that way until Trace shouts, "You can't go home—"

My head shoots up and I nearly hit the tray in his hands. He lowers it to the table. There are at least fifteen shot glasses on the tray.

"—you have to help me drink these."

I can't help but smile. "Shit. I thought you were gonna go easy on me."

He hands my card back to me. "I did. No worries. These are yours." He slides two glasses off the tray toward me. "The rest are mine."

I shake my head. I'm in for a much longer night than I had anticipated if Trace is drinking the rest of this. "What is all this?"

"One of everything from the top shelf." He's beaming.

"Why in the world . . ."

"Just to piss him off."

I look up at Trace, mouth open in indignation. "I don't want to piss him off!"

Trace's smile fades and he stares at me, serious all of a sudden. "He upset you. So he deserved it."

I shake my head and look at the table. "It's at least kind of my fault he lost his last job. I feel shitty about it and I wasn't prepared to see him. That's all it is. He didn't *do* anything to me."

I look at the bar. Jamie's hidden by the crowd, but I can see the top of his head moving back and forth behind the bar. I'm glad for all the people vying for his attention, so I can hide in the crowd.

"Oh," Trace says, sounding like I scolded him. He recovers pretty immediately. "Well, nothing I can do about it now. Let's get this party started. How in the hell can I tell what's what?" He scratches at the shaved side of his head.

"No idea. But that's kind of the point, right?" I grin at him, pick up a glass of what looks like whiskey, and hold it up, then throw it back. I cringe at the sweetness and burn.

He echoes me, picking up a glass, holding it out in a toast, and shooting back its contents. And then he picks up another.

"I can't feel my face," I say, smooshing up my right cheek.

Trace laughs and reaches across the table to press the left side of my face. "I can't feel your face either."

I drop my hands and let my head drop against the table. It hits with a thunk, and I sit up, rubbing at the point of impact.

"Shit, dude. You okay?"

I giggle and nod. "Uh-huh. I told you I can't feel my face."

I'm as drunk as I can ever remember being, and my three drinks are a fraction of what Trace had. My meds topped with alcohol are an ass-kicker.

"Your turn. Come on. Help a brother out. You can handle another one." Trace nods at the remaining drinks. He's shit-faced.

I groan and shake my head. The movement makes me dizzier. "I don't think I can."

"You can't wuss out on me now! I've made it this far. I just need a little help." He holds up his hand and tries to show how much help he needs with his thumb and forefinger.

"But I'm so drunk." I rest my chin on my hands and grin at him.

"Yeah, lightweight, you are. But you're not a quitter."

I pick up a glass without looking and swallow its contents with a grimace.

"What was it?"

I shrug. "No idea. I can't feel my taste buds anymore either. I gotta pee." I scoot out of the booth. "Come and get me if I'm not back in a half hour."

The bar's mostly cleared out now. The band finished up a few minutes ago, and the only people left are those finishing their drinks. I weave-walk to the hallway at the back of the bar and open the bathroom door, then stumble when it flies open, my push too forceful. "Oops."

I pee with my head in my hands, fighting a wave of nausea and closing my eyes to stop the room from spinning. I'm going to hate myself tomorrow.

I trip through the bathroom door and into a solid wall of person. I hold out my hands to steady myself. It's Jamie.

"How do you *still* smell like coffee?"

His hands are wrapped around my biceps. "Do I?" His voice more cheerful than earlier, but only just.

"Uh-huh." I nod against his chest. "You do. It makes me thirsty."

"I think you've had enough to drink tonight. How many of those shots did you have?"

I shake my head and hold up a hand. My fingers don't want to cooperate. "Three" comes out all slurry and garbled. The drunken scene I'm making has to be ridiculous, and his uncomfortable smile confirms it.

"I fucked up."

His smile fades. "Yeah. You did."

"I didn't mean to."

"Maybe not."

Even with my brain all swimmy, I know I don't want to have this conversation with Jamie. He's not the one I need to talk to. "I gotta go, though. Trace is waiting for me."

"No, he's not. I put him in a cab."

I pull away from him and end up stumbling back into the wall behind me. "Why'd you do that?" I wag a finger at him. "He's my friend."

"I know, Kyle. I'm about to do the same thing with you. The bar's closing."

"Oh." I rub my hands over my face, too hard. "I'm drunk."

"Yeah, I know that, too. Let's go."

We walk back into the main room. I slide my hand along the wall to steady myself and stumble when the wall runs out.

Jamie reaches out and catches me. "You okay?"

"No." I start to shake my head, but the motion makes my spinning head worse. I stop and drop my head into my hands. "What happened, Jamie?"

"You don't need me to tell you. You already know."

"I guess I do." A tear falls off my cheek.

"Aw, shit, man. Don't cry. I can't stay mad at you if you cry."

I hiccup and more tears fall as I look up at him. "I'm sorry. I really didn't mean to hurt you guys."

"Okay," he says.

"I couldn't say yes, Jamie. The doctor wouldn't have let me."

"Oh." From the one noise, I can tell he didn't know about Booth's part in things.

"Where did he go?"

"I don't think I should tell you that, Kyle."

"At least tell me he's okay."

"I definitely can't tell you that."

I reach for Jamie's arms to shake him, insist he tell me what's wrong, but fall into him instead. "Please, Jamie."

He takes the opportunity to move us closer to the front door. "Come on. Your cab should be here any second."

"What's wrong with him, Jamie? You have to tell me."

Jamie pushes us through the front door, then turns us so that my back is against the adjacent wall. "You broke his fucking heart, Kyle. That's what's wrong."

"But—" I stop. I don't know how to finish that sentence. A cab pulls to the curb next to us with a squeal of brakes.

"Go home. Sleep it off and forget you ever met him. That's the best thing for both of you."

I start crying in earnest. Even if I weren't sloppy drunk, I think I'd do the same. "I can't. I know I hurt him because I hurt myself, too. I know I hurt you and Fiona, too, and I'm just as sorry about that, but there's things that I don't think you know, Jamie. I need to see him."

Jamie reaches up, pinches the bridge of his nose, and groans. "I can't let you hurt him again." He looks up and levels his gaze at me. "He's been through enough."

I do my best to match the seriousness of his stare. "I know. I want to take care of him, too."

Jamie arches an eyebrow. I understand his doubts considering the state I'm in, but I do my best to stand straight and look as serious as possible.

The cab honks its horn and breaks our staring contest.

"You need to go."

I open my bag and fish through the bottom until my fingers find a pen, then pull it out along with my journal. The book opens automatically to the page of drawings and recipe ideas from the day of my first visit to The Coffee Shop. I've looked at the page thousands of times since then. I write my phone number in a blank space between the scribbles and circle around it. Then, I rip out the entire page and hand it to Jamie.

"Give him this." I look up at him. "Please."

The cab honks again, and the driver yells out the passenger window. "You comin' or not?"

I hold up a finger and return my attention to Jamie.

"I'll think about it. I'm not going to promise anything."

"Thanks, Jamie," I say, then stumble to the cab and get in.

I give the driver my address and watch Jamie through the window until I can't see him anymore.

* * *

I feel like shit and wake up confused: the last thing I remember is sitting at the table with Trace. My stomach flips. Oh. The shots.

"Ugh." I groan into my pillow and bury my face against the bright sunshine coming through the window. It's a good thing I don't have to work today.

I start to sit but immediately give up. My head's pounding. I think I might still be a little drunk.

There's a flash of the cab dropping me off, then—wait—*Jamie.* I gave him my phone number. He said he'd think about giving it to Jackson.

I guess I know where to find Jamie again, to plead my case when I'm sober.

In the kitchen, there's coffee waiting for me thanks to the timer on my machine, but it's cold. The coffee maker turned off hours ago. I pour a cup anyway and drink it black, just hoping for a wake-up jolt.

I pace the apartment, trying to pull a more solid memory of last night from the fog.

Jamie was really and truly pissed, not that I blame him. But I'm left with another takeaway, too: I know the decision I made was the right one. Even if I felt like I could pull it off, Booth would never have allowed me to work for Jackson. And, let's face it, I couldn't have pulled it off. I was—still sort of am—a goddamn mess.

Jamie said he'd think about it, though. So at least there's hope. And that's something I haven't had much of lately.

CHAPTER TWENTY-EIGHT

It's been a month since I gave Jamie my phone number. Still no word from Jackson.

The despondency of depression is creeping in again, blurring my edges, turning my mind all staticky. I get ready for work, going through the motions of dressing without noticing I'm even doing it. Next thing I know, I'm at the corner waiting for the bus and not remembering how I got there. Depression is a powerful drug.

The day at work is the same blur as the rest. I'm lost in my mind's buzz when there's a tap on my shoulder. I jump.

"Dude. I didn't mean to scare you. What's up with you these days? You seem checked out."

I shake my head and take a deep breath to try and settle my pulse. "Nothing. I've just got a lot on my mind."

"No shit," Trace says, smiling his goofy gap-toothed grin. "You wanna go next door?"

I haven't been out with him since that night at the bar. Shit, I haven't done anything but go to work or the grocery store since that night at the bar. My life looks just like it did before Hope House but without the random drunken hookups. Hell, without the drunken hookups, my life looks a lot like it did *in* Hope House. I'm pathetic.

"Nah, I'm gonna head home. I'm beat."

"Of course, you are," Trace mutters under his breath.

I heard him plain as day, but I still say, "Huh?"

"You heard me." He levels a stare at me, the goofy grin gone.

I turn back to my worktable and go back to cleaning up. I don't have the energy for a confrontation.

"We're friends, right?" he asks.

"Yeah," I whisper. Saying it out loud feels strange. I've been a totally shitty friend lately.

"Well, friends don't let friends fall down. And you, my friend, have fallen flat on your face."

I lean forward with my elbows on the table and put my head in my hands. "I know. I'm sorry."

"Shit, I didn't come in here to make you cry. I just—I guess this has something to do with that bartender, right?"

I nod into my palms.

"Well, remember there's other fish in the sea and all that bullshit."

I blow my nose into the kitchen towel in response. "I know. I just really wanted that fish."

"Yeah, I know the feeling." He stands behind me, quiet, for a few more seconds. "Well, I'm gonna go get shit-faced. You're always welcome to join me."

"Thanks, Trace." I turn to face him. "You're a good friend."

"See you tomorrow?"

"Yeah. Bright and early."

He turns and walks out the kitchen's swinging doors. I throw my now-snotty towel into the laundry, grab my purse, and walk through those same doors.

*　*　*

I'm looking at my feet, going up the three steps to my apartment building, and run right into someone. Hands grab my upper arms to steady me and a voice says, "We've really got to stop meeting this way."

It's Jackson.

I look up, dazed and bleary-eyed from the earlier tears. His face is worried, eyebrows pulled together.

"You've been crying."

"Yeah."

All this time worrying about whether I'd ever see him again and I can't think of a single other thing to say. My brain's still as blank as it has been for the past month.

"Are you okay?"

I shake my head. "Not really, no." I take a gulp of air. "What are you doing here?"

"I needed to see you."

"Why?" I look at the ground because looking at him hurts too much. I thought I'd be excited if this moment ever happened, but I'm not. In fact, I want to double over from the pain. I knew this last month of silence hurt me, but I didn't know just how much until right now.

"I've missed you." His hands squeeze my upper arms.

Immediately, the hurt is forgotten, and I'm pissed. My throat burns with rage, and I bite my lip hard enough to taste blood. I want to make him feel a fraction of the pain I do. I look at him and glare. "I'm right here. Been right here for the last fucking month, actually. Your phone broken?" I spit the words like venom and load them with all the spite and anger I can muster.

He at least has the decency to look embarrassed. Now it's his turn to look at the ground. "I know, and I'm sorry."

"A month ago, there was nothing in the world I wanted more than to see you. But now, I've gotta get over it. Because if you felt even a fraction for me of what I felt for you, it wouldn't have taken you a day to call, let alone a month." My heart's about to beat out of my chest. My face is hot with flush and anger. I point a finger in his face. "Go home, Jackson. You lost your chance." I immediately want to take that last part back.

"I know I messed up, Kyle. I just— I couldn't face you yet. I had to get better first."

I stumble back against the building. Of all the things he could have said . . . That . . . That . . . I'm at a loss for words, even in my mind, because that's the one thing he could have said that would make any sense to me, serve as any sort of apology worth listening to, make the month of waiting comprehendible to me, make my indignation vanish.

"Shit," I exhale, the word more the sound of my breath than something I've said.

He steps forward as he sees my rage extinguish and stands right in front of me, so close we're nearly touching. "I wasn't . . ." he stutters and stumbles. "I haven't been okay since you left."

"Why?"

"I was lost. For a long time."

"I know that feeling."

"I know you do. I also know that it doesn't excuse me. I was a dick."

I don't think I've heard Jackson use anything even approaching a curse word before, so the last sentence leaves me flabbergasted. I laugh, even though I don't want my facade to crack just yet. He might have said the perfect thing, but I'm still upset at his silence. "Yeah, you were."

His feet shuffle him an inch closer. I look down and watch his shoes—the same scuffed brown boots he wore at The Coffee Shop.

"Can I come up? I'd like it if we could talk. I only have a few minutes, so you don't have to worry about me overstaying my welcome."

I peek up and look at his face, look for anything but sincerity in his expression, and come up blank. Jackson's looking at me the same as he did that day in The Coffee Shop with his father: like he's desperate and drowning.

I take a deep breath, hold it, and count to five. "I guess so," I say on the exhale. I fish through my bag until my fingers land on my keys and pull them up to the apartment door with a shaking hand. Eventually, I get the key into the lock, go inside, and head up the stairs.

I don't look back at him, unsure if I've made the right decision to let Jackson in, all the way to my apartment and keep on not looking once we're both inside. I toss my bag on the floor and go into the kitchen to put some distance between us. "You want something to drink?"

"Nah. I'm okay."

"Well, I'm going to have something." I grab a beer and take my time popping the top. I take a long pull from the bottle.

Jackson hasn't moved away from the door but has his back pressed against it like he's waiting for a chance to get away. Or maybe he's as terrified of what I'm going to say as I am about what he will.

"So . . .?"

"Thank you, Kyle." Well, one thing I can say for him is he's surprising the hell out of me. "And I'm sorry."

"For what?"

"I've been awful to you." He takes a deep breath and closes his eyes. He looks like he might cry.

I stare at him. "I was pretty awful to you, too."

He shakes his head. "No. I understand. It took me a while, but eventually I got why you said no. I shouldn't have put you in the position I did. It was stupid and desperate."

I don't want to hash this out now, while I'm still a little angry, but there may not be another opportunity. "It sucked having to say those things in front of your father. That was majorly fucked up. But our timing was bad, Jackson. Why'd we have to meet while I was living in that stupid place? While I was under Booth's thumb? If not for that, I might have said yes."

"But if you hadn't been in that place, we never would have met."

I huff a laugh. "And I'm sure you're just thrilled about that."

"I am." He nods, unsmiling.

"But how could you be? It has to be at least partly my fault the shop closed. I don't know how you could forgive me." The tears well, and my anger is officially gone.

"Kyle." His tone is pleading. "I do forgive you. It hurt when you said no, but I get it now. You didn't do it to be cruel. You said no because you had to."

I nod once. "I did. But it was still horrible."

He walks over to me, grabs my hand, and squeezes. "It's okay. I didn't come here for your apology."

I pull my hand out of his. I may not be mad anymore, but I'm still hurt at the last month's silence. "Good. I wasn't intending to apologize to you." I blink back tears that are threatening to spill over while I finish off my beer, then put the empty bottle down on my table harder than necessary. I want to cover my face, but won't. I want to act as strong as I felt before running into Jamie, so I cross my arms and say, "I'm mad at you."

Jackson bites his lips and fights a smile. "I know. You should be." But there's laughter in his voice.

"I'm serious." I stomp my foot like an angry toddler.

"I know you are." He's fighting laughter now. "You're very serious and angry." He grabs one of my hands again and sandwiches it between his.

I lose the battle. A tear falls.

"Hey, please don't cry. It'll be okay. Once we get back to the willy-nilly hand-holding, no one and nothing can stop us."

I giggle through the tears. "Don't try to distract me. I *am* mad at you."

He squeezes my hand and straightens his face to something more neutral. "I'm sorry. I just . . . I missed this." He lifts a hand and waves a finger back and forth between us.

"I missed it, too," I admit.

We look at each other for a long time. My breath is stuttery at first, but eventually calms. "Not to ruin all this willy-nillyness—" I nod at our hands "—but why'd it take you a month to show up?"

He pulls his hand away and walks to my door again. "I wasn't kidding when I said I needed to get better. When the shop closed, it was either move back in with my father or be homeless. So I went back and just . . . shut down. Living there, my father's pressure to go to law school was relentless. Eventually I caved, just to make life bearable. He was thrilled. I've been miserable."

I know how much he hates the way things have turned out, and my first instinct is to ask why he didn't call if things were so bad. Maybe I could have helped. I bite my tongue when I realize how damn hypocritical the idea is.

"When Jamie showed up with that page from your journal, I ran to my phone. I swear I must have stared at it for hours trying to dial those numbers. But, Kyle, I just . . . I couldn't."

"But *why?*"

"I had to get my shit together. Come to some kind of terms with where my life has ended up. The last thing you needed was me bringing you down when you were finally doing better."

"How would you know I'm doing better?"

"You had to be, right? I knew you'd be amazing once you got out of that place. That much was a given."

I huff a laugh. "Well, that's the greatest overstatement of all time. Surprise: I'm a fucking mess."

He turns to face me, his expression suddenly grave and serious. "Really?"

"Jackson, you don't want to hear that stuff."

"Actually, I do."

"Well, what if I don't want to tell you?"

He smiles. "I'm not going to force you. I wish you would, though. How about this? Tell me what you're doing now. I know you're still working at the pizza place."

"Yeah. That's about it."

"How is it?"

"Okay, I guess."

"That wasn't very convincing."

I chuckle. "I guess not, huh? It could be worse."

"So you're baking pizza now?"

"Nope. I just make the crusts. Not really, though. I get about a billion pounds of pizza dough every morning that some other guy makes at night, then I make it into crusts. Over and over and over again. I work alone. All day, every day, it's me and a big pile of dough."

"They don't have you making it?"

"Uh-uh." I shake my head. "The night guy does. He's the only one who knows the 'family recipe.' And he's been there for something like thirty years."

"I guess that makes sense, but . . . why would they get you a job where you're not baking anything?"

I shrug. "Who knows what Booth was thinking."

We're silent for another minute, studying each other.

"Hey." Jackson looks at his watch, then says, softly, "I have to go. I have dinner plans with my father and some attorney buddy of his about an internship."

"Then go." The anger comes roaring back. The stops and starts that seem to make up our entire relationship are wearing me out. One step forward, two steps back.

"I really . . . Well, I really came to give you this." He pulls an envelope out of his back pocket, then walks over and lays it next to the beer bottle on my table. "I'll call you, okay?"

He comes to me, picks up my hands, squeezes them, then walks out my door.

I sit down hard on my bed and stare at the letter like it's combustible. Something tells me I don't want to read whatever's inside.

Well, at least now I know where to find him.

CHAPTER TWENTY-NINE

I stare at the envelope for a long time but can't bring myself to open it. So I go in the kitchen and bake. I make two pies and four dozen cookies before I run out of steam. My brain is such a mess after the past month. I'm emotionally wrecked. I don't know if I can handle whatever he wrote.

Once, Jackson mentioned that the boathouse at Humboldt Park was his favorite place. It's not far from here on the bus. It's only a couple of hours until sunrise, and I've given up on sleep.

The bus stop is on the opposite end of the park from the boathouse, so I start down the path. Other than a couple of joggers, it's quiet this early. He was right; it is peaceful. The sidewalk takes me along the edge of the lagoon. This end is a narrow strip of water bordered by reeds and tall grasses. At the boathouse, the lagoon opens into a larger, semicircular pond. I know that the path cuts all the way around, but I walk through the middle arch of the boathouse to the dock, climb onto the railing, and sit.

A sheet of fog rests on the water. The city is a little lost from here. There's a busy street a few hundred feet away, but I don't hear it.

I've carried Jackson's letter here, and I've been staring at the precise blue lines spelling out my name and address on the front, unblinking, blurring the letters into nonsensical shapes. The envelope is a creamy white, heavy paper. It's expensive, and reminds me of something Jackson's father would use. It probably is if Jackson's living with him now.

I slide a finger under the flap and pull it open slowly, trying not to tear it, even though I want to rip it open.

Kyle,

I miss seeing you in the window at Hope House. There's a stranger in your room now. It's not your window anymore. That it's not your room is a good thing. I am glad you are doing better and are well enough to have regained your freedom. I know you must enjoy being unrestrained. You deserve to live a life unfettered, suffused with beauty.

I lay the letter on my lap and look across the water again. It feels like he's here with me, whispering these words into my ear as I read. The first few sentences leave me feeling gut-punched, and I'm not sure if I can handle the whole thing. I wipe away a tear and resume reading anyway. I'm not sure if I could put it away at this point either.

All of my adult life, I've tried to live with reasoned passion. But I find, even with the time and distance, I cannot temper my longing for you. I wonder if your own has waned.

Most people cannot see it, but all of my behaviors and decisions are ruled by my passions. I used to be driven by that fervency without offset. Over time, I learned that I need a counterbalance, an armor of sorts; a protection against people like my father and former fiancée. They used my enthusiasm to manipulate me. For years, I held all my passions in my heart, hidden from others who would use them against me like they did. But I'm certain that on your first day in the shop, you saw past my armor. You saw the enthusiasm inside of me as soon as you took your first sip of my coffee. At the same time, I saw so much of myself in you—I saw your armor, but I could also see your passion.

The next morning, I got the first cakes. Those cakes held your passion the same way my coffee did mine. I didn't know it then, but looking back I must have been blind. How did I not realize you needed your armor as much as I needed mine?

I am truly sorry for trying to strip you of its protection. I bear the blame for putting you in the horrible position that day with my father, the fault for chasing you away. I never should have burdened you with that guilt.

And the day you ran to me? The day we hugged and held hands and went to Fiona's show . . . as soon as you put your arms around me, telling you all of my truths became a necessity. I wanted to give you all of my secrets and take yours in return. I want to protect you with all that I am but lost that privilege with my impulsivity. What I wouldn't give to have all this time back. Are you afraid of me? My father? Do you think that you need to protect yourself from me? From my father? Do you still want to know me, as I know you?

Jorge Luis Borges wrote, "Being with you and not being with you is the only way I have to measure time." I hadn't read that poem since college, but I can't stop thinking of it now. Without you, Kyle, time has no meaning.

Ten months ago, an extraordinary girl walked into my store, and then I forced her away. I wish she would come back. Regardless of whether she does: I wish her a life filled with passion, a life without the burden of armor, a life unencumbered by grief and doubt, a life of meaningful time.

Yours,
Jackson

Tears splash onto the letter. Holy shit. There are so many emotions bubbling up right now I'm honestly not sure what to do next. I wish I could text him. I want to tell him that I read his letter, and it's the most beautiful thing I've ever read, and how I hate that so much time has passed and it's my fault, too, because I saw his heart and didn't want to take it for granted and would have until I got better. And now I'm rambling in my head. I hate to think what it would sound like if I tried to talk to him.

I shuffle back to the bus stop, wiping tears and snot with my forearm and not caring that I look absolutely unhinged.

Back at home, I get in bed and curl myself around his letter. I hold the paper to my nose, hoping to catch a whiff of Jackson. It's there: the coffee and sandalwood. Or maybe it's just in my mind. Either way, it's real to me. I carefully refold the paper and cradle it against my chest, then lie still, staring at the wall.

Jackson. The Coffee Shop was never my quiet place to come up with new ideas. It was him. It has been him this whole time. He's the final item on the list.

Now I just have to hope he comes back.

* * *

"You made me beer pie? That's fucking awesome!" Trace dances a little jig and digs into the dessert with a fork straight out of the restaurant dishwasher.

"That was supposed to be for everybody," I protest.

"Then you shouldn't have given it to me when nobody else was here." He shovels in another bite. "Dude, this is really fucking good. Why are you working here, again?"

I walk into the dough room, frowning. What *am* I doing here? Even if I can't bake for The Coffee Shop, there has to be somebody out there I can bake for. Probably more than one somebody. How many somebodies would it take for me to call it a business? I start mentally tallying costs and prices.

Ten minutes later, Trace yells, "You need this dish back?"

"Yes, please. Just bring it in here. I'll wash it."

"Here you go." Trace is standing right next to me, and I startle. He's waving the empty pie plate around.

"Did you seriously just eat that entire pie?"

"Yep." He rubs his stomach. "That was the most awesome thing ever. Nobody's ever made me a pie before. Thanks."

"Nobody's ever made you a pie? Like, ever?"

"I mean, I've had pie before, you know, at Thanksgiving and shit. Nobody's ever made one just for me, though."

"Well, if you want to get technical about it, nobody has yet. That was supposed to be for everybody, remember?"

"I'm just gonna pretend you didn't say that. Let me live under the delusion you made it just for me, okay?"

I giggle. "Don't let it go to your head."

"No worries. Thanks again. Gotta get to work."

* * *

For six hours, my hands keep to the task in front of them: turning chunk after chunk of dough into pizza crust. My mind, though, hasn't given a single conscious thought to anything but the idea of my own business. Eight. If my mental math is correct, that's how many somebodies I'd need to pull it off. Eight regular, repeat customers.

By the end of my shift, I have a business plan of sorts and want to tell Jackson.

Hell, I want to do more than tell him; I want to claim him. I want to look at him every day from now on. Or for at least as long as he can put up with me and my crazy.

CHAPTER THIRTY

Patsy Cline's "I Fall to Pieces" played in the living room. The knife slipped, and I cut my arm. It didn't hurt, so I did it again, and again. The blood flowed down my forearm and onto the linoleum. The stream reached the edge of the hardwood and pooled at the boundary. The edges of my vision blurred.

"Kyle."

Jackson? Was he coming to save me?

I wake up clutching my left arm, scrabbling at the scars. The lines are still there but have faded into slightly paler streaks instead of the angry things they were a few months ago. I'm wet with sweat, as much from the summer heat as the dream. Having the windows open is nearly counterproductive, as hot as it is tonight. I go to the bathroom and splash cold water on my face, then hold the towel to my face and groan into it.

I walk back into the living room and turn on the light. I'm blinking through the brightness when the front door buzzer goes off.

My finger shakes against the button before I press and ask, "Hello?"

It's the middle of the night, and there's only one person I want it to be. If it's Trace, shit-faced and looking for a place to crash, I'll kick his ass.

"Can I come up?" Jackson's voice comes crackling through the speaker.

I don't answer but hit the button to open the front door instead.

I put my ear to the door and listen. A few seconds later, footsteps run down the hall. I open the door before he can knock.

Jackson's flushed and shiny with sweat. The pulse throbs at the base of his neck.

"You're all sweaty," I say. "Did you run here?"

"Yeah."

"Why?"

"I couldn't sleep."

"So you . . . ran here? In the middle of the night?"

"Yeah. I didn't want to wait any longer."

"Well, I . . . come in." I move aside to make room and close the door, then lean against it. He's close. Closer than I expected. Although the fact that he's here at all is pretty out of the blue, so I probably shouldn't be trying to guess what's coming.

"I'm sorry I had to leave earlier."

"It's okay."

"It didn't seem okay."

"Well, it wasn't at first. But it's okay now."

He smirks. "I missed this, too."

"What's that?" I raise my eyebrows.

At first, I think he's going to tell me what he means, but then he takes the step and a half over to me, grabs my hips, and pulls me up against him.

I tilt my chin up to look into his eyes.

He closes the remaining few inches between us and crushes his mouth to mine. This isn't the slow, sensual experience of our first kiss; this is a feral thing, a carnal attack. He lifts me off the ground, and I groan at his strength. My slightly open mouth gives him the opportunity to take a bite at my lower lip. I tease at his teeth with my tongue, and he gives me his. As soon as our tongues touch for the first time, he groans, and I throw my legs around his hips, giving me leverage to loosen my arms and explore. I run one hand down his back, feeling his muscles flex, and the other up the short bristles of hair at his nape. I fist into the softness.

He presses me against the door, then grips my ass with a not-at-all-tentative squeeze. We both groan, and then? He changes the kiss. He slows, changing it from animalistic to caring. One more swipe of his tongue and he removes his mouth from mine. He feathers tiny kisses on the corner of my mouth, then nuzzles into my neck, still pecking and ghosting hot breaths as his hand moves up, up, up. He reaches my ribcage, slowing down more, seemingly palpating each ridge. He stops just as his wrist touches my breast, his thumb resting just under it.

He freezes and loosens his grip, forcing me to stand up. As soon as I'm on my own feet, he lets go, pacing away a few steps. He puts his hands to his face and rubs. He took all my wits with him, so I stand there silently.

It feels like a million minutes pass with the two of us recovering from that, frankly, epic kiss. I break the silence: "I read your letter."

"Yeah?"

"Uh-huh." I nod, even though his back is still to me, and continue, "It was so beautiful, and no one has ever said anything like that to me, and I will keep it forever. Did you know I think you're extraordinary, too?"

He turns around.

"You overwhelmed me," I said.

"Well, if you haven't figured it out . . . I'm quite infatuated with you."

Is swooning really a thing? If it is, I'm sure I just did it. "Oh," I breathe. "I think I might know that now."

"I'm sorry if I ever made you doubt that. That's something that's never changed."

I yawn, a very unladylike, noisy thing. Jackson smiles. "Sorry. Apparently I'm sleepy."

"No need to apologize. It's the middle of the night."

"What are you doing here, Jackson? Other than kissing the hell out of me."

"I just couldn't wait another minute." I form an O with my mouth but don't make a sound. "Can I ask you a favor?"

I nod. "Anything." After that letter, I'd give him a kidney if he asked.

"Can I lie down with you?"

"It'd make me a lot happy if you did that."

He holds out a hand and leads me across the few feet to the bed. "I like this. It reminds me a little of mine."

"That's why I bought it. It reminded me of your rain-forest bed."

He grins, sits down, and starts unlacing his boots. I climb into bed and crawl to the opposite side, leaving plenty of room for him. "Roll over," he says as he gets in.

He slides an arm under my head and pulls so that he's flush against my back. It's so much like that first time we did this when I was in Hope House, I shiver in spite of the heat.

"Are you cold?"

"No. Just thinking about the first time we did this."

"Is that good or bad?"

"A little bit of both, I think."

He sighs. It's a sigh of understanding. I'm not sure how I know that, but I do.

"So, what else have you been up to? Besides not baking pizzas?"

I start to say "nothing" but change my mind as I open my mouth. "I've been working on a list."

"A list?"

"Yeah." I swallow. "A list. Booth had me make it. Actually, I wrote it the second time I went to The Coffee Shop. It was a list of things I wanted in my new life. You know, my life after Hope House."

"Okay." His breath whispers over my ear.

"So, I made this list of four things. I thought it was kind of stupid at the time. I didn't really understand how these things would make any difference. Then at an appointment with Booth, we were talking about you."

"Me?" I feel his head lift a little.

I nod. "We talked about you a lot. Mainly Booth telling me to stop seeing you, but this conversation . . . it was different. We talked about how unworthy of you I felt."

"But—"

I roll over to face him. "You may not feel that way, but I do." I close my eyes. "At least I did."

"You . . . *did*?" His voice lifts with hope on the last word.

"Well, I'm working on the 'did' part. I'm doing the things on that list."

"Okay. So what are the four things?"

I go through the changes I've made to my apartment and how I've made friends with Trace. I tell him I'm looking for a new job but haven't found a new place to hang out yet. He listens without saying anything.

"And you think these things are going to make you worthy?"

I sigh. "No. But I think doing them is making me better, and getting better might make me worthy. Just doing these four things has helped me realize how messed up I've been for a long time. That I ignored how screwed up I am."

Jackson sighs. "We're all screwed up, Kyle."

I smile. "I know. That was part of the problem. I assumed I wasn't sick. That I was just screwed up like everybody else. I'm just now really figuring that out. That I am actually sick."

"Ah," he says, a flicker of a smile on the corners of his mouth.

"So, the list . . . I think I'm done with it."

"Yeah?"

"Well, maybe. A lot of that's going to depend on you. At first, I had the place to hang out all figured out—The Coffee Shop—but then . . . well, I fucked that up." He starts to say something, but I cut him off. "I realized today that it wasn't the shop at all. It was you, Jackson. *You're* my place."

The look on his face just about kills me. The wash of emotions is just about too much. "Can I ask you a question?"

I nod.

"Why me?"

"I could ask the same thing of you."

"Says the woman who's all torn up over the unemployed barista living with his parents."

"Who says I'm torn up over you? Besides, throwing yourself at a mental patient isn't exactly a model for good decisions," I joke, trying to lighten the mood.

"Well, it's just a guess, but if you feel anything like I do . . ."

I close my eyes and sigh. I'm thrilled he's here but not ready for any soul-spilling declarations. I need to know he's planning on staying put. He said he likes my brutal honesty, so I go for broke. "When you say things like that, Jackson . . . it's crazy, and everything anybody would want to hear. But you and I . . . we're not very good at this." I wave a finger back and forth between us. "How do I know you're not going anywhere? If we do this . . . I need to know you're in it. Like, all the way in it. You know? Because no one in my life has ever wanted me around. Not really, anyway."

He wraps his arms around me and pulls me to him. I nuzzle into his chest. "Well, then you never made cookies for them."

I close my eyes and shake my head. I don't think I'll ever get used to goofy Jackson. "See, now you're making jokes. I'm serious."

"I know you are. I'm being serious, too. I'll stick around forever as long as you promise to always make me cookies."

"You're ridiculous."

"Or am I incredible?" He laughs, his chest shaking against me.

I laugh, too, keeping my eyes closed. "Both. You also scare the shit out of me."

"Why?"

I sigh. "I've never been in a relationship before. Unless you count Shawn Mathias, my boyfriend for two weeks in tenth grade. I have no idea what I'm doing. And it's terrifying"

"You think I do? I've fought against my father for years, only to be left with no choice but to do as he asks. You, Kyle . . . you don't ask anything of me other than to be myself. Do you know what a relief that is? To relax? To breathe? You're my greatest gift."

And here I go, swooning again. But shaking my head at the same time, doubting him. This beautiful man with his beautiful words.

"Are you really afraid of me?" he asks.

I nod.

"Why?"

"I'm afraid of everything."

"Me, too."

We lie there, silent for a while. I need to get some sleep if I'm even going to think about making it through the day at work tomorrow. Without a word, I roll back to my side, and Jackson spoons against my back. Eventually, his breathing slows, and I'm pretty sure he's fallen asleep.

I'm awake for a long time, enjoying him next to me and hoping it'll last longer than tonight.

CHAPTER THIRTY-ONE

I roll my shoulder, trying to ease the knots from my day at Frank's. After doing the job for this long, I've built enough strength to get rid of most of the aches and pains, but not all of them. The tension and nerves over waiting for Jackson aren't helping either.

He told me to meet him at his father's after work, but it's been over an hour with no sign of him. I need to go home. It's not impossible that he's changed his mind since last night. He was gone when I woke up this morning, after all. There was a note on my dining room table, right next to his letter, telling me to meet him here, with his phone number at the bottom. But he's not answering my texts.

"Miss Davies," comes from behind me.

I startle and squeal. It's Jackson's father.

"Sorry to sneak up on you. You here to see Jack?"

"Um, yeah. Sure." I stumble over the words and immediately lose the opportunity to play it cool.

"How's the job? You've been there, what? Nearly a year, right?"

"Yeah. It's good. Um, how did you know that?"

He smiles. It's like a shark going in for the kill, all teeth and shiny menace. "We were formally introduced on your first day, I believe."

"Oh." I look at the sidewalk. I don't want to think about that day, but the memory slams into me anyway. His answer doesn't entirely explain how he knows I'm still there—well, other than the flour all over me—but I don't say anything. I don't want to voluntarily prolong our interaction.

"How's Zach?"

I raise my head. My brain spins through my mental Rolodex and comes up blank. "Zach? I don't think I know—"

He cuts me off, laughing. "I believe you know him as Dr. Booth."

"You know Booth?" I'm dizzy all of a sudden. One thing I can say for Mr. Turner, he's good at surprises. I knew Booth recognized Jackson's name on the phone but never connected the dots that Mr. Turner and Booth actually *know* each other.

He nods. "From the charity circuit."

"Of course. I'm afraid I can't tell you how he is. We don't share a circle these days." Well, that came out really fucking snippy. Oh well.

His lighthearted expression vanishes, and he glares at me. "You're out."

"Yes. I am." I look straight into his eyes, being as confident as possible. "Since right after we met, actually."

"You're not here to do something foolish, are you?" He slides his hands into his pockets. His pose is suddenly casual, a contrast to his threatening words.

I have to choose my words carefully. Or, you know what? Maybe I don't. My first instinct is to cower and hide, just like I've been doing for the past hour out here on the sidewalk. "I'm not sure." My answer is honest, at least, but I don't think being with Jackson would be foolish. Having to deal with this ass again just might be, though. "But I don't think so."

"Well. I hope you're smart enough to see reason. Jack can be so damn stubborn when he sets his mind to something. Eventually, I hope he'll come to his senses and settle down with a choice woman. Now that this silly coffee thing is done with." His eyes sweep me from head to toe. The displeasure is clear.

I pull my hands behind my back and clench my fists, fighting the urge to throat-punch this douchebag. "A choice woman? Well, that's the uppitiest thing I've ever heard."

"Mind your tongue." He stands, chest puffed out a little, feet spread. It's aggressive. Bullying.

"Oh, I'm not the one who needs to mind their tongue, Alderman. If you knew your son at all, you'd know a 'choice woman'—at least one you'd approve of—is the last thing on his mind."

"I think it's time for you to go, Miss Davies. I won't tell Jack you stopped by." His shark smile is back.

I shake my head. "I'll catch him later."

I turn and walk away but call over my shoulder. "By the way, his name's Jackson." I don't look back for Mr. Turner's reaction to my final jab. At the bus stop, I sit on the bench, take three deep breaths, and try to calm down.

* * *

Two and a half hours later, I'm pacing in my apartment and torn over what to say to Jackson. He ditched me again. Not only ditched me, but left me in a position to have to deal with his father.

I want to call him, tell him about my run-in, but I don't want the alderman to overhear. Those few minutes on the sidewalk left me with so much anger. Again. The fury wells up and makes it hard to breathe.

Fuck Alderman William Fucking Turner! And fuck his choice women, too! And fuck Jackson Turner, too, if he can't make up his fucking mind. I'm done with all this bullshit.

I pull my phone out of my pocket and text, *Where are you?*

The reply comes after a few seconds. *My father's. Sorry about this afternoon. I can explain.*

It says so much about the situation that, even though he's living in the house, he doesn't call it home. *Come over.*

Be there as soon as I can. Okay?

Okay.

*   *   *

He's standing at my front door and looking . . . what's the opposite of unruffled? Ruffled? Relief washes over his face when he sees me.

My anger wanes. "Hey. Are you okay?"

He nods, then throws his arms around me. After a second, I hug him back. He kisses the top of my head, rubs circles between my shoulder blades. "Hi."

I pull back. I'm still mad at him, and there still hasn't been any explanation. "Hello."

"I've missed you."

"Yeah?"

"Yeah. And I'm sorry."

"You should be. Your father's an asshole."

He pulls back and studies me. Apparently, dear old dad was true to his word and hasn't told him about our conversation. "Where's that coming from? I mean, yeah, he is, but . . ."

"We had a little talk this afternoon. At his house. He turned up while I was waiting for you."

Concern washes over his face. "Jesus, I'm sorry. What did he have to say?"

"It doesn't bear repeating."

"Did he try to scare you off?"

"Keeping me away from you was clearly on the agenda."

He nods. "What did you have to say about that?"

"Quite a bit, actually."

His eyebrows rise.

"He pissed me off. Granted, I was already pissed off since I was in the middle of being stood up . . ."

He rubs a hand over his face. "Shit. I'm sorry. That's all my father's fault, too. He sent me on another interview this afternoon and didn't bother telling me it involved spending the afternoon on the golf course."

My eyebrows shoot up. "I didn't realize they confiscate your phone on the golf course and forbid you from texting anyone so they know where you are and that you're running late."

He grimaces. "Okay. It's not all my father's fault. Honestly, I was just so angry at him that I sort of had blinders on. That wasn't fair to you. I'm sorry. I'll do better."

I sigh. At least he knows how to apologize. "So . . . You golf?"

"Hell, no. I just followed the other guy around and listened to him talk about himself for four hours."

"That sounds awful."

"There are no words." He puts a hand on my lower back, all gentlemanly, and we walk toward my dining room table. "What did my father say to make you angry?"

"Oh, some bullshit about you coming to your senses and finding a choice woman. What does he think, you're going to buy one at the store?"

He laughs as we sit. "Probably."

"Does he know anything about you at all?"

"Sure. He just refuses to listen. He's got a PhD in willful blindness."

I look him in the eyes and put my hands on his shoulders. "I don't think that your coffee is something to come to your senses over. I'm sad you're not doing it anymore. And I'm sorry for what I had to do with that."

"It would have happened eventually, whether you said yes or no. But thank you. I really was desperate at that point."

"So, your letter . . ." I sigh, a little dreamy, a little stressed.

"Yeah?" His expression turns serious.

"I love it."

"That's good. I went through about a hundred drafts before that one. I needed it to be perfect."

"Well, it was. I mean, I'd be crazy to not love it, but . . . Jackson, did you mean it?"

He nods and reaches for my hands. "Every word."

"Because, Jackson, if we're gonna do this, you have to be all in. I can't keep stopping and starting. Like when I was waiting for you this afternoon. It's really doing a number on me."

He looks solemn. And then, his face blossoms into a blush. "Me, too. But you have to know, if you didn't already: I've been all in since that day you hugged me on the sidewalk."

A rush of self-doubt floods my mind. "I'm not sure why."

"If only you could see what I see," he sighs, squeezing my hands. "You'd understand."

"Maybe someday you'll have told me enough times for me to believe it."

He leans in and kisses me softly. "I'll tell you as many times as I need to."

"So. Aside from your father, we've got one little thing standing in our way. Dr. Booth still has legal control over me. He can put me back in the hospital whenever he wants. I have no say in it."

"How on earth did he manage that?"

"When I was first admitted, he was the doctor on call. Since I don't have any family, there was no one able to make decisions for me. He swooped in and petitioned to be my health care proxy. Pretty much all he had to do was prove to a judge that I couldn't be trusted to make sound decisions and I was a danger to myself. Which, since I had tried to kill myself two days before, I was. If it were happening today, I would have fought it. But I didn't care what happened to me then. It was the shittiest possible place, mentally. I signed the papers without thinking about the ramifications."

"So what do you have to do to change that?"

"I can petition to have the order rescinded at any time, but I have to prove that I'm capable of making better decisions for myself. And I am. I'm so much better." I sigh bitterly. "The one thing Booth insisted on, though, was that I shouldn't be in a relationship with you. Well, any relationship. But he was adamant that pursuing anything with you, specifically, should be avoided."

"Well, we've definitely managed to avoid it. No relationship here." He holds up his hands in mock surrender.

"Yeah, but that was a good thing."

His eyebrows draw together.

"We weren't ready. Maybe being glad I tried to kill myself is stupid and backward, but I am. Because if I hadn't slit my wrist, I might not have ever known there's something really wrong with me. As much as I hate Dr. Booth, he was right about a lot of things. I needed to work on me before giving anyone else my attention. Even you. Even though I wanted to be with you more than anything. I needed to figure out how to make myself happy first, and I think I've just about cracked it."

Jackson grins. "Yeah?"

"You know what makes me happy? My baking. And you."

"Oh yeah?" His eyes have gone all twinkly, and there's a hint of a grin dancing around his mouth.

"Oh yeah."

Jackson stands and puts a hand on my shoulder. "You make me happy, too. And I'm pretty enthusiastic about your baking myself. So . . . I don't want to be pushy, but what does all this mean?"

"That you're stuck with me. At least for a while."

"That's a good start."

"Yeah. So, we'll spend time together and, um, I'll make you cookies. Maybe every day. That depends on if I can get a different job. I mean, a different job's not necessarily a problem, but I have an idea. I'm not sure if it will work. I do know I won't be happy rolling pizza dough for the rest of my life."

I scoot forward in the chair, knees between his thighs, and work my arms around his waist, relishing the ability to do it. "You know what would really piss off your father?"

He pecks a kiss on my forehead. "What's that?"

"Him pissing me off is the reason you ended up here. So, essentially, this is all his fault." I slide a hand up to his neck and pull him toward me.

"I'll be sure and tell him that. He'll hate it." He smiles and kisses me.

There should be a list of the kinds of Jackson kisses. There's the sweet, closed mouth passes of our first kiss. The wild, feral second kiss, complete with grasping and a little biting. Then there's this one. I'm not sure how to describe it, except somewhere in the middle of those others, but I think it's my favorite. He starts slowly, with those closed mouth passes across my lips. Little wisps of touch that leave me grabbing at the nape of his neck and pushing toward him for more. The intensity builds. His arm is banded around my torso to hold me in place, the other on my neck, positioning me. It's slow and forceful and beautiful and everything I've ever wanted or needed a kiss to be.

His lips move across my cheek, then down my neck, leaving a path of heat and damp in their wake. I think I moan. The room is spinning with his sensory assault. His left hand scratches across my shoulder blade.

I'm fighting to get closer, but there's only so much I can do without climbing into his lap. I want to take my time, explore every cord of muscle. Maybe pick a favorite.

He's sucking and nibbling a line down my collarbone. Then he stands, pulling me with him, mouth not stopping, and walks me backward. "Is this okay? Just tell me, and I'll stop."

"It's more than okay. But I'm pretty sure I know where this is headed, and I need to tell you something first."

He freezes, probably thinks it's more hugely devastating, separate-us-for-months news. That's how it's always gone before.

"Nothing bad. Not really." I pull back a little, then angle his chin so I can see his whole face. I laugh.

"What's so funny?"

"You've got some flour on your nose. And your forehead. And your chin." I wipe a finger over the spots as I list them. "I was just going to warn you not to put me on the bed until I've had a shower. Coming home covered in flour is an occupational hazard."

"Oh, is that all?" He pushes me back onto the deep green covering, and I could swear a puff of flour rises around me.

"But –"

He looms over me, a hand on either side of my head. His thighs bracket mine, holding me in place. "You see, there's this little thing called a washing machine. Maybe you've heard of it?"

"Oh, so now the funny comes out, huh? I'm serious. You have no idea. It'll get everywhere."

"You said I'm stuck with you, right?" I nod. "Then you're stuck with me. Let me hold on to you for a while. I can buy more sheets. I can buy another duvet."

"I don't want to ruin anything. They're so much nicer than anything I've ever had before."

"Then we'll get you a backup set. We'll get ten more if it means you'll quit worrying about getting flour on the bed while I'm trying to show you how crazy I am for you."

I hold up a hand to shake on it. "Deal."

He nips at the end of my finger, then nudges my hand away with his face. He slides a hand under my shirt and rests his hand over my heart.

I shift. My want for him still makes me uneasy. "I need . . ." I have no idea how to finish that sentence.

"What do you need?" His fingers shift over my heart, mirroring my agitation.

I lose my train of thought. "I have no idea." That's a lie, though. Right now, I need him.

"What about this?" he asks as he brushes his lips over my cheekbone.

I squeeze my fingers into his back as an answer. I can't make my mouth form words.

Another sweep of his lips down my jawline, from ear to chin. "Or this?"

I shiver.

"Maybe this?" He whispers a kiss on my lips.

Oh, my. This. This is what I need. How did I go without his kisses all this time? I grab a handful of T-shirt over his heart and sigh. Jackson takes my antsy hands as a green light, or maybe a yellow, and keeps kissing—ear, nose, forehead, collarbone. The open-mouthed passes of hot breath are overwhelming.

"You," I breathe. "I need you."

CHAPTER THIRTY-TWO

"You want pizza or Chinese?"

"I may never want pizza again."

"Never? Come on. You're a Chicagoan. We're weaned on deep dish," Jackson teases.

"Maybe if it's deep dish. And I don't have to make it."

"Nope. No more pizza making for you today."

"I always want Chinese."

"Hunan Palace or Mr. Wong's?"

"*That* I don't care about. Depends on if you want spicy or not."

Jackson comes up behind me, slides his arms around my waist, and nuzzles my neck. "You know I can't turn down a little spice."

"Ha-ha. Dude, get back, you're seriously gonna mess these up. They're for that coffee shop on Wabash. The one you hate with all the novelty lattes."

"You're gonna bake for *them?*" There's a sneer in his voice, and I have to bite my tongue to keep from snapping at him.

"Maybe. If they want me."

"Well, they'd be stupid not to. But I'm not sure they're all that smart." He walks around to the other side of the counter where I'm decorating shortbreads to look like rainbows and unicorns.

"You know, I wouldn't have to bake for them at all if I just started charging you, Jamie, and Fiona for all the stuff you guys eat."

He shakes his head, turns, pulls out his phone, and calls Hunan Palace.

"So, not spicy, after all?"

"Not in the mood anymore." He sits on the couch, crosses his arms, and makes an exaggerated pouty face, his lower lip poking out.

"Don't pout."

"I'm not pouting. I'm sulking."

I put down the piping bag and go over to him. "What's wrong?"

"Nothing. Just pretending so I could get my girl to quit making cookies and pay attention to me for a little while."

"Your girl, huh?"

"Yep."

"Well, your girl has to finish these outlines. It's gotta set before I can fill them in." I return to my work. "I told you it wasn't going to be any fun over here tonight. You should have stayed home."

"I know what you said, but I'd rather be here talking to you than sitting at my father's house."

"Aren't you the sweetest?"

"Yep." He picks up a book and flips to a page toward the front.

"What are you reading?"

"*Problems in Contract Law*," he says blandly.

"Sounds exciting," I tease.

"Very. Wake me up when dinner gets here." He fakes sleep and a snore.

Jackson started his second semester of law school at Northwestern this month. His father is ecstatic; Jackson's not. He's also not about to become a politician on the other side of things. No need to tell Mr. Turner about that little detail, though. "It'll keep my father off my back until I decide what to do next," he told me while he held me in bed.

"I meant to ask: How did you get my address?"

"Huh?" he asks, confused by my out-of-the-blue question.

"Your letter. My address was on the front. How'd you get it?"

"After The Coffee Shop closed, I kept an eye on Hope House, and every day there was this twitchy guy who came and went. I figured there was no way he was on staff, so he was as good a bet as any."

"Eddie."

"Yep. I didn't have anything to lose, so one day I stopped him on the sidewalk and asked about you."

"He couldn't have known anything. We weren't exactly buddies. Eddie's not friends with anyone." I immediately want to take back what I just said. Eddie *might* be my friend. Well, at least as much as he's capable.

"Well, it turns out, Eddie's my friend. For a hundred bucks."

"You gave him a hundred bucks? For what?"

"He volunteered to do it," he says, too quickly. "He offered to bring me the whole file, but I told him I only wanted your address. He thinks I'm nuts for not snooping, and that's fine with me. I didn't get the feeling he cared about having your information for himself."

"You had Eddie steal my file? And he didn't get caught?"

Jackson shakes his head. "Apparently he does it all the time and thinks it's funny. He probably read your file months ago."

"Of course, he did." I shake my head, too. "You know, I kind of miss him."

"Why?" he asks, laughing.

I shrug. "I don't know. He was an ungodly pain in the ass ninety-nine percent of the time, but he made me smile sometimes. I wasn't doing much of that while I was there." I don't think he knows what to say about that, and I realize, too late, that he might have thought I was talking about him. "I'm smiling now, though."

I go back to my piping, shaking my head and grinning. It's been two great weeks. It's not that long in the scheme of things, but they've been monumentally good. I glance at my refrigerator and look at the business plan Jackson helped me put together. It's stuck right next to the court order restoring my medical proxy.

Booth didn't fight me when I asked, just sent me a letter informing me of the court date. The hearing took all of three minutes. Booth didn't even show up. His lawyer handed the judge a signed piece of paper, and it was over.

There's a strange lack of closure, not seeing the doctor. After all of it, I'm not sure who's responsible for how well things are panning out—him or me. Was Booth's treatment plan so effective that I had no choice but to end up on the right path, or did I make this happen myself? The self-doubt gnaws at the corners of my mind all the time. I'm doing my best to shove it back.

Eight coffee shops. That's how many we figure it will take for me to pay my bills. I have my first meeting at ten in the morning, and I'm waiting for phone calls from three more. I had to ask for the day off at Frank's to pull it off. Trace was pissed when he found out why I asked for time off, but he'll have to get over it. I told him I'd train whoever he finds to replace me. He said he knew he couldn't keep this "whiz kid" around forever. Besides, it was the only time the coffee shop owner had available.

I stop icing cookies long enough to inhale the world's greatest Peking shrimp. This carton is full of some wicked voodoo magic. I imagine the chef at Hunan Palace throwing shrimp, peas, eggs, and garlic into a wok, then waving his hands and calling on the gods.

I finish the five dozen cookies for tomorrow at two in the morning. I'm dead on my feet, but contentment washes over me when I walk over and find Jackson in my bed, an arm stretched out waiting for me to cuddle up. I oblige and push back against him, molding myself as close as possible. He makes a little happy sound.

"Thanks, Jackson." I kind of hate waking him up, but I need to say it again. Really, I can't tell him enough.

"For what?" he mumbles, then kisses the back of my head.

"Being here."

"Hmm." His hum vibrates against my back and makes me grin.

I didn't figure he'd say much; he's getting sick of hearing it. I've switched to thanking him instead of apologizing, and that's progress. There are a million "sorry"s on the tip of my tongue every day.

His arm that's draped over my waist inches up and rests just below my breasts. His breaths even out and deepen as he falls back asleep.

I rest a hand over his and breathe deep. I lie there, awake and content, until Jackson's alarm goes off at six thirty.

It's a strange thing, contentment. All this time, I thought I was looking for happiness. Feeling through the darkness of my mind for this magical euphoria. I was wrong. This feeling of rightness washing over me? *This* is the stuff. My brain's default is still a dull hum, but now the pitch and tone have shifted to something pure and clean, rather than an atonal mishmash.

I'm not delusional. I know it won't last forever, but I'm going to enjoy it as long as it does.

* * *

"Morning."

"Hey." He stretches and yawns. "Go back to sleep. I'm going to Jamie's."

"Really? Why?" I roll over, nuzzling into his chest.

"Dunno. Something about needing to help a friend move. He texted last night." He yawns again and curls around me. "Maybe I can be late. I don't want to leave this spot."

"Do you want me to come with you?"

"Get some more sleep before your meeting."

"I do need my beauty sleep. Just in case I need to flirt to seal the deal."

He squeezes me, and I kiss across his shoulder. All this access to him can be overwhelming, but this morning I relish my freedom to touch him.

"Uh-huh. Don't start that," he scolds as I kiss up his neck. "I really, really don't have time. Why don't you try to get some more sleep?"

"I don't think sleep's in the cards. I'm too antsy. The meeting this morning has me on edge."

"You'll do great. They'd be stupid to not buy your desserts."

"Thanks. Now, get out of my bed and quit tempting me with all this shirtlessness. I'm not sure how much longer I can control myself."

He laughs, stands, and stretches, exaggerating the movements and sweeping a hand over his torso. "What? This?"

I laugh and throw the blanket over my head. A minute later, the shower turns on.

I stay under the blanket, grinning like crazy.

Maybe it will last.

AUTHOR'S NOTE

Dear Reader,

Thank you for reading *Closer to Okay*. I hope you enjoy reading it as much as I've enjoyed writing it.

Although all of my book and the characters therein are a work of fiction, I felt it was important to include a note about just what, exactly, takes its cues from the real world: namely, Kyle's illness, which belongs to both her *and* me. Her profound and unshakable sadness and how it sounds in her head are mine. Her anxiety tics are mine. The way she clenches her fists to calm down? I do that, too. Also like Kyle, I suffered much too long before seeking help. I dealt with untreated depression for years and assumed that was how everyone else's brain worked. It's funny how the default for us as humans is to assume that the way we work is just how we're supposed to work. The way my brain was working wasn't going to get better just from the trying harder to be happy. Turns out, anti-depressants can be miraculous things. Imagine my surprise when at thirty years old, I found out that not everyone walks around wanting to die. Can you believe it?

So, Kyle's depression and anxiety are real, almost as real to me as mine. Still, it needs to be said I am not a doctor or psychiatrist or psychologist or therapist. While I hope that some of you will feel seen and supported in these pages, please do not look to my book for advice on how to treat your own depression. And although I tried to treat the illnesses represented accurately and sought out sensitivity reads from individuals who cope with everything described, I am by no means a mental health expert. I implore you, though, if you see yourself in Kyle, Joey, Mary, or even Eddie, get help. Don't use the actions in my book as a guide but, rather, seek help from a licensed mental health professional. It can make all the difference in helping you be okay.

Amy

ACKNOWLEDGMENTS

I already thanked him once since I dedicated the gosh darn book to him, but Eric deserves a huge, squeezy hug for not telling me I was crazy the day I came home and announced out of the blue that I was writing a novel. And then putting up with me while I actually did it. I'm so glad you're my person and really don't know what I'd do without you.

My parents deserve a billion thanks for never doubting that I could do any of the occasionally oddball things I set my mind to. Your love and faith in me mean the world.

My agent, Jon Michael Darga . . . there aren't enough words. Thank you for taking a chance on me and my slush pile manuscript. You helped make my story a million times better than it was when I gave it to you. You saw Kyle and Jackson the same way I did from the very beginning, and this book wouldn't be what it is today without your humor, intelligence, empathy, insight, and, let's face it, patience.

Acknowledgments

Thank you to Tara and everyone else at Alcove Press for making my writerly dreams come true.

And lastly, thanks to my friends, coworkers, critique partners, baristas, and coffee-drinking neighbors. So many people had a hand in making this book happen, and I couldn't begin to list you all, but you have my love and gratitude. You all know who you are.

BOOK CLUB QUESTIONS

1. Have you ever been in a situation when you felt at the end of your rope and without hope, as Kyle does in the book? How did you get past that? Who did you lean on for help?

2. Discuss the other members of Hope House. Why are they all there? Do you think they all deserve to be committed to a halfway house? Did you relate to any of them?

3. Do you think it was a good idea for Kyle to enter into a relationship with Jackson, or did she need to give herself more time? Did she do the right thing in walking away from his father's offer to have her help with The Coffee Shop?

4. Discuss the role that food and drink play in the book. What do you think their significance is? Do you have something that serves the same purpose in your life as baking does in Kyle's?

5. Near the end of the book, Kyle drinks more than she should, even knowing that alcohol will interact dangerously with her

medication. Why do you think she does this? What is her thought process like in that moment?

6. Early in the book, Kyle mentions that she is still trying to figure out if Dr. Booth is "good" or "bad." What do you think? Are all of the decisions he makes for Kyle in her best interests?

7. Kyle admires Jackson for being brutally honest with his customers, often at a cost to The Coffee Shop's business. Do you agree with her stance? Is his behavior true to who he is? Or is it a defense mechanism? Or both?

8. What do you think happens to Kyle and Jackson after the book ends? Do they have a Happily Ever After?

9. Do you think Jackson makes the right decision by giving in to his father's demand that he become a lawyer? Even if closing The Coffee Shop was inevitable, should he have gone to law school or made a different decision altogether?

10. Just before Kyle leaves Hope House, we find out why Eddie is there. And how long he's been there. Knowing those things, did you look at him differently in terms of his illness and motivations? Was he really as bad as he seemed, or was there more behind his actions than just messing with the other patients?